The Magic Barks

Proof Read: SB Proofreading

ISBN 9798566948874

Back Cover Photographs

Inset, Gilbert and Margaret on their wedding day.

Main Photograph, Court One, Firth Road West Melton.
Gilbert was born in number 38, the last house in the row.

The Magpie Barks

The Magpie
One for Sorrow
Two for Joy
Three for a Girl
Four for a Boy
Five for Silver
Six for Gold
Seven for a Secret
Never to be told

The Magpie

'I walked to the church, and back, the day I got married.

When we got home, the cat had had kittens and the coal had been delivered. So, just two hours after setting out in our finery, I was in my pit clothes shovelling coal into the cellar while Margaret was in her pinny scrubbing blood and cat placenta from the kitchen flags.

Not the ideal way to start a marriage you might think, but let me tell you, becoming one with Margaret Beadling was the best thing that happened in my entire life.

She was the gaffer in the kitchen. It was spotless, always hospital-clean, and the meals she cooked on that tiny gas stove would bring queues to the door as the smell drifted into the Yard. How she fed what became the six of us through the war years, was nothing short of miraculous.

But she knew more ways to a man's heart than through his stomach. When she went upstairs and took that pinny off, she was something else again. I still remember the time I said 'Not again luv, I've got to be underground in an hour.' She poked me in the back, gently chiding me in her sing-song Geordie lilt 'Gilbert Law, would you leave your woman wanting, when she is going to be all alone in this house for the next twelve hours?'

Jesus wept, it's hardly surprising I'm so thin.

My favourite times, before the kids came, were when we turned the gas mantle off and sat in front of the coals. In our own little world, defined by the guttering glow from the fire as it spluttered and flared, we would talk. She could make the mundane seem marvellous, find humour in the dullest place and even make our neighbour, old Howard Arnold, interesting.

On a Saturday night, when we stepped out for a pint, she was always at the centre of the conversation, her stories decorated with infectious laughter. But, oh, please, never cross her. There has been more than one occasion when I have known her test the strength of her argument, by seeing which would break first, her fist or a man's chin.

Anyway, let's not get ahead of ourselves… because her story starts miles away from Yorkshire, at the home of the bare-knuckle fighter, Thomas Beadling, in Benwell, the centre of Newcastle, literally on the northern bank of the River Tyne.'

One for Sorrow

March 1931

The sun glinted on the river making the water gleam, giving the gap at the bottom of the terraces a golden hue. An illusion of contentment. A stark contrast to the dismal reality of dark red brick, grey flagstones and charcoal tarmac. Black patches on the pavement showed where coal had been delivered and then shovelled into cellars. Rain was yet to wash the dust down the street to where it could meander across the dock road then into the slowly moving Tyne.

Margaret strode down the street with a purpose that belied her tender years. At ten years old she was still learning her role and responsibilities. Today she was to shop and then make a pie for tonight's dinner plus the beginnings of a stew for tomorrow. Saturdays may not involve school, but her education continued.

Rounding the corner, she walked alongside the Tyne as it made its way to the sea. Boats seeking coal and steel fought their way up river against the flow of the tide, their rugged outlines dwarfed by the carcasses of the liners being constructed at the dry docks. The constant pounding of metal reached Margaret's ears as riveters smashed hot metal into holes to hold the huge frames together. The acrid fumes they generated joined with sea salt to combat the stale scent of the waste of thousands slowly drifting out into the North Sea.

Sawyers' butchers was the first shop in the row and Margaret pushed the door open to new and more appealing smells. As she walked up to the counter the butcher came over and looked across the sterile glass counter.

'Half a crown of corner lift and a pack of suet, please.'

'On Susannah's slate?'

'Aye, please Mr Sawyer.'

'What's on the menu tonight then, young Margaret?'

'Meat and tatty pie, Mr Sawyer.'

'Lovely, can I have an invite?'

'Aye, if you brings your own bait. At your prices like, there'll hardly be enough for mi da!'

Wrapping her order in paper, Frank Sawyer smiled. The Beadling family were well known in Benwell and Margaret was the sharpest knife in the box. He looked at the young girl. Her hand-me-down dress was at least two years too big for her, while the washed-out cardigan she was wearing showed a hole where the pocket should be. Her hair was brown with a ginger tint, taking it to an attractive auburn shade which offset sensitive hazel eyes. Yes, in a few years' time young Margaret would be a looker and would make some young man very happy.

'Here we go then. Give my regards to Susannah and I bet your meal is the tastiest in Benwell.'

'Ta, Mr Sawyer. See you.'

Tucking her package under her arm, Margaret started back. At the bottom of the street she put her head down and shortened her stride, for number 122 was near the top and Violet Street was a steep climb. When it rained water ran down it at a furious pace and if kids played ball they must be wonderfully adept, because should they miss it, the chances were the ball would race down the hill and be lost in the river.

The row of terraces ran straight down the hill, doors and windows all painted blue – a sign they were owned by Carr and Cochran Ltd, the owners of the Charlotte Mine. Each house consisted of four rooms. A front parlour and back kitchen divided by stairs, one set down to the cellar and one set up to the two bedrooms above. Outside was a small yard separated from the back alley by a toilet and a lean- to for the dust bin. Every man who lived there worked for the company. Even though there were pot holes, leaking pipes, broken walls, and ill-fitting doors where the wind whistled through, there was never any outstanding rent. It was deducted from the men's pay packets every week. Before their wages were paid.

After a few strides Margaret lifted her head and looked up. Unusually there was a truck on the street and it was parked outside her house. Margaret squinted and realised it was the pit ambulance. An old van first used in the Great War but bought by the Newcastle colliers' union to help injured miners. She remembered seeing it on the street once before when old man Siddall broke his leg down the mine and they brought him home in it. Now she realised the front door to her home was open. The front door was never used, everyone came in through the back.

A feeling of dread crept into her chest. She pulled her package tight and started to run up the hill. Out of habit she ducked into the entry, onto the back alley, burst through the gate into their yard and flew into the back room.

'Mam, Mam, what's happened!'

'Wait there Margaret, your da's been hurt. Give me a minute.' came her mother's voice from the front parlour.

Margaret started to open the door between the two rooms but a strident yell from her mother stopped her in her tracks. 'I said, stay there, Margaret, and I meant it. Dunna give me any bother, I've got enough here.'

Muffled voices and the sound of furniture being moved came from the parlour. Margaret heard the squeal of a heavy object scraping across the lino. After what seemed an age her mother appeared, looking fraught and worried.

'Your da's had an accident underground, pet. They've brought him back in the ambulance and the doctor's on the way. Be a good girl and put the kettle on to make them men a cuppa.'

'But I want to see Da.'

'Not just yet, Margaret. He's taken a bash to the face and he don't look too bonny. Let the doctor sort him out then you can go in. Promise.'

'But, Mam'

'Please, Margaret. Do as I say make them men a drink.'

'The doctor's here, Mrs Beadling.' A strong deep voice came from the parlour.

'I'm coming love. The tea, Margaret.'

Her mother disappeared back into the parlour, Margaret filled the kettle and stoked the coals. Her dad was in trouble and here she was making tea. It was all wrong. But when Mother said, you did and if Mother said please, you double-did. So, tea it was.

The men were long gone and the tea brewed to treacle when her mother reappeared.

'The doctor's just going to finish cleaning the wound and dress it. Then you can go in and see your da.'

'Right, Mam.'

'He'll also tell us how to look after your da, because he'll need both of us for a while.'

'Right, Mam'

'Now, lets' have a cup of that tea and get the dinner started. Young Jack will be home soon and he'll need feeding.'

'Right, Mam.'

Dr Stuart Hardy looked down at Thomas – it was not a pretty sight. Stuart was used to seeing messed-up faces as he often acted as the official doctor at bare-knuckle fist fights where, only a few years ago Thomas had been one of the star attractions on the circuit. Not a pretty man to start with, the fights left Thomas with several scars and Stuart could remember at least two occasions when he had reset the nose on the face he was looking at.

Thomas was a big man with hands the size of shovels, but his knuckles were scared and swollen with arthritis – the result of years punching bags and men. His left ear was puffed up and looked chewed, while scars across his eyebrows gave him a mean almost evil look, which belied his true character. For despite his appearance Thomas was a kind man who loved his family more than anything. The fights were simply to supplement his income and support his family. They were not for fun, malice, or pride.

Stuart took a quick look around while he placed his bag on a small wooden table. As well as the table there was a sideboard pushed up against the back wall, a sofa, and an armchair. Apart from a mirror hanging above the fireplace there was no other furnishing in the small room. The hearth itself was spotless, Stuart guessed it had not been used since last Christmas – most likely the only time in the year the room was used. Life in these terraces was conducted almost exclusively in the back room. He could see the scrapes on the lino where the ambulance men had moved the sofa out of the way and noted how they had put the armchair Thomas was in under the window, so he could see the injury clearly. He made a mental note to thank the men for their foresight then turned his thoughts to the task in hand.

As Benwell's doctor for many years, Stuart thought there was nothing that could shock him, but this was different. The men told him Thomas was underground when he walked into a rusty metal rod protruding from the roof. Thomas must have been walking at a fair rate – possibly running, because the rod had penetrated his nose, smashed the bone alongside and entered his face. There was a gaping hole where

Thomas's left nostril used to be and a bloody mess behind. It looked like Thomas's natural reaction had been to pull away, or perhaps he had fallen back from the rod, ripping it out of his face. Whatever the cause, the skin around his nose was badly torn, adding to the deep impact wound.

The rod had obviously penetrated a long way and despite the nasal cavity being a buffer there was a small chance it had reached the brain. Stuart believed weaker men might have died of shock after the impact but, from his days as a bare-knuckle fist fighter, Thomas was ring-hardened to blows around the head. Even taking this into account, he was amazed Thomas managed to walk from the ambulance into the parlour. The men were ready with the stretcher but Thomas had refused their help.

Stuart diligently cleaned the wound and fixed a dressing by winding bandages around Thomas's head. It was the best he could do, and it was now literally up in the air whether or not the wound became infected. Unfortunately for Thomas, the air in Benwell, where people lived on top of each other, was dank, fetid, and soot infested.

Stuart shook his head, there was a lot of tragedy in Benwell, but if there was one family attracting it, it was the Beadlings. He recalled being present at the death of Thomas's first wife, Elizabeth – the all too familiar story of a woman dying during child birth; but to add to the misery, the baby had been stillborn. He was called, too late, to their first daughter when she died of pneumonia. But even worse was the death of Martha, Thomas's second daughter; she contracted Potts Disease, a variant of tuberculosis, which left her paraplegic. Her left arm became infected and turned gangrenous and Stuart had to amputate at the elbow. A beautiful seventeen-year-old girl ravaged by disease; it was heart-breaking. Thomas broke down and cried like a child as he held her during the operation. Stuart heard that he needed supporting during the funeral, the loss too great to bear – and now, here he was, a hard man, forged in the pit, toughened in the ring and seasoned in the trenches of Flanders. Stuart knew this could be the biggest challenge of Thomas's life. Infection was the enemy and it was as insidious as it was invisible.

For now, though, Thomas was calm and quiet, breathing slowly through his mouth. The doctor tiptoed from the parlour into the back room, gratefully accepting a mug of tea as he sat down. Both mother and daughter looked at him expectantly. Stuart knew his next words would determine their lives for the foreseeable future. He needed to pick them carefully. Facts first.

'The good news is that Thomas is comfortable and was able to walk from the ambulance, but he took a nasty blow to the face. A rod entered his nose. The rod was rusty and dirty. I have cleaned the wound as best I can but there could be some bone splinters further in, where I cannot reach. They will do no damage and I could do more harm than good trying to get at them. The wound, however, is large and will leave a scar when it heals. Thomas will not be winning any beauty parades after today.'

The doctor took a huge intake of breath. The attempt at levity was the prelude to bad news.

'The biggest problem is likely to be infection. You must keep the wound clean. I have removed all the dirt and stitched it closed. Clean the wound every day, use clean bandages and do not let him outside until the wound is sealed.'

His audience of two was captivated by his voice. He realised the trance he held them in was not one of his doing; it was the work of a rusty metal rod and years and years of gentle leadership from Thomas. But now came the stark reality – his reality. There was hardship everywhere in Benwell, dirt, disease and decay on every corner. Just as the men underground or in the ship yards toiled to feed their families, Stuart needed to feed his; but their food was paid for in the pain and despair of others. So, Stuart delivered the practised line everyone knew and no one liked before quickly moving on to practicalities.

'Susannah, the Union paid for this visit and I will leave bandages and disinfectant, but if I am needed again, I'm sorry but I will have to charge. Thomas is a fit man and at a guess will be back on his feet quicker than most, but he will suffer a severe headache and possibly some vomiting. He needs plenty of rest. Don't let him get up too soon, don't let him kid you he is feeling well; but the most important thing of all is to keep the wound clean.'

He kept his face expressionless. Susannah's was a riot of different emotions while the girl was watching them both intently with tears brimming in her eyes as she rolled the pastry. He could do no more.

'If there is nothing else, Susannah, I'll be off.'

Stuart stopped at the door looking back at the woman and girl who were both staring at him. The pleading in their eyes was soul-destroying. The big man in the front room was their world, without him fit and working there was no income, no food, and a queue of men waiting to take his job.

'With luck Thomas will be up and about in a few days' time. Just keep him clean and get some food and lots of water down him.'

As he closed the door behind him, he heard the silence broken. It was the first break in the tension which held the pair of them paralysed.

'Can I go in and see mi da now, Mam?'

'Aye love. I'll make a fresh brew and fetch him a cup.'

April 1931

The man moaned as Billy pulled the rope tight around his wrist. They had lain in wait for two hours before he eventually left the pub at closing time and started his walk home. When he passed the entry behind the pub three of the brothers jumped on him, a few slaps from Charlie stopped him protesting and he fell silent. Harry waited for their signal, then drove the lorry around to the back road where they bundled him into the rear. The two younger brothers stayed with him, while the two elder brothers sat in the cab.

Heading towards Bedes Burn a five minute drive took them through Jarrow and into the countryside. After they crossed the burn Harry made a sharp left into Jarrow Cemetery, one hundred yards further, deep inside the cemetery, Harry stopped the lorry and turned the lights off. There was a glow in the background from the lights in Jarrow but under the trees it was almost pitch black. Blood was still pouring from the man's nose as they dragged him from the back of the lorry. Billy brought more rope from the cab and, spreading his arms out as if crucified, retied him by his wrists to the drop-down sides of the lorry.

Harry nodded at Charlie and Jimmy. They were only fifteen years old but their size belied the fact. This was their first debt collection with their elder brothers and it was important they played a major part, so at Harry's signal the two younger twins moved forward and started punching the man in his stomach and chest. With nowhere to go and no way of their victim riding the blows, they landed with devastating effect. In less than a minute he was sagging in a heap, held up only by the ropes around his wrists. Harry signalled for the boys to stop. He pulled out a packet of cigarettes and passed them around while they waited for the man to recover.

The aromatic scent of the tobacco mingled with the damp smell of yew and grass as they listened to the wind and a late-night coal train chugging down the track to Newcastle. Jarrow Cemetery itself was silent. The nearest house was the other side of the mud flats of the River Don as it meandered down to the Tyne. Harry and Billy were frequent visitors to the cemetery. It was a favourite place to bring their customers and there were several graves occupied by more bones than the headstone declared. There was only one way in, which was easily watched and, while it seemed to lead to a dead end, if you knew the way, at the far side of the cemetery there was a track across the river bed at Low Simonside which would take their lorry at low tide. High tide was a different matter, so Harry only chose to come here when the tide was out.

Using the sporadic glow of the cigarettes Harry watched the man. He owed them money. Not a lot but enough for a message to be sent. He had ordered a dozen crates of illicit whisky and, promising to settle up in one month's time, sold the bottles around the local pubs. Somehow, he forgot to pay; the Blacks were keen to remind him, and to use the opportunity to send a message to their other customers.

A groan indicated the man was back to his senses and Harry knew those senses would be screaming given the pummelling just inflicted upon him. He moved across, grabbed him by the chin; pushed his head up. Billy tapped him gently on the side of the head with the starting handle from the lorry, showing him a sinister lop-sided sneer.

'Well now, my friend, it's good to see you again. You have been rather elusive since we last met.' Harry took a pull on his cigarette and stared at the face in front of him. The nose had stopped bleeding, although there was blood all down his front, while the eyes were wide and terrified. His breath coming in pants.

'Now tell me, when did you intend to pay us a visit and settle your bill?'

'Please, Harry. Time. Give some time. No got it yet, got to… Harry give me a week and I'll pay in full. Honest. One week'

'Unfortunately, that is not the answer I want. Either you have it or you don't.'

'A week.'

A punch to the stomach from Billy stopped the pleading and Harry continued:

'You agreed to pay us two weeks ago, that was the term of our arrangement. You did not, and now you want another week? Well, me and the boys are going to be extremely generous – you will pay us in full in seven days' time or we will be paying you another visit. Next time we won't be as generous – you won't survive, and, sadly, we'll be forced to ask your mother and father for the money. If they don't have it, we'll have to go to your wife, then her parents, then your brothers and sisters – until we do have the money. And each time we fail to collect we will

17

leave a message.' Harry signalled to Billy who thrust a diesel stained rag into the man's mouth and grabbed one of the roped hands.

'Today we're going to start with a message to you.' With that Harry pulled a knife from inside his jacket and seized the forefinger of the hand held out by Billy. The man kicked and jerked but Billy held his hand still while Harry slid the knife into the webbing under the finger and started to cut through the skin, tendon, and muscle around the base knuckle. He pushed the knife under the bone and stabbed, the finger came off, without looking at it he threw it over a headstone at the side of the road.

'There, that's my message. Now, would you like to say a few words Billy?'

Without saying a thing Billy let go of the hand and picked up the starting handle. He took a step forward and swung the handle hard onto the man's knee. There was the sickening sound of a knee cap smashing and the man fell unconscious again.

Billy signalled to the two boys, they released the ropes and threw the limp bundle of rags back into the lorry. The two men climbed into the front and they set off. After retracing their route, Harry stopped outside the entry where they had collected the man, banging on the glass panel behind him. The boys picked up the heap from the floor, removed the rag from his mouth and threw him out of the lorry. Harry engaged the gears and they moved off into the night. He had no idea if the man was dead or alive, he didn't care. When he was found everybody would know what had happened, the message would be loud and clear, all around Jarrow. A missing finger was Harry's calling card while a smashed knee cap was Billy's. The younger boys had yet to develop their own style, but they would, in time.

The saucepan was hot and heavy; Margaret carried it with care. She poured half its contents into the teapot before spooning a small teaspoon of tea leaves into it, giving the pot a vigorous stir. She looked into the caddy, there was probably another two brews in it, if you classed the dust that was left as tea. Margaret moved carefully and quietly, her mother was asleep in the chair she was now using as a bed. It seemed an age ago since either of them managed more than cat naps but Susannah was breathing deeply, with small snores. Margaret had a pang of jealousy when she thought of Jack staying at his Auntie Megs, eating two meals a day and a posse of other kids to play with. *Stop it, it wouldn't be right for him to be here.*

Margaret took a small pile of filthy bandages putting them into the sauce pan, returning it to the hob to boil for a few minutes before slowly adding cold water until her hands could bear the heat. Then with a rapid scouring motion she scrubbed the bandages, removing what puss and blood she could. There was no soap any more. Wringing them hard to remove the surplus water, she took them into the front parlour and placed them on the window sill to dry fully in the sun.

Her footsteps echoed in the room. The bare patches, where the furniture had been, showed darker than the rest of the old sun-bleached lino. Just under a week after Thomas's injury her mother sold all the furniture to a new neighbour and used most of the money to buy laudanum and fresh bandages. But these were now all long gone.

Margaret returned to the kitchen, poured the pallid tea into a cup and picking up a spoon she started up the stairs. From the bottom step she could hear the rasping rattle of her fathers' breathing. Bracing herself, she entered the bedroom.

The stench was now all-pervading, a sour sickly odour thickening the air like a greasy invisible fog. A grating sucking-in of breath was followed by a stifled moan before the inevitable groan came from the bed. Thomas was propped up on pillows and a folded rug. If he lay down, fluid from his wound ran into his throat which meant breathing became nigh on impossible. The chamber pot stood at the side of the bed – unused. Margaret could not remember the last time, two, three days ago?

She sat on the side of the bed and held his hand. 'Da, it's Margaret.' she whispered as she gripped his fingers. Thomas had not spoken in over a week, his last communication was three days ago when he squeezed her hand. She looked at his face. The swelling had increased yet again. He had been unable to see since his eyes closed ten days ago. Then the wound burst open and Margaret and her mother gave up on the pretence of keeping it clean. They ran out of bandages instead they were washing old ones, simply using them to wipe the puss from his face whenever they could. The sores, at the corner of his mouth, where his left nostril used to be and under his left eye were permanently damp and oozed a snot coloured fluid. The rest of the skin across his swollen, ball shaped face was taut and violent red. He was constantly hot; his temperature the warmest thing in the house for days. How he was hanging on no one knew, Thomas was fighter – and showing it.

Picking up the spoon, she dipped it into the weak tea attempting to pour a spoonful into his mouth. The liquid stayed in for a second then, as Thomas breathed out, it ran down his chin, thicker and tainted with slimy yellow green puss. Margaret dabbed at his chin with the bandages and tried again. Thomas had not taken anything but fluids for days, his emaciated body looked bony and wasted through his old pyjamas.

Wistfully, Margaret remembered the day when he tied a heavy punch bag onto the clothes post in the Yard and trained until the sweat was rolling off his lean but well-defined body.

'Come on Mags, let's see what you've got. Six pennies if you can knock the bag backwards.' She ran at the bag and hit it as hard as she could, but it only hurt her hand.

'That's no good, you only give it a slap, come on let's show you how to do it.'

For the next half an hour her father showed her how to stand with her feet apart, swing her arm back, move her weight forward onto her left foot and punch with her right arm bringing all her weight through.

'Punch through the bag and don't forget to twist your fist at the last second, it gives extra bite to the punch.'

She hit the bag with all her might and still it stayed rock solid.

'I can't do it, Da!'

'There's no such thing as "can't", Mags, there's only "try again". Take a rest and we'll have another go tomorrow. You'll see, I'll have you knocking this bag out o' the yard afore the end of the week.'

This started regular sessions, where father and daughter took turns smashing a bag, until they hugged, exhausted and laughing like demented school kids, on the day when Margaret finally made the bag move.

She looked down at him now, a mere shadow of the man he once was, his face unrecognisable, his breathing a constant demonstration of torture. Margaret knew her own face was drawn, with shadows where her cheeks should be, the deep bags under her eyes framed in black. Sleep was a luxury for the moment; worry was constant and food was scarce. They did not have long in the house, though the Coal company would not evict them while Thomas was suffering; but even now, their coal allowance was forfeit in place of the rent they owed. Neighbours were bringing them buckets of coal enabling them to cook and heat water, even so, they used the little they received with care.

Thomas suddenly coughed and sat up spluttering, he drew a huge breath releasing a terrible wail. Margaret ran to the door.

'Mam, Mam!' she yelled. 'Get up here quick, Mam, Mam!'

Susannah leapt from the chair and sprinted up the stairs, uncertain on her feet and confused at suddenly waking from a deep sleep. She took it all in though as she entered the bedroom. Margaret was standing terrified, with her back against the wall, while Thomas was sitting upright in the bed making the most appalling noise.

Susannah crossed to the side of the bed and grabbed his hand.

'Thomas, it's me, Susannah. Calm down, pet, you'll be hurting yourself. Come on now, let's make you comfortable.'

Thomas opened his mouth wide, splitting the sores around his lips, adding blood to the puss dribbling down his chin. Screaming, he began waving his arms violently. As suddenly as he had started, Thomas fell back onto the bed, a painful moan emanated from his face, a gasping splutter followed by a groan.

Then he was silent.

Margaret stared at her mother as she held his hand again. Susannah's colour was draining quickly and Margaret thought she might faint. She turned her attention to her father, his face was waxy with a sweaty glaze upon it, the taut red skin taking on a lighter shade. His head was flopped forward, his chin resting on his chest and there was not a flicker of movement across his face. Margaret knew by the tension in her mother's back and the silence from the bed that it was over.

Thomas had left them.

She did not know whether she felt grief... or relief. For the last ten days, Thomas suffered his injuries without any respite after the doses of laudanum ran out. He had screamed in agony for two of those days then settled into a moaning groaning rhythm of agonised breathing.

Now it was over.

Susannah sank to her knees at the side of the bed, still holding his hand. Margaret moved from the wall and held her mother's shoulders from behind until finally Susannah broke the silence.

'Be a good girl, Margaret, and go tell the doctor your da has passed away, ask him to make the arrangements. Oh and on your way out, can you pull the curtains closed in the parlour? There's a good girl.'

From there on it became a blur. Doctor Hardy came and filled in the certificate for Thomas, telling Susannah the Funeral Director would be along shortly and that he would also need a copy of the certificate. Within an hour, the men from the funeral company came with a horse-drawn trap – they asked Susannah if she would be paying for a church funeral. When she said no, they became brief and efficient.

Margaret and Susannah stood by the bedroom window as the men first placed ropes across the bed, then unfolded a grey canvas sheet which looked as if it had seen service on a sail boat, on top of the ropes. They carefully eased Thomas onto his side and slid the canvas under him, laying him on his back and folding his arms. They folded the left side of the canvas over, then the top and bottom into the middle and finally folded the right side over the top of it all. Finally, they tied the ropes securing the canvas around Thomas's body. They carried him down the stairs placing him on the trap before their boss came back into the house.

'There'll be a funeral on Friday at ten o'clock, I reckon Thomas will be one of them, Missus.' From the moment she said there would be no church service, Susannah knew that Thomas would have a pauper's funeral, a mass burial in an unmarked communal grave. A sad end for a proud man. Susannah nodded her understanding and the men left. Mother and daughter sat in the kitchen and Susannah made them both a pot of tea.

'Mam, am hungry.'

'I know pet, I know.' Susannah cut them each a hunk of bread with some hard cheese. They ate in silence with the coals burning down.

'Mam, it's so cold,' complained Margaret, finally breaking their self-imposed quiet.

'I know, pet, I know. Come here.' Susannah patted the armchair, cuddling Margaret into her chest wrapping her blanket around them both, their body warmth consoling them.

22

Margaret whispered, 'Mam, am scared.'

Barely breathing Susannah held back her tears and quietly replied.

'I know pet, I know.'

After the clock had ticked for an interminable ten seconds, she silently mouthed.

'So am I pet, so am I.'

May 1931

The chant drifted down the corridor in waves.

A clutch of immature Yorkshire accents in a timeless mantra. A monastic rhythm moving up and down, its hypnotic effect permeating the thick brick walls before reaching Gilbert. The chant came into his head, unbidden: one six is six; two sixes are twelve; three sixes are eighteen… His voice was broken now and he knew if he chanted the rhyme the sound would not match the notes in his head. His piercing steel blue eyes glazed while he listened with his head slightly bowed. His light-brown hair was short at the sides, but too long on top and flopped over his forehead trapping a long straight nose between it, and a proud, prominent chin.

A late spring sun shone through the window in shafts of hard light, as if trying to spear the dreary interior of the room – to remind the occupants the world outside was better. The rays piercing the gloom glistened with sparkles of even whiter light, the chalk dust from the black board dancing through the air, seemingly in time to the rhythmic chant. Gilbert thought it looked like fine snow on a calm cold day or perhaps dandruff from Wilfred Coley's shoulders after someone slapped him on the back.

He turned his attention to the redoubtable Mrs Mountfield booming out the benefits of a good and virtuous life in the shadow of Jesus in a voice capable of penetrating reinforced steel. The black board cleaner in one hand, a baton of chalk in the other for finer details, she demonstrated her points with huge waves of her arms, sending even more chalk dust waltzing in a merry pattern through the air in the sun beams. Not long now he thought.

Bum cheeks aching from siting on the hard-wooden bench for the past hour, he wished for the padding Mrs Mountfield carried, but none of the kids in the class enjoyed any spare flesh. Packman was not the place for excess as demonstrated by the clothes they all wore – hand-me-downs everyone. Thin, worn, grey jumpers over slightly less grey but supposedly white shirts, patched-up grey or black shorts for the boys while the girls all wore skirts, not a pair of matching socks in the room and the only two pairs of shoes standing out like beacons between the

24

backless, homemade wooden clogs. Gilbert was determined that when he got a job, and his own money, he would buy the best clothes. They would all be quality and he would have a pair of shoes shining like the paint work on Dr Brown's car, and in his mind that day could not be far away now.

Last Tuesday had been his thirteenth birthday, which meant he could leave school when he obtained the necessary number of attendances, this morning was his final one. Gilbert knew he was not coming back. Looking around the room, which had contained the biggest part of his life for the past eight years, he felt no regrets. Sure, the dinners were great, but sitting for hours listening to stories about kings and queens – he may as well have been listening to fairy tales for all the relevance they had to his life. Maths and new inventions were fascinating, but written English was as different and foreign to the talk in the Yard as the man on the wireless. Still, he enjoyed reading the newspapers, could write a good letter, and now he was ready; the world needed Gilbert Law. He was not going to disappoint.

Finally, the Headmaster rang the bell in the corridor – time to go. Without a second's hesitation or one single look back, Gilbert was out of the door, straight down the corridor, out of the main entrance and down the drive to the school gates. His mother, Sarah, stood by the gate a proud smile on her face.

'Right then Gilbert, you'd better get a crack on, Jack'll be waiting outside pit yard – he'll show you what to do.'

'Right. Thanks, Ma.'

Gilbert took the battered snap tin and water bottle, which had been his father's until only four months ago and turned left down Brampton Road. Every day for the past eight years he had turned right, then right again onto Firth Road where he was born, then right at the Cottage of Content into Packman Road where they now lived. A four-hundred-yard rectangle encompassing his entire life. But today he turned left into enemy territory. For years Brampton Ellis School had been a no-man's-land where the kids from Brampton and Packman went to school and a truculent truce was declared under the watchful eyes of the teachers. But once out of the school gates no one from Brampton turned right without consequences and no one from Packman turned left without the same.

Unfortunately, the quickest route to Cortonwood Colliery was up Brampton Road and along Manor Road – deep in the heart of Brampton.

Without hesitation Gilbert marched up the road. He was a man now, on his way to work and above childish territorial games; although if you had asked him at the time, he would have admitted a few nerves. Approaching the colliery gates, Gilbert saw his older brother Jack. He was married with kids of his own, and, while he lived outside the Yard, he still called in on his mother every other day. It was Jack who suggested Gilbert try for a job on the haulage at Cortonwood, as a reliable hard worker with a good reputation, Jack's word was enough to secure Gilbert the job.

'Eyop Gilbert. Ready? Come on then, let's show you to Fred.'

Jack turned, walking through the gates, crossing the Yard to the squat, ugly, brick-built building opposite. Without knocking he opened the door and walked in, not bothering to see if Gilbert was following.

'Fred, this is our Gilbert, come for his first shift. I'll leave him with you.' Jack turned and looked at Gilbert. 'Gilbert, Fred's pit bottom foreman. Listen to him, he'll show you what to do. I've got to go, but I'll see you later.'

Gilbert looked up at Fred. He was an old, one armed, barrel-chested man who Gilbert knew had grown up in Packman but now lived down Wath, the next village. He did not know him personally but all the men who worked at the pit spoke highly of him. He was a genius with ponies and once he lost his arm when it was crushed between two tubs, meaning his shovelling days were over, the colliery manager put him in charge of the pit bottom where his talents were best used.

'Come on then, young Gilbert. Are you as good with hosses as your kid?'

'Better, Mr Stevenson I've been helping at Dyson's Carters with their horses for last two years.'

'Well, let's put that to good use then. Sign here and let's get going.' Fred ignored the boast, he had seen dozens of youngsters come to work with the pony haulage before going on to become hewers or rippers, and all of them thought they knew the job before they started. But the first day underground was an assault on the senses as they experienced the mine for the first time. Not the beer bravado of their brothers or neighbours but the harsh reality of the muck, noise, smell and clamour,

26

which would make up their lives for at least eight hours a day from here on in.

Together they walked across the pit yard to the check room where Gilbert was allocated his pit number and two metal checks with his number stamped into them. Except for today, when his pay started from the time of his registration, it would start when he handed the banksman his tin check as he entered the mine and finish when he handed the banksman the brass check when he left the mine. But today he needed to be fitted out to work underground.

Cortonwood Colliery was one of four owned and operated by the Fitzwilliams. The Earl was ridiculously rich and lived in Wentworth Woodhouse, which, despite its name was in fact a huge stone mansion famed for having three hundred and sixty-five windows, its own deer park and a bigger frontage than Buckingham Palace. The Earl employed the most brutal of game keepers and protected his lands assiduously, yet was known as a kind and generous employer. During the last miners' strike he had paid for all his miners' children to be fed daily, and, while he stuck to national pay rates, all his workers received an extra-large coal allowance on top of their wages. Everyone wanted to work at one of his mines where the atmosphere at each could almost have been described as happy.

One of his innovations was that each new employee was fitted out with sturdy boots and a belt with hooks for their snap tin, water bottle and lamp. The first issue of these was free; the men could have a refit every two years or they could pay a small amount each week to get quicker replacements. Fred took Gilbert across to the stores. Here, he entered a small high room with a counter running the length of the wall at the far end. He strode to the counter and yelled:

'Frank, I've got you a new customer.'

After an age a face appeared behind the counter. Both the face and Gilbert almost jumped back.

'You all right Frank, you look as if you've seen a ghost. This here's Gilbert. He's starting today and needs some kit. What shoe size are you, Gilbert?'

'Don't know, Mr Stevenson.'

'Well stick your foot on there,' he said, pointing to a block of wood with lines ruled across it.

27

'Right, you're a seven but I reckon we need a nine to give you chance to grow. So, can we have a nine please, Frank, and a belt? For God's sake, man, stop gawping like you've seen bloody King's brother.'

The face disappeared back into the gloom and Fred turned to Gilbert

'That's Frank Trenham, he's the storekeeper but I don't know what's up with him, he nearly jumped out of his skin when he saw you.'

'Yeah, Mr Stevenson, I know Mr Trenham, and I was as surprised as him.'

'So, why did he jump?'

'It's a long story.'

'Well, we'd best go for a cuppa then, while you tell me it. I ent seen Frank jump like that afore and I could do with a wet.'

The storekeeper returned with the boots and belt. Fred checked them while Gilbert signed a docket and they left an ashen faced Frank Trenham, who had not said a word during the whole process.

Fred led Gilbert around the corner and into the blacksmith's forge. The furnace was standing at ease with a teapot balancing on the side of the coals. Fred nodded in the direction of a man in a huge leather apron who was pulling a metal rim from a wooden wheel. The man was topped with a shock of black hair, the start of a dense black beard and his forearms were covered in a mat of tight black curls. Gilbert thought he looked more like a bear than a man and felt a moment's pity for the wheel he was wrestling with.

'Arthur, just going to get a brew with young Gilbert here, be out of your way in a minute or two.'

'Aye, ok, Fred'

One at a time Fred took two mugs down from a shelf filling them full of tea from the pot. The tea was almost black and as soon as he filled the cups Fred poured more water into the pot from the sink at the side before placing it back on the coals. It was a non-stop teapot. Gilbert looked at his mug – it was chipped and stained dark brown with the evidence of years of use, but the tea was welcome.

'So, come on then, young Gilbert, what is it with thee and Frank?'

Fred stood with his back to the furnace while Gilbert sat opposite him in an old arm chair, which was so battered all the cushions had been replaced with black, shiny, rag rugs.

'Well, Mr Stevenson, it was last year, you know, when it were right hot last summer, and me and mi dad was sat outside on a bench taking turns to whittle a nipsy. Ma were getting washing in off the line when we hears this crying and wailing, and young Eva Brown comes round corner, bawling her eyes out. Ma runs to her and she's got cuts above her eye, blood running from her nose, a bust lip and welts down her arms and legs. Ma picks her up and cuddles her and carries her through Yard to her house.

'I don't know if you know the Browns, Mr Stephenson, but they are right nice people. Mr Brown were in Great War and stayed over there at the end cos Huns might still not sign a peace treaty, and he met Mrs Brown and they got married. She's a German but she's great, always happy and always helping.

'Any road, after a bit, Ma comes back and tells mi Dad it was Amos Trenham, that's Frank's youngest lad, who done it to Eva just 'cos her mother's from Germany—'

'And young Eva, how old is she?' interrupted Fred.

'She's only about five or six, just started school. As bright as a button and blinking good at football.'

'And Amos?'

'Why he'd be fourteen or so then. He stayed on at school to get his qualifications so's he could get an office job.'

'He didn't last long here,' interjected Arthur who joined them with a mug of tea. 'He worked in office during summer holidays, but word is, he made a pass at Winifred, colliery manager's daughter, and she reported him. So, same day Manager booted him off site. I doubt he'll ever get a job at a Fitzwilliam mine again.'

'Were that Frank's lad? Bloody 'ell he sounds a right pain. Carry on, young Gilbert.' Fred encouraged.

'Well, you're from the Yard Mr Stevenson and you know Packmanites don't like Bramptonites, any road Amos is from Brampton and he was their top dog. Well I weren't right happy so I stood up and waved mi mate, Shudder Madeley and we went out of the Yard on an Amos-hunt. It took us about an hour, but we found Amos walking up Pontefract Road with a couple of his mates. We didn't mess about, me and Shudder, we grabbed some stones and ran at em, throwing as we went. They turned and ran away, surprised that we were there, but Amos was oldest amongst us by a bit and he turned back and stopped and put his fists up. I ran at him and dove on him knocking him over and Shudder jumped on top. Other two ran hell-for-leather and we didn't see them again.

'We pushed Amos onto floor, pulled his belt off then tied his arms behind his back with it. Next, quick and quiet as we could, we marched him back through fields until we got to Brampton Road where we cut through Cadman's Yard and down their fields at the back of Manor Road, until we could cross Packman Road and into the Yard. We thought we were right clever because we never saw nobody all way back.

'Any road, when we got him into the Yard, we marched him to our clothes post and using mi ma's washing line, we tied him to it. We tied him good and proper and left him there. By now everybody in the Yard knew what had happened and they ignored him. People walked past him to go to toilet, Mrs Moore got her washing in, and me and mi dad sat on the bench whittling again. Nobody said a word to him when he shouted at them. After a bit, he got right idea and shut up.

'We ate our dinner and still he was there, then, just as light were starting to fade, Mr Trenham come running into the Yard screaming, 'What's going off? Who's done this? Who's done this?' His face were a right shade o' red and there was spit everywhere as he screamed. Ah thought, Uh-o I'm in a bit o' trouble 'ere.

'Mi dad started to get up from bench and began to shuffle across, you know, how he did in them days, when old lass Thicket strode into the Yard—'

'You mean Jane Thicket?' interrupted Fred. 'Blimey I thought she were dead years ago; she was old when I was a lad. Go on, young Gilbert. What happened then?'

'Well, Mrs Thicket marched up to Frank and shouts at him. "Stop it Frank, just stop a minute." And he did! Then she says: "The question you should be asking is not who did this, but why? That's what you should be doing. Follow me and see for yourself, then you can rant and rave all you wants."

'She marched across the Yard with Frank in tow and stopped outside the Brown's.' She called Eva to come out; the door opened and Mrs Brown stood on their top step with young Eva hiding in her skirts. Mrs Thicket asked Eva to turn round, and Mrs Brown slowly turned Eva by her shoulders. Her eye were all puffed up and swollen, the cut on her eyebrow showed flesh underneath, there was blood still coming from her nose; her lips were split and cracked while them welts on her arms and legs were starting to turn into bruises. Mrs Thicket pulls herself up, straight as a die and says in his face: "There's the why, Frank. Proud o' your lad are you?"

'Mr Trenham stood stock still, I've never seen change like it. One minute he were raving, next minute his shoulders slumped nearly to his knees and he were almost crying. Then, he changed again, straightened up, his face got a red fury on it once more and he marched over to Amos. He never said a word, he just gave Amos the biggest flat handed slap across the face I ever seen. I reckon they could've heard it in Barnsley. It made Amos's head snap back and there was a massive red mark of a hand across his cheek. Mr Trenham turned to old lass Thicket and said: "Let him go when you think he's had enough." Without another word he walked out of the Yard.'

'About half an hour later when it was almost dark, Mrs Thicket and Mr Arnold cut Amos down; he hobbled out of the Yard, and that was the last time I seen him or his Dad, until today.'

'Well, well, well!' said Fred 'There it is, from hoss's mouth.'

'I heard Frank kicked his youngest lad out of the house and he went to live with Frank's mother on far side o Brampton, but I didn't know why,' offered Arthur.

'Aye, but if what Gilbert says is even half true we mustn't say owt, else Frank'll get hump on, and from what I've just heard he did nothing wrong.'

'Aye right Fred, but I've got to get back to work.' Arthur turned around and resumed his wrestle with the wheel. Fred stood up, swilled both mugs out under the tap and put them back on the shelf.

'Come on then, Gilbert, we haven't got all day, let's get you down pit and trained in haulage, else the Earl will be stopping both our pay.'

Fred marched Gilbert across the yard again, this time into the lamp room where he showed him how to fit his lamp, snap tin and water bottle onto his belt. Gilbert put his new boots on and felt somewhat ridiculous, clomping his way towards the shaft with huge shoes like a clown and his pants being pulled down by his weighted belt, no matter how tight he cinched it.

31

When they got to the shaft Fred stopped and said in a serious but gentle voice 'This is the hard bit Gilbert; first time inside the cage is scary for everybody. Big men have shaken like puppies in here. There will only be me and you on this ride, so don't try to put a brave face on if you're worried. Everybody is first time. I've seen it all and told nobody. You'll be fine, come on.'

Fred walked forward and gave his check to the banksman; Gilbert copied his actions. The banksman pulled up a heavy iron, mesh curtain which covered the entrance to the cage. Fred ducked and entered, turning to encourage Gilbert. The cage itself was a heavy, metal construction with two floors. The sides were open except for a metal grid which formed the frame. The floor was a tighter metal grid which allowed air through but also showed the black void beneath their feet. Twelve hundred feet of absolutely nothing below them. Once they were both in and holding onto the straps dangling from the roof the banksman let the mesh curtain fall before pressing a button on the wall at the side.

The cage creaked and groaned, then simply dropped. The sun light coming in through the open door to the yard vanished and darkness enveloped the two riders. Air sped past, getting faster and faster, the fringe of Gilbert's hair was whipped up until it was standing vertical on his head. Sounds echoed but were distorted and swallowed by the noise of the rushing wind. Breathing through his nose felt impossible so Gilbert grabbed gulps of air from the torrent as it raced past. Occasionally there was a whoosh as an old adit or opening was passed in the fall. Halfway down they passed the other cage coming up the shaft. The air compressed forcing itself through the gaps in the mesh as the two cages crossed at speed. For a second it was too hard to breathe. Gilberts ears popped and his heart pumped wildly. Apart from Fred's lamp there was no light, the rushing walls flying past were a blurred impression of grey and brown.

Finally the cage started to slow, Gilbert felt his weight increase as his feet tried to find their way up through his knees and his knees up through his hips. He steadied himself looking at the wall through the bars as it started to take on definition once again. Then with a hard bump the cage stopped. There was a rattle and the onsetter pulled up the mesh curtain revealing the pit bottom.

32

They stepped out into a different world; a world Gilbert had heard about every day of his life, but he imagined nothing like this. His heart was still pounding with blood rushing in his ears as he tried to take in the sights and sounds around him.

The light was a contradiction, it was a harsh hard white but subdued. Dust swirled around in tiny whirlwinds or billowed in clouds like a nest of wasps on the move. The air was heavy and dry and hot, and after only a few breaths Gilbert could feel his mouth and throat constrict until he needed to swallow to enable him to talk. But he was speechless. The taste of dust and coal and sweat and grease fought to compete in his parched mouth, his nostrils were clogged almost immediately, giving him some relieve from the sensory invasion he was suffering. The cage behind him banged and rattled as it started its ascent, while rail tubs clattered and clashed in front of him. Fred said the cage ride would overwhelm him – but compared to this it was nothing.

Fred stood back to let him take it all in. The lad had not flinched during the ride down the shaft and that took some bottle. But now they were in a new environment, one which, if he took to it, would become the mainstay of Gilbert's life for many years to come. There was no rush – let the lad adsorb it, before he became part of it.

After a short wait Fred led Gilbert forward. He took him to one side and started to show him all the tricks of the trade. How to lock off a tub wheel, how to use his brake stick, how to ensure the connecting chains did not cow horn, how to change the points and the myriad other little tips he needed to know. He took him in between the rails where the tubs were going backwards and forwards to the cage.

'This is *the* most dangerous place in pit.' he informed a bewildered Gilbert as tubs clanked and rattled and groaned as they passed by on either side. Men and lads pushing or pulling or connecting the rope haulage shouting to each other in a code only they understood. 'There are more accidents and injuries here than anywhere else. Put your foot or your hand in the wrong place and you'll be at least a finger or toe short. Get your clothes trapped and you'll be pulled into places God hasn't seen. Keep your wits about you at all times, your eyes open and your ears wide. This is your workplace, Gilbert, and it is work, it's not fun; take it serious every minute and you'll be fine, but turn off, and we'll be carrying you out in a bag.'

Fred eyeballed Gilbert as hard as he could; he felt a responsibility to every youngster who came into this environment but the reality was, if they could not look after themselves they would be out in one piece or many and the next lad would be in their place.

'Come on then Gilbert, let's meet ponies, they smell a bit but they are better company than this lot,' he said waving his arm at the rest of the pit bottom lads.

Gilbert walked slowly down the road, his face was black with his eyes showing as white stains. His old clogs were back on his feet and he was carrying his new boots along with the empty snap tin and water bottle. He put his index finger alongside his nose and blew hard to clear one nostril, then repeated it for the other. Taking a final swig from the water bottle he swilled the water around his mouth and spat the residue onto the grass at the side of the road. Then he coughed and spat a thick black glob of phlegm into the field. It was hard to believe, but this morning he walked to school a boy and tonight he was walking home from the pit an absolutely exhausted, but elated, man.

The last rays of sunshine were falling below the horizon as he pushed open the door to No 7, Top Yard. The smell of bacon assaulted him and his mother smiled as he entered.

'Well, Gilbert, how did it go?'

'Fine, Ma. Mr Stevenson showed all what I've got to do and I've got to report to him in pit bottom tomorrow.'

'That's good. Sit down, there's a cup o' tea ready and I'll have your dinner in a minute.'

Gilbert put his boots, snap tin and water bottle down and looked round the room. There was only one place set at the table, his father's.

'Ma, why is Dad's place set?'

'It's no longer your dad's, it's yours.'

'But Ma!'

'No but's, Gilbert. You're the man of the house now, you're fetching in the wage and you'll sit at the top of the table as befits the man of the house.'

'But Ma!'

'I said no but's, Gilbert. You may be man o' house but you'll not answer your mother back.' Sarah said almost slamming a mug of tea onto the table.

Gilbert sat down sheepishly. He was used to sitting behind the table, furthest away from the fire, and it seemed strange to be sat at the head of the table. The heavy green cloth was covered, as usual, with a white table cloth, the hard-backed chairs in their usual place. His father's comfy chair was opposite the highly polished sideboard. Everything was exactly as normal, but different.

He tried to think of something to say but words failed him as a plate of new potatoes, bacon and baked beans – all smothered in bacon fat, was placed in front of him. Without a word he attacked it, swallowing gulps of tea on the way and wiping the plate clean with a piece of bread.

'Ma, best dinner I've 'ad in years. Is there another mug of tea in pot?'

As instructed and without argument he moved to the comfy armchair and sat back with his belly fit to burst while another mug of tea appeared in front of him. His new vantage point allowed him to scan the room and he looked across at the mantelpiece over the fire. When his Dad died, four months ago, his mother had placed a photograph of him in his uniform in pride of place on the mantelpiece and tonight it seemed Elias was staring at him with a look of satisfaction on his face. His medals and the shrapnel dug from his back were in a tin box alongside.

Not knowing why, Gilbert said, 'I weren't born so I didn't know mi Dad before the war, Ma, and I was little when he came back, he's always seemed old and small. Not like in that photo.'

'Yeah, he was different alright. Before the war.' replied Sarah. 'He was a good-looking man, fit as a flea when he went and when he came home from Somme he weren't too bad. Just a minor scrape he kept saying. It looked like a big bullet hole to me. They never should have sent him back. Ypres did for him. I don't think he ever recovered. Blown to smithereens, same week as you were born. A weaker man would've given in after seventeen months in hospital, but not your Dad. Not your Dad. I reckon he wanted to see you. That's what kept him going.'

Sarah dropped into a deep reflective mood and Gilbert regretted bringing it up, but everything today was strange and surreal. He remembered his Dad's final days. Elias had been underground, working near where Gilbert had stood in shock today. A tub came off the track spilling its load. Elias helped with pushing it back on and shovelling the coal back in, but after the tub was sent on its way, Elias collapsed and was carried out of the pit.

When they got him back home, he sat in the chair where Gilbert sat now, his face a picture of agony. In spite of his protests, Sarah insisted on Gilbert fetching the doctor who inspected Elias. Gilbert remembered his words and the emotions that raced through his body and exploded in his mind as the doctor said to his father:

'Elias, I think you have reopened your wounds. There is no outward sign but your stomach is starting to swell and you are in considerable pain. With nothing for me to see I am not sure how bad it is, but see how you go over night, I will come back in the morning.'

The following morning it all kicked off. The doctor came in and was alarmed at how much Elias's stomach had swollen overnight.

'Elias I am going to make a small cut to relieve the pressure.'

The doctor took out a small scalpel; washed it in alcohol and made a tiny nick in Elias's belly. Instantly, pus oozed through the hole and the doctor jumped back. He took Sarah to one side.

'This is beyond me, Sarah. He's had those wounds for years. I'm going to phone the army surgeon to come and have a look.'

The army surgeon appeared and immediately diagnosed the reopening of the wounds exactly as the doctor thought. He arranged for Elias to be taken to Leeds Military Infirmary where he could be treated by experts. The ambulance collected him and took him to Sheffield railway station for the onward journey to Leeds. The last time Gilbert and Sarah saw him he was unconscious while being stretchered into the ambulance. He died in the Infirmary a week later from blood poisoning due to infection from the old wounds. Possibly the last victim of the Great War to die from his wounds.

Although four months had passed the void he left was still palpable, but Gilbert was stepping up and would now be earning as much as his father. Due to his injuries, the agonising shuffle which Elias used to move around meant he could not work like the other men down the pit. He was found a quiet but poorly paying job, opening and closing doors after rail tubs passed by. Until the day he tried to help.

Gilbert stared at the photograph. *Yes, Dad, I am going to make you proud.* His chin hit his chest and he fell fast asleep with the mug of tea still in his hand.

Friday 13 August 1937

It had taken an age, but baby Doris was sleeping at last. For the best part of half an hour Margaret had rocked her as she screamed and cried with teething pain, but now, finally, she was away. Jack and their other step-sister, Brenda, were fast asleep in the other room, while Susannah was outside in the toilet. Barney was nowhere to be seen, as usual.

Margaret sighed and put the kettle on with her free hand, holding Doris in her other arm. She turned at the sound of her mother opening the door, her face ashen white and her eyes sunken into her skull. Morning sickness, what a title – it was ten o'clock at night, how could that be called morning sickness? But there was no doubt Susannah was pregnant again. It seemed Barney was going to keep her permanently pregnant until she bore him a boy. Well, third time lucky.

'You alright, Mam?'

'Aye, just the same old story. Seems babies don't want me to eat, so I've just emptied my stomach down the toilet again.' Susannah replied with a wry grin.

'Cup o' tea then to wash your mouth out.'

'Aye that'd be good. Thanks, Margaret.'

Margaret turned back to the fire and picked up the teapot as the door opened again, this time with a clatter. Barney strode in. He was not a big man, only just taller than Margaret, but he could make an entrance. He threw his jacket over a chair.

'I'll be having a brew, Margaret, and some dinner, Susan,' he proclaimed. With a stagger to the left, he flopped into a chair and lit a cigarette, beer fumes filling the kitchen.

Margaret put a cup in front of her mother and went back to the fire once more. *Here we go again!* Barney had a couple of drinks inside him so was going to be cranky all night. It was not unusual and becoming more regular, though on the plus side it also meant he spent more time out, which was a relief.

'We've not made dinner, but there's some bread and cheese,' offered Susannah.

'Get me something proper – and you'll not be needing this 'cos you'll be busy,' said Barney as he picked up Susannah's tea cup and started drinking.

'But Barney, pet, can't you make do – just the once?'

Barney slammed the cup down, spilling half the contents, jumping up, grabbing Susannah by the throat. 'Did you not hear me?' he screamed. 'I said I want dinner!' He pushed Susannah's head into the table with one hand and balled his other into a fist.

'Did you not hear me?' he yelled again, but didn't get any further as Margaret, dropping Doris into the armchair, launched herself at him. As the baby started crying, Margaret slammed into Barney, knocking him off her mother. When Barney staggered back, she pushed him upright with her left hand throwing an almighty punch with her right, just like her dad had shown her. Punch with twist. It caught Barney flush on the chin, knocking him backwards against the wall, a look of shock and surprise on his face.

Before he could recover Margaret pushed herself at him, trapping him against the wall, grabbing his shirt with both hands, she thrust her face into his. Baring her teeth, she snarled: 'Touch my mam again and I'll break every bone in your body. Every single one! Do you hear?'

Barney looked at the young woman in front of him with undisguised hatred, she was only a stripling but there was a way about her which belied her frame coupled with a determination no one could match. He hauled himself back to his full height, and, puffing up his slight frame, looked into her eyes.

'You will regret this,' he said, in slow individually articulated words.

'Not as much as you, if you ever does it again,' she said, completely unconcerned with his threat.

Barney pushed her back and picked up his jacket. 'I'm going out for a pint. I'll get myself something from chippy on mi way back. Don't wait up… and get this bitch under control!' he instructed Susannah, storming out of the door.

Margaret turned and put her arms around her mother who was still sitting at the table in a state of shock. Doris increased the decibel level, demanding attention from the armchair, but Margaret ignored her and cuddled her mother. Susannah smiled and placed her hand on Margaret's arm.

'Thanks, pet.' Then with false bravado and sad humour she repeated the mantra which, ever since she had married Barney, they both used in private to sustain them through the bad times: 'Better than the workhouse, hey?'

The door to the cellar creaked as he opened it. Reaching in Amos took the jar from the shelf. The one labelled biscuits: the one he watched her take money from when he collected the hire purchase payments. Lifting the lid, he examined the contents. There were several notes and lots of coins. He left three ten shilling notes and about half of the coins, taking the rest. Leaving enough so as to not raise suspicion.

Replacing the jar, he closed the door, carefully avoiding the figure laying in front of the fire.

Walking quickly across the front room his hands were shaking as he replaced the key on the hook at the side of the door. Exactly where he stole it from earlier. This meant he could not lock the door behind him when he left, but the old girl was becoming forgetful and an unlocked door would raise fewer questions than a missing key.

He looked through the window checking up and down the street. Nothing. There were no houses opposite, the only pavement was on this side of the road. Everyone not at work should be asleep or in the back room but this was the risky bit. If he was seen now there was no way out. He counted to five, composed himself, opened the door a crack and listened. Silence. He opened the door fully and peered out. Clear.

Closing the door behind him he stepped out into the dark. Moving quickly uphill he passed the entrance to the yard. A few more strides and he would be clear. His heart was pounding, his ears pulsing, his eyes probing the darkness. A few more strides that's all he needed.

Two hundred yards further on he stopped, looking back. There was no one. The dark was complete. Now he took the time to rub his singed hands, the hairs on the back of them gone. A couple of knuckles were blistered, the skin burnt off by the fire. He would need some lard on the burns when he got home and he needed to think of a reason to explain them. But overall tonight was a success. He counted the money. Seven pounds seven and six.

Amos grinned. Revenge and enough money to keep him in beer and fags for several weeks. It was too late for the pub so he would open a bottle in celebration when he got home. That was one of the benefits of

living alone since his Nan passed away. He was his own master. He
started back, whistling. The smile on his lips kept stopping him from
whistling so instead he allowed himself a hop, skip and a jump to try to
get rid of some adrenalin. That didn't work either.

If he couldn't whistle, he could hum and he matched his tune to his
pace as he marched.

Surprisingly, Doris seemed to be over the worst of the teething and an
uncomfortable truce settled over the family during the next few days
though it was difficult to live without tension when there were six of
them living, eating and sleeping in two rooms. Life had been good at first
when Susannah married Barney, his job installing radios in ships in the
dry docks was well paid and they moved in with him. It was a relief from
poverty and the prospect of the workhouse, while his strange Yorkshire
accent was amusing. But, when Palmer's closed and Barney became one
of the many unemployed, a new reality developed. Susannah blamed the
stress as Barney became more and more distant, constantly on edge and
unpredictable while his ego struggled with what he perceived as his
failure.

Jobs along the Tyne were scarce, competition fierce. They lost the
house they were renting and conditions slowly spiralled down until the
family were now renting rooms in Blandford Street, in the centre of
Newcastle. Blandford Street was the transient centre of Newcastle; there
were families from all over England alongside Irish, Scots, Poles,
Germans and even Russians, crammed into six-roomed terraces. Two
rooms were regarded as a luxury, in some cases there were families of
five living in one room. The outside toilet was shared, as was the scullery
– for both there was often a queue, though people tended to pick their
times.

For a while Margaret worked part-time mending nets on the dock. It
was the only work she could find. Though it was a hard boring job
paying a pittance there were women queueing to take the place of anyone
who slacked. Margaret's young fingers were nimble and quick while her
bright mind handled the complicated patterns easily, but even so, the
number of days when she was sent home without work increased as the
fishing fleets dwindled, the fishermen concentrating their efforts on the

better markets in Scarborough and Grimsby. After they moved into Blandford Street there was no work to be found.

She was sixteen now and probably grown as much as she would. To say her frame was sparse was an understatement. Walking up and down two flights of stairs for water, coal, or the toilet, meant her legs, while lean, were sturdy. Her hands were callused and scarred from work and burned from cooking over an open fire. Her feet were always black and coated in tough hard skin as she never wore shoes, unless she was outside of the yard.

It was Friday night, the truce seemed to have developed into a full blow peace treaty when Barney surprised them all by buying fish and chips for the whole family. There were full bellies and a feeling of contentment.

Meal over, Barney appeared from the other room in his best trousers and jacket. Margaret watched as he picked up his cigarette case, checking the contents. Secretly, she shook her head; here they were living in a hovel while Barney had a silver cigarette case engraved with his name. He bought the cheapest fags available, put them inside his case and threw the packet away. Who was he fooling? You could smell the tobacco was cheap – the silver case disguised nothing.

'I'm going for a pint. Back later,' he announced, standing in front of the mirror, licking his hand then using it to stick his hair down. The feeble thin strands would not cover his growing forehead as he wanted them to and he took his time to get them in place.

Margaret smiled inwardly. Two steps outside and the wind would undo all his pathetic, vain efforts. But she kept quiet. If Barney was out, she and her mother could have a peaceful night mending clothes while chatting.

It was getting late. Barney had still not returned and Susannah was uncertain whether or not to climb into bed or wait up for him. All the kids, with the exception of Doris who slept in the armchair, were in the other room – hopefully sleeping. A small pile of mended clothes was folded neatly by the wall, showing the results of a productive night, for the first time in a while she and Margaret had been content with life, chatting or laughing most of the evening. Susannah even managed to keep her dinner down.

42

She heard heavy footsteps hesitating outside and braced herself for Barney's entry. The door swung open and a slim, white-haired man shouldered his way into the room. Susannah stared, the man was younger than her but had the whitest hair and eyebrows she had ever seen. His clean-shaven face was the colour of alabaster, while his eyes were the strangest combination of blue, piecing grey blue in the centre and a ring of deep dark blue around the edge. His black suit was immaculate and probably cost more than Susannah had seen in her life time, underneath the waistcoat a crisp black shirt was held in place at his throat by an immaculate red tie. Black shoes shone underneath the smartly ironed turn ups of his trousers.

'Where is he?' the white man demanded as two more men, staggeringly large, with hair and beards blacker than night, barged in behind him.

'What? Where's who?'

'Your husband, who else? Barney, blue-eyed, Trenham. Where is he?'

'He's... why he's out,' stuttered Susannah, totally bewildered.

The man raised his hand and pointed a slender finger at her. 'You had better not be lying.'

Margaret, hearing unfamiliar voices from the other room, was instantly awake and came to the door, her hair tussled from sleep.

'Mam what's wrong? Who're they?'

'And who might this be?' questioned the man sitting at the table while the other two stood by the door.

'That'll be none of your business,' bristled Susannah placing both arms around Margaret's shoulders. 'What's going on here?'

'Ah, that is the question I want to be asking Barney. What is going on, hey?' He stretched his shoulders inside the jacket pulling the material tight to enable him to put his elbows on the table.

'What is going on? Let me tell you, missus – what is going on is a question I will get answered, and if I don't get the answer I want, me and my younger brothers here will be taking Barney for a walk. A walk he won't like, if you get my drift.'

Susannah stared back and forth between the ghostly white, immaculately dressed man at the table and the dark giants by the door. Both wore mops of black hair above full black beards while their clothes were the dark jackets and trousers of dock workers with handkerchiefs tied at their throats. The ghost flicked a wrist in their general direction.

'Same Pa, different Ma,' he said nonchalantly. 'Now, why don't you put the kettle on and get me and my brothers a drink while we wait for your husband to come home, hey? All nice and friendly like.'

'You can't just walk in here and demand tea! Wait outside if its Barney you want,' blustered Margaret.

The man looked at her as if she had fallen out of the sky.

'I did not ask you anything, but if you want to get involved, you can come and sit on my knee.'

'Stay there, Margaret,' instructed her mother. Looking back at the man she said, 'I'll make tea, if you're civil, but you tell me what this is about.'

'Now there's the attitude, missus. You, keep quiet young 'un.'

No one moved or spoke, all eyes following Susannah while she put the kettle on and made three cups of tea. She set them down in front of the man then sat down at the opposite end of the table. He signalled to the two brothers, who joined them. As they sat, one of them took a chisel from his jacket pocket and started to carve his initials into the table top.

'Well?' Susannah asked.

'Your husband's been messing about with our sister. He's taking advantage of the poor girl while her fella spends a bit of time in one of His Majesty's hotels. So, we are here to stop him. Does that answer your question?'

'No, it doesn't!' burst in Margaret. 'You can't come in here like you own the place, just 'cos you thinks Barneys been flirting. This is our home, if you want to talk to Barney, wait outside!'

'Flirting... flirting? Oh, it's a lot more than flirting, young 'un. Pregnant is a lot more than flirting, and...' flicking his wrist towards Susannah's protruding stomach, '...it seems Barney is very good at that part. Now you, missus,' he said pointing at Susannah with an index finger that was so smooth it could never have seen work, 'are nice and polite; but this one...' he turned the finger towards Margaret, '...this one is a right little fire-brand who ought to learn some manners and we are just the boys to teach manners, aren't we lads?'

44

The two giants smirked, looking Margaret up and down. The ghost picked up his tea cup and drank delicately. Margaret stood behind her mother and wrapped her arms protectively around her. A painful silence engulfed the room as the five of them were lost in their own thoughts while the clock ticked and Doris snored gently.

Ten o'clock became half past... half past became eleven – and still no Barney.

'What time does he get back?' asked the suit.

Despite the tension, Susannah seemed in a world of her own, unable to grasp what was happening or how to deal with it and the comment obviously startled her. Margaret answered for her.

'Around half ten, after closing.'

'Well, let's give him another half an hour then.'

At half past eleven the ghost stirred.

'Right, I reckon he's not coming back tonight and we have other jobs to do, so you tell him Harry Black and his brothers was here and we will all be back, unless we see him before. You...' he pointed to Margaret '...are lucky this time, but if we have to come back then me and my brothers are going to have a bit of fun with you, to help you learn some respect. But for now, we need to leave Barney a message.'

He signalled to his brothers who jumped up and grabbed Margaret and Susannah – one each. The one holding Susannah sat back down at the table, holding her in his lap, pulling her arm onto the table forcing her hand down. Harry picked up the chisel and placed it on Susannah's ring finger.

'Now, Barney appears not to have any respect for marriage so we'll teach him some.'

He turned to the fire, picked up a heavy iron pot and slammed it down on the chisel. The blade bit through Susannah's finger slicing it off. Susannah fainted and fell to the floor, Margaret screamed and fought free, throwing herself on top of her mother. Jack and Brenda, woken by the noise, stood terrified, holding hands, at the door. 'Stay there!' Margaret yelled at them. A brother pocketed the chisel while Harry pulled a thin wedding ring from the severed finger, put it in his pocket and threw the finger onto the fire.

'Remember, young 'un, to tell Barney. We will be back,' he said calmly. 'And remember, if we don't find him, you are next.'

The three of them walked slowly through the door leaving it wide open so Margaret could see the men saunter past open doors where concerned neighbours looked on.

Margaret held her mother, reached behind her and grabbed a shirt from the pile of patched-up clothes and wrapped it around Susannah's bloody hand. She knelt and cuddled Brenda, then Jack. 'Jack, can you be a good boy and take Brenda back to bed, please, pet? I'll be in in a minute, when I've sorted Mam out.'

'But what's happening Margaret?' the boy asked.

'I don't know, pet – but let me sort Mam out, then we can talk. Ok?'

Jack took Brenda's hand and led her through the door. Despite everything, she was nearly asleep.

Margaret turned to her mother who was still lying unconscious on the floor. There was a noise at the door; Margaret froze and a shudder ran down her back as she thought of the three men returning. But underneath grey hair pulled up into a greasy bun, there was a concerned face peering in through the open doorway.

'Can help?' she said in a strange accent. 'Was nurse in war. Can help.'

Margaret nodded and the woman knelt down at the side of her mother. She unwrapped the shirt bandage and looked at the wound.

'Ok, hold like this,' she said, holding Susannah's hand up high. She picked up the poker, rattled the fire and pushed the poker into it. 'Keep up, I back quick.'

Margaret held Susannah's hand in the air and watched as the woman hurried out of the door. She was sure she had passed her in the building before but people tended to keep themselves very much to themselves in the crowded conditions. It could have only been a minute and Margaret thought Susannah was starting to stir when the woman returned with a tin of cream in her hand. She immediately ripped the ruined shirt into strips discarding the ones covered in blood.

'Ok, will hurt but needs to do.'

She took the hand from Margaret and still holding it up high pulled the poker from the fire. Before Margaret could react, she pressed the gleaming red poker onto the finger stub and held it. The stench of burning flesh filled the room; Margaret held her hands to her face in panic. The woman dropped the poker onto the hearth, opened the tin of

46

cream and smeared the wound with it and expertly wrapped the finger and hand in the strips of shirt. Susannah did not stir throughout.

'Ok, all good,' she confirmed. 'Will hurt for two, three day but will heal. Ok?'

'Thank you,' said Margaret. 'Thank you.'

'Is ok. You sleep.' The woman picked up the tin of cream, threw the bloody strips of shirt onto the fire, smiled at Margaret and left, closing the door behind her. Margaret took the cushion from the armchair placing it under Susannah's head. She rammed the door wedge under the door to stop anyone from coming in and went into the other room. Brenda was fast asleep but Jack sat up, staring at her.

'Is Mam alright?' he asked.

'Aye, I'm guessing she will be now,' replied Margaret. 'Jack, I really don't know what happened tonight, but some bad men have hurt Mam and are blaming Barney for something. I've jammed the door so they can't get back in. When Barney comes back, we'll find out what's going on. Try to get some sleep now and I'll look after Mam.'

She put her arms around him for a second or two, ruffled his hair and went back to Susannah. Cuddling the sleeping Doris, Margaret sat in the cushionless armchair listening to her mother breathing – slowly and softly. She took some comfort from the fact that at least her mother had not felt the pain of the burn, but Barney had a lot to answer for. These were her last thoughts as she drifted into a hazy sleep.

Susannah opened her eyes and saw Margaret, above her, asleep in the chair. The house was quiet. Her hand throbbed, as she looked at it the memory flooded back: the three men; the chisel; then nothing. She held her hand noting the bandaging. Where did Margaret learn how to do that? She cradled her arm carefully and sat up slowly, a tiny groan announcing the movement, but Margaret slept on.

What would I do without you? Susannah's eyes passed from the bandages to the sleeping girl. Standing, she saw the blood and the initials carved into the table. Jesus it had all been real. They were coming back! Panic hit her like a runaway train as she remembered their last words, they were coming back for Barney and if not for him, Margaret. *Oh my God!* She staggered and slumped into a chair. *Oh my God what can we do? What have you done, Barney? What have you done?*

47

She never wanted to see Barney again, she would even take him to the Blacks herself – but then what? Her hand ached and throbbed as she laid her other arm on the table and rested her head against it. She could not remember falling asleep, but she must have done. Thoughts raged around her head, pain pulsed in her hand every time her heart beat, her dreams were filled with ghosts and screams and red. Red blood, red embers and red pain.

It was early morning and someone was trying to get in through the door. Margaret grabbed the poker from the hearth and moved behind the door. She saw her mother wake as she said, 'Who's there?'

'Margaret, ssshh, it's me, Barney. Open the door and keep the noise down.'

Margaret opened the door slowly, the poker raised above her head. Barney slid through. She closed it behind him ramming the wedge back into place. Barney looked in horror at the poker in her hand, then at Susannah, her hand bandaged and blood staining the table and floor.

'Oh my God, what happened?'

'You know what happened, Barney. Three men happened! They come to pay you a visit, but you weren't here, so they left a message through Mam. Bloody chopped her finger off they did. Her wedding-ring finger. Is that enough of a message? Hey? I ought to knock your brains in here and now – save them a job,' spat Margaret, advancing on Barney with the poker held high.

'Stop it, Margaret' cried Susannah 'don't make bad worse. Barney, I can't think straight, but you've done something; you didn't get home last night and them men don't waste their effort. You'd best explain yourself and tell us how we get out o' this mess.'

Barney collapsed into a chair. 'I didn't come back 'cos I was told Black Harry were after me – they told me in pub – he'd been in there looking, so I stayed away. I don't know what I've done or why he is after me. I never even met him.'

'Bullshit, Barney!' shouted Margaret. 'Don't mess about. They're after you because you've been messing with their sister!'

'No, No, it's a lie. I've not, on mi mother's life.'

'Your mother's dead Barney, so don't try that one,' snorted Susannah. 'Look, we can talk all day and I promise you, me and you are

48

gonna talk some more Barney Trenham, but what're we going to do? They're coming back and if they don't find you, they promised they'll take it out on me or Margaret.'

'Let me think a minute, woman. There must be something we can do. Let me think.'

'Margaret, pet, can you stoke the fire and put a kettle on? I think we could use a cuppa and the kids'll be up soon any way. Now, Barney – who is Harry Black?' Margaret was seething, but the calm Susannah exuded was infectious so she turned her anger and the poker onto the fire rather than Barney.

'Harry Black is the leader of the Jarrow crowd. Him and his brothers are smugglers and run on the other side of the Tyne. I haven't been the other side of the river since Palmer's closed. I don't know why they're after me, I don't know why they come north, but I do know they hurt people real bad and some of them they do hurt don't come back.'

'Aye, well, I've seen some of that already, first-hand you might say and more is promised. You're a born liar, Barney. There's more to this, but we can leave it for now. What we going to do?'

Margaret watched Barney stare at the table, the carved initials, the blood stains and Susannah's bandaged hand. His despair was transparent, his fear naked as he replied.

'Susan, we need to leave.'

'Barney how're we gonna leave? We can't even afford this place and it's the cheapest in Newcastle, how we going to do it?

'It don't matter how we do it, this…' he pointed to her hand, '…can't happen again. We have to leave.'

'What you means Barney, is it can't happen to you.'

'No, no, it's just… just… Jesus Susan, we have to go. Can your Meg look after Margaret and Jack for a bit, hey? If she can, we can go to Yorkshire, to mi dad. He'll put us up until we sort ourselves—'

'No. I am not leaving Jack or Margaret on their own with them nutters about. Absolutely no chance!' Susannah's green eyes pierced Barney like lightning bolts.

'It's just… well Susan… it's just, the more of us there are the harder it is.'

'No, Barney, we're not splitting the family. Understand? We'll find a way, together, understand?'

49

Barney was sweating as he emptied his pockets onto the table.

'That's it... that's all I've got. Use it, use it all, but let's go now... to Wath. At least then I can borrow money from mi Dad 'til we're sorted.'

Margaret looked at the money on the table. She was unsure how much it would cost to leave, but there was more money than she expected. There could be as much as six or even seven pounds there. That should be enough. It had to be enough.

'Margaret, what do you think?' asked her mother.

'Let's go before them men come back.'

'Ok... ok... Right. What we need do is get on the train to Wath and maybe we'll find somewhere for all o' us straightaway. If we can't we'll have to bunk at your Da's until we do. Ok? But let's get going. Now. Right away.'

Two for Joy

Saturday 14 August 1937

With the decision made, Susannah seemed to be in a daze, but Margaret acted quickly. First, she picked up the money, counted it and gave most of it back to Barney. Next, she made a large breakfast for everyone using as much of the food as possible, with the little left over made into sandwiches for the journey. Jack and Brenda were woken up and fed while Barney started packing.

'Jack, pet, I need you to run to Auntie Meg's and tell them there's an emergency in Yorkshire and we're having to go there. Tell her, me and Mam will write as soon as we can to let her know where we are and what's happening. Fast as lightning, Jack, no dawdling, no chatting at Auntie Meg's. Straight back. Do you hear?'

Jack raced out of the door with a slice of bread crammed into his mouth.

'Mam, I'm going to the station to find out when the trains to Wath are. I'll be as quick as I can. Right then, Barney, help Mam, you can see she can't do much.'

Margaret put her shoes on and took the stairs two at a time. Although the railway station was less than four hundred yards away from Blandford Street it was not a place Margaret was familiar with. She walked at a quick nip and entered the vast building. The place was teeming with people despite the weekend and the early hour. Every kind of person was there, all walking as if they knew where they were going. Margaret stood bewildered – there were stone columns, walls full of arched windows filled with offices, wrought-iron stairs, platforms where huge trains stood belching steam into the air, men in railway uniform scurrying around and besieged postal workers dumping huge sacks of letters in piles near the trains.

She walked up to the man with the smartest railway uniform.

'Excuse me Mister, can you tell me what time the next train to Wath is, please?'

'You need to ask the Station Master for that information, young miss. See the office over there, go inside and ask at the first counter. He'll be able to help you.'

'Ok, thanks Mister'

Margaret crossed the concourse; there were a couple of men wrapped in tattered blankets sleeping under a set of stairs, but two policemen were descending to move them on their way. She pushed open a stiff heavy door and walked into the room. There was a counter running the length of the opposite wall with several openings with queues at each. She joined the queue for the first clerk and waited impatiently. Finally, she reached the front where she repeated her question.

'Ahh Wath, that'll be Wath-upon-Dearne,' said the friendly face behind the counter 'I think you have to change at Doncaster… let me see.' He pulled a book full of lists of names and numbers from a drawer under the desk running his finger down the columns. 'Yes, that's right. You need to get the train to Doncaster, then change there. The next train is at nine o'clock, then there is one on the hour, every hour until six. Do you want tickets, miss?'

'No thanks Mister, but mi Mam will later. Thanks.'

Margaret left the station walking back with a long, positive stride. She ran up the steps and burst into their room. The change was encouraging. Susannah was wrapping cups and plates in clothes then packing them with incredible care into their suitcase and struggling one handed to sort out Doris while Brenda was in the armchair kicking her legs into space. Barney stood over blankets and sheets laid on the floor with piles of clothes stacked in them. Margaret could see a blanket left spare for her clothes.

'Nine o'clock to Doncaster then change to Wath,' she blurted. 'That's the first, then every hour after that.'

'Ok, if Jack gets back in time we'll try for the nine o'clock,' said Barney. 'You need to wrap your clothes up Margaret, there's a blanket over there.'

By the time Jack returned they were ready and it was still only a quarter past eight. Susannah picked up Doris, but that was all she could do with her hand strapped up and obviously still causing her considerable discomfort. Jack carried the kettle and a saucepan with a rolled up blanket stuffed with his clothes tied around his back – military style. Margaret carried a similar blanket on her back, another blanket balled up with clothes in it in one hand and Brenda, who held a pillow containing several items of clothing in her other hand. Barney laboured with two blankets tied up in balls with a rope joining them together passing under his left arm and over his right shoulder to allow them to dangle at his waist. Tied to the rope were the remaining pots and pans while he carried the suitcase full of crockery in his right hand.

Margaret looked around the room. There was nothing left of any consequence, the family's whole life was on their backs. They left, shutting the door starting down the stairs. As they passed the next floor a door opened and a familiar bun-topped face looked out.

'You go?' she enquired.

The family paused and Margaret said to them: 'It's all right. One minute, I'll catch up with you.'

She stopped by the door and said to the woman 'Aye we're going. Thank you for your help.'

'Wait!' the woman instructed and disappeared behind the door. A second later she was back.

'Here. Take. On each day. Ok? Each day.' She passed Margaret the small tin of cream.

Margaret grabbed the woman and gave her a big hug. 'I can't thank you enough,' she said. 'Thank you, thank you!'

The woman smiled in embarrassment 'Goodbye. Hope ok. Schwarz, bad man. Hope ok.' She said closing the door.

Margaret thrust the tin into her coat pocket and launched herself after the others, who, burdened with all their belongings and Brenda's small legs, had not made much progress. Margaret watched them from behind as she started to catch up. There was no doubt they were running. Many families did a moonlight flit to avoid debt and from behind they looked every bit the part. Barney's head was on a permanent swivel as he looked for any sign of the Blacks. What he could have done, with all those bags wrapped around him, Margaret simply could not imagine.

At the station Barney left them on one side in the concourse and went into the ticket office. After a long ten minutes, he returned with a sheaf of tickets in his hand.

'Right, Platform 6. We've ten minutes to get over there or we'll have to wait another hour.'

They picked up their belongings and started across the station. Access to Platform 6 involved climbing a flight of wrought-iron steps, crossing a bridge, then down another set of steps. When they arrived the train was nowhere to be seen, but there was a crowd waiting. After five minutes, the rails started to rattle then hum and a deafening blast on a whistle signalled a dark thunder cloud trundling down the line, gaining shape as it moved towards them.

The large, black main-line engine breathed out steam and smoke. Margaret and Jack used to sit on the embankment watching trains like this pull in and out of the station, but they had never been so close to one. A long line of dark-red carriages with gold lettering on their sides snaked past before the train finally came to a halt in a scream of brakes from its wheels accompanied by whistles from the conductors at the side. Barney looked at his tickets then the carriage numbers. 'This way,' he called.

They set off down the platform passing crowded carriages, as the people inside looked out at them. At first there were ladies in expensive coats and hats with feathers in them. Men with Homberg hats smoking cigars; all of them seemed to be laughing or joking. Then there were fewer hats, more caps and fewer ladies as they moved down the platform. When, eventually, they came to their carriage the family climbed on board into the third-class section – with its slatted wooden bench seats facing each other, forwards and backwards to the direction of the engine.

Sitting down, Jack could hardly contain himself – his eyes were as big as the train wheels, scanning first the platform then the other passengers, casting Margaret an occasional glance as if to communicate his excitement. It was the first time on a train for both of them and Margaret, in spite of the circumstances, felt a tingle of anticipation. There were two soldiers standing in the doorway, with the window down, knapsacks at their feet, chatting to two pretty girls standing on the platform. Inside the carriage, most of the seats had been taken, largely by men wearing cloth caps and clutching suitcases, but there was another family at the far end. They too were carrying suitcases, but no one else carried blankets or pots and pans.

There was a shrill whistle and the train jerked as, carriage by carriage, the engine pulled the train into motion. Margaret watched Barney let out a long breath and visibly relax. Jack's nose was pressed against the window as they left the station and started through Newcastle. The train worked its way slowly over bridges, through embankments, between church spires and chimney pots, underneath plumes of smoke

56

rising from the houses and factories. After crossing the Tyne on a huge metal bridge, it continued to wind through blackened red-brick terraces, the white steam contrasting with the black smoke from the city. Once the imposing stone-fronted buildings of the city centre fell behind them, it seemed the suburbs would go on forever, red brick after red brick, grey slate after grey slate, tarmac road after tarmac road. It was all Margaret had known and, while the layout was unfamiliar, the setting had been the backdrop to her life.

When the train broke free from the bricks and tarmac and built up speed, they started to see green fields and trees. The leaves on the trees were at their finest and the corn beneath was stacked into sheaves having been attacked by men driving tractors or horses pulling ploughs. Cows and sheep watched them pass, chewing the cud; interested only for a second or two.

The scenery fascinated Margaret and even after Jack lost interest she continued to stare at the landscape as it whizzed past. The rhythmic pattern of the wheels crossing the tracks started to have its hypnotic effect on the passengers and one by one they dropped off. Barney, resting on his blanket bags, while Jack sprawled across the seat at the side of him. Susannah slept with Doris in her lap while Brenda was on the seat sleeping across Margaret's knee.

Margaret looked at them all and wondered what was in store for them. Yes, Blandford Street had been its own hell but at least it was a familiar one. Barney was a pain but he knew where they were going. They had to trust him. She remembered how scared she was when her father died. How Barney saved them. He was the reason they were in this mess but he was also their route out of it. They needed him. She tried to stay awake, but eventually the ker-clunk, ker-clunk, ker-clunk of the train lulled her into sleep.

'Doncaster next stop.' shouted the conductor walking through the train. 'Next stop, Doncaster.'

Margaret jerked awake picking up her blanket, shaking Brenda. Jack was back on duty peering ahead through the window as the train slowed down. It went under a bridge and through a tunnel, before emerging into a station like the one in Newcastle, but much smaller. A vaulted roof protected the passengers from the elements, while the platform was lined with the same offices and waiting rooms. Men dressed in the railway company uniform stood with trolleys waiting to take the bags from the first and second class carriages. No one waited at third class.

The family climbed down from the train and stood on the platform bemused, watching people walking with purpose towards the exit or across bridges to other platforms. Barney looked at the tickets but could not decipher them, so he approached a bag attendant who had missed out on the other passengers. The man directed them to another platform, where they sat on benches for thirty minutes before a smaller train pulled in and they clambered on board.

Twenty-five minutes later they were leaving the train again, this time at Wath Central. For such a grand name, the station disappointed. It was a single platform with two lines running through it; however, the views were more than imposing.

Looking back to the east, in the direction of Doncaster, the tracks from the station joined others, which travelled around the outside of the station towards the industrial might of Manvers. A soap and oil factory puthered out smoke, which an adjoining glass works tried to smother with its own dark black offering. Beyond these were the winding gear to Manvers Colliery while behind this was a coke and gas works where the scene ended in the glorious fog it created. Margaret was mesmerised. What were they coming to? It looked like a piece of hell had been cut out and dumped by the tracks. Newcastle seemed another world.

She turned to the west and the view there was smoke free, but the head gear for Wath Main Colliery dominated the sky line, while in the foreground the railway tracks split time and time again until there must be a least fifty or sixty sidings, all crammed with coal wagons. A huge sign announced they were looking at wagons waiting at Wath Hump. There were well over a thousand wagons on view all with exotic names on their side, Cortonwood, Elsecar, New Stubbin, and Barnburgh.

For a few seconds the family took it all in, before Barney led them away. From the station they turned right between a cricket pitch and two football fields, then they turned up Pit Lane away from the pit into Wath itself. As they approached the town, they passed the public baths and crossed a stone humpbacked bridge over a canal where a barge was puttering past, full of coal. It seemed there was coal everywhere. After the bridge, the lane was flanked by terraces built from soft, beige coloured Yorkshire sandstone – giving a warm, homely feel in contrast to the harsh red-brick of the houses of Newcastle. They emerged onto the High Street by the Post Office and turned right past a toy shop called Tommy Tesh's which Jack was entranced with. A few yards further on, Barney opened the door to William Davies Estate Agents and ushered the family inside.

Behind the large oak door, a high oak counter with several glass panels ran along one side of the room, while on the other side a pew-like bench ran from the door to the back wall, giving the room a tunnel like feel. Barney knocked on one of the glass panels and it slid open.

'Ah yes, how can I help you?' Said a heavy-jowled elderly man with spectacles perched on the end of his nose, the raised counter enabling him to look down on Barney.

'Afternoon Mr Davies,' said Barney. 'I'm looking to rent somewhere for me and my family, do you have anything available?'

Margaret felt Davies looking across at the family, taking in the two young children, the obviously pregnant woman with the injured hand and the blankets carrying their processions. The signs were not good, she had already learned that the more desperate people were, the more likely a profit would be made from them. She felt vulnerable, helpless, lost in this strange new environment.

'Right, right, well you've come to the right place. Now what is your name and where are we all from hey?'

'I'm Frank Trenham's lad, Frank junior. You'll know Frank – he's the storekeeper at Cortonwood and we're all back down from Newcastle,' replied Barney.

'Well, well, well Frank's lad, hey? He's a good man is Frank and no doubt he'll vouch for you?'

'I'm sure he will, Mr Davies.'

'Right, right, good, good. Well let me see…' Davies turned, picking up several large books flicking through them. 'Hmmm, nothing much at the moment, but I do have a two-bedroom terrace coming up next Thursday or Friday. It's in Packman Road, Number three Top Yard. Do you remember Packman?'

'Yeah, just past Brampton church, but how much would it be?'

59

'Well, the rent will be ten shillings a week, with four weeks as deposit, so I would need two pounds and ten shillings in order to reserve it and get it ready for you.'

'Aye Mr Davies. That would be fine.'

Margaret's jaw dropped. What was Barney playing at? He hadn't even tried to haggle the rent. She could see by his face that Davies was delighted – he was obviously making a killing here. There must be something they could get out of this. Before Barney could say any more, Margaret joined him at the counter and interrupted. 'Why can't we have it earlier, Mr Davies?'

'Well, well, it's just… well…' stuttered Davies, obviously unused to being challenged. 'It's a sad story, you see, Mrs Thicket, the lady who lived there, well she died in Mexborough Montague Hospital last week and we still have to have the house cleared.'

Barney said nothing. Margaret however was in full flow.

'So, when will you empty it and clean it, Mr Davies?'

'Well, the carters are booked for next Tuesday, and the cleaners next Thursday.'

'What'll happen to the furniture, Mr Davies?'

'It will go to auction, on Thursday – at Flavell's.' Davies was now becoming uncomfortable at the interrogation.

'But that makes no sense – why don't we buy the furniture from you, Mr Davies? It'll save you the cost of moving it and selling it and me and mi mam are good cleaners. So why don't we save you the bother and do it ourselves?'

Davies looked at the girl with fresh eyes. Here was the chance of a profit without any effort and profit without effort did not happen very often. He also knew he would have problems renting the house to locals. Jane Thicket's death had not been easy, she had fallen inside the house, head first, into the fire. She was barely recognisable when first found, with no signs of life, but he wasn't exactly lying when he said she died at the hospital. She was declared dead when she arrived there but everyone knew she died inside the house. Locals knowing the story would be reluctant to rent the house. These nomads from Newcastle were a God send and he could not miss the opportunity. His thoughts distracted him and as he hesitated the girl was in full flow again.

60

'If we go and look at the house and furniture, I'm sure Barney and mi mam can come to an arrangement with you and if not, we'll be having the house next Friday anyways – so you don't lose either way. What d'you say?'

Davies thought hard and fast. The office was quiet and his apprentice Roger could handle the arrangements. If he drove up and if they were quick about it he would have time to call for a pint in the Plough before he came back to close up, so yes, the idea was appealing.

'Yes, very well, young lady… if your mother and father agree, I'll meet you up at the house in one hour's time, but I need a deposit now, Mr Trenham.'

Margaret and Barney looked over at a pale, drawn Susannah who had hardly moved and not spoken during the whole episode; the journey and the pain evidently draining her. Eventually, Barney said: 'Let's have a look. It can't do any harm and if it's not right, we're on the way to me dad's, anyway.' Susannah simply nodded her agreement. Talking was beyond her.

To Margaret, it seemed to take Davies an age to produce a rent book and a receipt for the upfront payment from Barney. Eventually, he looked up, 'Right. You know the way? I'll see you up there in an hour.'

The family filed out of the office and into the street. Barney led them to the right again, past the Red Lion pub, a newsagent, a fruit and veg shop, a pawn brokers and three banks. All the buildings built in the same Yorkshire stone – some relatively new, looking mild and warm while some were stained black from the smoke pouring out of the factories and houses in the distance. They stopped at a bus stop in the centre of the town and waited the twenty minutes for the next bus.

It was dizzying. To Margaret is was all new, the sights, the sounds, the smells. It all looked so normal, so peaceful, yet Harry Black was out there somewhere. He would be looking for them but here! She recalled his ghostly features, the huge dark menace of his brothers and shivered. Surely they were safe now. As they boarded the bus two strangers, a man and woman, helped them with their bags, making sure Susannah was comfortable. She smiled and thanked them.

It was only one and a half miles to Packman Road with the bus route taking them through parts of Wath, then West Melton, to the edge of

Brampton. The story of stone-fronted terraces continued until they passed a church on the edge of Brampton when the ubiquitous red bricks appeared once more. Firth Road and Packman Road were almost the same as the terraces in Newcastle, except some had tiny front gardens; but the further they went up the hill these disappeared and the terraces fronted straight onto the pavement. The family got off the bus at a pub called the Cottage of Content, which brought a smile to Margaret's lips. *I hope so!*

Barney led them up the road, through an entry, into a large triangular shaped Yard shared by all the terraces around it. There was a row of terraces on the left-hand side with a smaller row across the top, forming the triangle, a pavement bordered the backs of the houses and an area of hard, compacted soil in the middle came to an end at the right-hand side, in a row of toilets and a wall. Beyond the wall was a quarry in front of a huge chimney piercing the sky above a brickworks.

Davies appeared from the other end of the terrace and started to fumble with a set of keys.

'Right... right... here we go... yes this is it. *Open sesame!*' he said, laughing at his own joke. 'Now I've not been in since Jane's sister, sorry, Mrs Thicket's sister came to take her personal belongings, so I don't know what state it's in.' They entered in single file.

The place was immaculate.

Mrs Thicket's sister had apparently cleared everything out and left it spotless. There was a fireplace, a gas hob, and a brown laundry sink in the corner to the left as they walked through the door. In front of the fireplace was a table with two chairs, an easy chair alongside. A sideboard pushed hard against the back wall. A large rag rug filled the space between the fire and the table. Opposite the outside door were two other doors, one either side of the wall. One led to the cellar steps with shelves lining the wall opposite the top step. The other door led to the front room and the bottom of the stairs leading to the bedrooms. The front room contained only a sofa, another rag rug in front of the fireplace with a small table under the window. Upstairs there was a double bed in the front room and a single bed in the back. There was not a sheet, a cup, a knife or cloth in the house. But everything was spotlessly clean.

Though she hid it from Davies, internally, Margaret beamed. The back bedroom could be for the kids. Jack and Brenda could top and tail on the single mattress on the floor while she could put the rag rugs on the bed springs. Barney and her Mam could have the double bed. They had enough sheets and blankets for now. No more sleeping on the floor.

'Well, Mrs Trenham, what do you think?' asked Davies. 'It all looks fine to—'

'Where's the toilet? asked Margaret

'It's the third one in from the end.' said Davies pointing through the window at the row of toilets across the Yard.

'Jack, go have a look and pull the chain to make sure it flushes.'

'Really, Miss. Trenham! I don't think there is any need.'

'Maybe not, Mr Davies. But now's the time to check, hey?'

Jack came running back. 'It all works, Mags.'

'Right then, Mr Davies, all looks fine, so how much do you want for the furniture?'

'Well, well it all seems in fine order, so shall we say thirty pounds at fifteen shillings a week?'

Susannah raised her head from the kitchen table where she was resting her arm. 'Mr Davies there's only two chairs at this table, a sofa in the front room, there's not enough beds for the family. We'll need more than this, we can't afford thirty pounds.'

'It's daylight robbery,' interjected Margaret. 'We're saving you the cost of taking it away and selling it, and on top of that, we're cleaning the place for you and you'll be getting an extra week's rent. Twenty pounds at five shillings a week is fair.'

'But… I have to pay the money to the family, it is my duty to get the best deal.' spluttered Davies. Margaret strongly suspected that there was no such payment due to the family and that Davies planned to pocket the money himself. Davies looked at Barney who simply shrugged his shoulders. Before he could reply, Margaret stepped in again:

'Barney, can me and you have a word? Just the two of us like.'

Confused, Barney repeated the shrug of his shoulders and walked outside. Margaret followed him out and led the way to the end of the Yard where a low wall overlooked a filthy pond. She looked down, the steep sides momentarily taking her breath away; recovering she turned.

'I don't know what you're thinking, but let me tell you what I think. You caused this mess and you're gonna get us out of it. I knows what money you got and none of us are sleeping on the floor while you got that kind o' money. So, Barney Trenham, you've got a choice – either you go back inside and get us a deal, or I will.'

She stared at him, daring him to challenge her; daring him to defy her; daring him to step forward. Her back was rock solid, her shoulders square, her feet set. Subconsciously she was adopting the fighting stance taught to her by her father. Barney met her stare and locked it. Seconds passed; people moved around them unseen. Barney broke the stare.

'Go on then, do it!' he spat and strode away from her. Margaret followed his every step, watching his back disappearing inside the door. *Come on then, girl, you asked for this!* She collected herself, following him in.

Susannah was still slumped in one of the chairs, exhausted by the journey. Barney dropped into a chair alongside, avoiding eye contact while Margaret strode purposefully into the middle of the room. She saw Davies smile. He thought they were trapped.

'Sorry Mam, but we need to get to Barney's da's. You gonna manage it?'

'Wait, wait!' implored Davies, the sudden change catching him off guard. 'Surely we can find a compromise.'

Margaret stared at Davies. How far could she push him? So far, they were out of pocket two pounds ten shillings, plus the rail tickets and bus fare. Barney still had knocking on four pounds. She couldn't let this chance slip. They needed to get the furniture out of Barney before he could slide out of it; but they also needed to eat and pay the bills until they could find work. No problem, they had gone hungry before.

'Twenty pounds at five shillings a week, that's it!' declared Margaret.

'Twenty-two pounds at five shillings a week, one week in advance,' bargained Davies.

Margaret looked at Barney with a slight nod. 'Ok, Mr Davies but you put it on the rent book and we move in right now,' said Barney.

'Done, my good fellow, done.' Davies appeared pleased to be dealing with Barney and not haggling with Margaret any further. He made the changes to the rent book, which Barney marked with an exaggerated signature then gave him a receipt for the deposit. Davies left after passing the keys to Susannah.

The door closed behind him and the family looked around their new home. Barney dropped his blankets onto the floor and placed the suitcase on the table.

'Well, here we are then,' he declared triumphantly. 'If you two want to get this place looking summat like, I'm going to nip to me dad's and let him know we're here. There's a shop at the bottom of the road, opposite the pub, where you can buy stuff for tea. I should only be a couple of hours. Want to come with me Jack?' Jack looked at Susannah who nodded her head and the two of them left through the door.

Margaret stood in disbelief, only sixteen hours earlier she had been asleep in Blandford Street, unhappy, but unaware of the problem about to blow into their lives in the shape of the Blacks. Now, less than eight hours after walking out of the door, they were about to settle into a house away from everything she had ever known, with a whole new world to explore. She looked at her mother, smiled and said: 'Running water, a toilet of our own, a gas hob and two beds – now that has to be better than the work house!'

Susannah smiled and hugged her daughter 'Nearly worth losing a finger for, definitely worth upsetting Barney for. Crikey, the man might have actually done us a favour! But aye, definitely better than the work house.' And they both burst into fits of laughter.

Monday 16 August 1937

Gilbert took a huge pull on his cigarette, the end sparked bright red as his lungs sucked in the tar and smoke. He carried on sucking until the flaming red ash was a quarter of an inch long, then held his breath. He could feel the nicotine tingling through his system, nerve endings starting to twitch before relaxing, his first pull of the morning taking effect. The first cigarette was always the best. He released the smoke in a long languid sigh and flicked the ash onto the pavement.

It was a glorious summers day, with the sun beating down from an almost cloudless sky. He could hear his mother behind him clearing pots and washing them. In front of him, as he sat on their back step, he could see the Yard coming to life. Several neighbours visited their toilets, nodding to him as they passed, while behind them he could see signs of Harry Hallets' brickyard about to start another firing. Having spent all his life living within two hundred yards of the brickworks, Gilbert did not need to see the men scurrying around or bringing in the wood and straw needed to start the furnace – a look at the chimney was enough. Small puffs of white smoke told him that the first fire of dried wood was starting to heat the chimney before the kiln itself was lit.

Yesterday was a lazy day, his first off for several weeks and he spent it sitting on the bank of Pottery Pond, fighting a battle of wits with a mean old pike who lurked at the far side. The pike won again, but Gilbert knew he would catch him… one day. Today was a late start because he was on the middle shift and not due at the pit until nine o'clock. He loved the late starts but unfortunately they only came round one week in four.

His mother spent most of breakfast telling him about the new family who moved into the Yard on Saturday. A Saturday move was an unheard of occurrence and, even stranger, Bill Davies let them in himself. He guessed it was something to do with the sad way old lass Thickett died. According to his mother their new neighbours were from Newcastle, which apparently meant they were 'magpies'. But the big news for Gilbert was that the man of the house was Frank Trenham's eldest lad, Barney. Gilbert and Frank were on decent terms now; nearly six years of working at the same place meant there could be no animosity and to be fair, Frank was a nice man.

He took another pull on his cigarette and looked down the Yard. He would have known there were new people in the Yard without being told. It being a Monday, the newcomers were doing their washing and several sheets hung on a line tied to their clothes post. No one else had any washing out – the reason being Hallets. The smoke from the chimney was getting thicker, soon it would erupt with a thick dark smog and the wind coming from the east would blow it straight into the Yard. Within seconds all the washing out on the line would be covered in soot. Even as the thought went through his mind he could hear doors and windows being shut. Yes, the old hands were wise to events.

There was a further noise and, beneath the hanging sheets, he could see a pair of legs starting to put more clothes on the line behind. As Gilbert watched he could see whoever it was, was barefoot. She stretched to hang the washing, her dress riding up her legs to a few inches above her knee. Gilbert was mesmerised. The legs were young, lean yet sturdy with a beautiful shape to them, which only got better when the owner stretched onto her tip toes to complete the hanging. He was torn – should he go and say something about Hallets or should he sit here and continue to admire the view? A compromise surfaced, he decided to finish his cigarette, while admiring the view, then go to advise the owner of the legs about the problem. He took another pull and Eva Brown came around the corner, fresh from the shop, with a bag in her hand.

'Hi Gilbert' she greeted, as he nodded she looked at the sheets hanging on the line. A quick glance at Hallets' chimney – even at eleven Eva knew. 'Gilbert Law, what're doing, why haven't you told them?'

Wagging her finger at him she strode past Gilbert and her own house, stooped under the sheets and started to talk to the girl behind. Gilbert heard a sing-song voice answer Eva before both girls disappeared inside. Within seconds they reappeared with a woman carrying a baby in one arm, holding a bandaged hand down by her side. The girls quickly collected all the wet washing from the line and took it inside. When the sheets came down Gilbert got his first view of the owner of the legs. She looked about sixteen and was of medium height. Her hair was a dark brown with a ginger tint and her eyes were a wonderful shade of hazel – sensitive, worried, but thoughtful. When she saw him sitting on the step she didn't look away, instead she looked him straight in the eye with an inquisitive, almost challenging stare, before carrying on collecting the washing. In Gilbert's eyes the Yard suddenly became more attractive.

The two girls bundled the washing back inside onto the kitchen table. Margaret was frustrated; if what the young girl said was true and she could see no one else was hanging any washing out, there was a pile of wet washing which now needed drying inside.

'Have you got any coal?' asked Eva 'If you have, I'll ask me dad if you can borrow our clothes horse, you can dry them in front of the fire.' While not ideal, this was the only solution and the cellar was the only place Mrs Thicket's sister had not cleaned out entirely, so they had enough coal to last a week or so.

Eva was back within a few minutes with the clothes horse. Margaret and Susannah watched a huge plume of black smoke drive through the Yard from Hallets' chimney. There was no doubt now – the young girl was right, her intervention saving them from a fresh wash. Margaret stoked the fire while Susannah made a pot of tea and all three sat around the table talking. From the conversation they learned that she was their next-door neighbour but one – living with her widowed father, which shop to go to for vegetables, which for soap plus a myriad other details to make life easier.

After a suitable break in the chat Margaret asked who the man sitting on the step, smoking a cigarette was. 'Ah that's Gilbert, Gilbert Law. He's great. He lives with his ma and works down pit, he's got an allotment where he grows veg and the like and he always shares it with everybody. If you want a couple of eggs, Gilbert'll let you have them from his hens – he's dead generous.' Margaret's thoughts were not, however, with veg or eggs, but she kept quiet knowing her mother could read her like a book.

Gilbert was inside; driven back by Henry Hallets' fog. His mother had made his pack-up – beef-dripping sandwiches wrapped in greaseproof paper and stored inside his snap tin. He picked it up 'Going to go early and spend an hour on allotment, Ma. See you when I get out of the pit.' Sarah nodded her head in response.

Gilbert went out of the Yard, across the road and through Cadman's field to the allotment. While fishing gave him peace and quiet away from

68

the pit and the Yard, the allotment enabled him to stretch his muscles, exercise his mind and see the end product when it appeared on his plate. More often than not, someone else would be working on their patch meaning tips, advice or a friendly conversation was never far away. But today Gilbert worked alone in a world of his own, his mind replaying scenes of bare feet, long legs and hazel eyes.

Margaret spent the day sorting out the washing. She felt she was starting to get the rhythm of the Yard. Susannah was doing more and more, the pain from her hand reducing by the day. Margaret was changing the bandages daily, using the cream every time and delighted to see the wound healing without any swelling or pus or infection. Barney was spending lots of time with his father who was trying to get him a job at the pit. It seemed that the move had been a good thing all round. Barney returned with his father Frank on the first day of their arrival bringing with him two chairs, a set of dishcloths and a brush. It looked as though Mr Davies had been right about one thing, because Frank was a lovely man who laughed a lot and even went to see Davies first thing on the Monday to give him assurances about his son.

When alone, Margaret and Susannah pondered the mystery of the Blacks; they told anyone who asked that Susannah damaged her hand in an accident at work – mending nets. No one mended nets locally so they could not question the logic. Barney stuck to his story that he didn't know the Black's sister and was bemused as to why they were after him. However, when questioned about where he got the money from, he did confess to buying and selling potcheen illegally, which all pointed to some connection to the Black brothers. As Susannah stated: 'Barney would lie to save a farthing, so I can't believe anything he says – there's more to this.' Nevertheless, the journey from Newcastle, the deposit on the house and furniture had all but emptied Barney's pockets, so the need for a job was becoming urgent.

Mulling everything over, later that afternoon, as the sun continued to burn bright, Margaret sat on the low brick wall at the end of the Yard, dangling her feet over the edge, studying the quarry falling away below her feet, as it dropped down to a pond then up again to the kilns, store rooms and the brickyard chimney. She became aware of someone behind her and turned to see Gilbert approaching.

'Mind if I join you?' he said.

'Not at all. It's a free world'

'Huh not if Adolf has his way'

'Well, that's a cheerful way to start a conversation!'

'Sorry. I'm Gilbert – I live over there,' he said nodding towards his house as he sat alongside her.

'Margaret.' Margaret saw no reason to enlighten Gilbert about the fact that she already knew who he was.

'This is dangerous isn't it?' she indicated the pond.

'What's that?'

'This hole with the water in the bottom. I mean, the sides are nearly straight and they go all the way up to that house at the end.'

'I s'pose we're used to it. It used to be a clay quarry but it's all gone now. They won't dig it any bigger and they've already started filling it with waste bricks and rubbish from Hallets.'

'Where does that filthy water go?'

'Nowhere. It just sits there. If it floods there's an overflow pipe to Abdy stream, but only when it floods and its always mucky. If you want to get rid of anything, tie a weight on it and chuck it in, you'll never see it again!'

'Does it always make that black smoke?' Margaret asked, pointing at the huge chimney.

'Yeah, but you'll get used to it. Any road, enough about Hallets, how're you finding the Yard?'

'It's a lot better than Newcastle, where we come from, but I'm a bit at a loss – I don't know my way around or where things are yet, it's all a bit of a mystery.'

'Well, I'm happy to show you around, do you want to go for a walk?'

'Do you mind? I need to get out. I've been inside the house for nigh on three days.'

'Come on then, but get your shoes on,' Gilbert said, looking at her bare feet.

He led her out of the Yard, down to the Cottage of Content, pointing out all the shops and bus stops and telling her where each bus went. At the pub, Margaret pointed to a tower in the distance. It poked above the trees on a hill, its flat top holding a strange tall dome, seemingly off centre.

'What's that?' she asked.

'Hoober Stand. It's a folly. The old earls were fond of building them and this one's the best.'

'What's a folly?'

'It's something that has no purpose, just built for fun, but Hoober Stand is a bit different 'cos the views from up there are fantastic. Do you want to go up and have a look?'

'Aye I'd love to.'

'Well let's meet on Saturday morning and we can walk up. I'll get me ma to make us some sandwiches and I'll show you about a bit more.'

'Right, I'll look forward to it,' said Margaret with a big smile on her face.

They continued their walk as Gilbert described how Packman was really only two streets forming the 'V' of a triangle around Hallets' brickyard. Trapped between West Melton and Brampton on the edge of Wath-upon-Dearne, it was liked by none and poorest of all. He showed her Chapman's chip shop, Brampton Ellis School and the church where his father was buried.

'See the building there?' Gilbert pointed beyond the church, 'well it used to be a right posh school years ago but they caught Headmaster forging pound notes, so they shipped him to Van Diemen's Land.'

'I'd take that risk!' declared Margaret. 'I really needs a job but I've no idea where to start.'

'Well, you could try at Hallets,' Gilbert offered. 'Me grandad is foreman – we can ask him if you want, see if he'll put in a word for you.'

'Do you think he would? 'Cos that'd be great!'

'Let's see. He only lives on Firth Road.'

They walked back past the church and the school onto Firth Road and turned right, into a yard with a terrace on one side only. Gilbert walked up to the last house in the terrace running up the hill, it was the house where he was born, banging on the tin bath hanging outside the house, he pushed the door open.

'Grandad, Gran are you in? I've got a visitor for you.'

Margaret walked into a room almost identical to theirs in the Yard except this had a lived-in and loved feel about it. There was an embroidered cloth over the table, lace embroidery over the sideboard, some horse brasses hanging on the wall and two photographs on the

71

mantelpiece. Gilbert's grandad, who was almost a spitting image of Gilbert, sat in an armchair reading a newspaper while his grandma sat opposite him knitting.

'Hello love, what you doing here? It's not dinner time you know,' teased his grandma.

'This is me Gran, she makes the best Yorkshire puddings in England,' informed Gilbert, 'and this is me grandad who in't as grumpy as he looks. While this here's Margaret, who's just moved into Yard from Newcastle.'

'Well, welcome love, do you want a cuppa?'

'No thanks, Gran we're just here to ask me grandad if there are any jobs at brickyard. Margaret han't got a job and don't know anybody, so I thought I'd ask for her.'

Alfred placed the newspaper on his knee and looked across at the two of them.

'Gilbert, you know only job I can give would be to clean out kiln at end of a firing.'

'Yep, but even so it's better than nothing, int it, Grandad?'

'Only just. Did he say your name is Margaret? Well, Margaret, just so you know, we start all newcomers cleaning out kiln first, if they don't complain and get on with it, we consider them for other jobs. But cleaning out kiln is horrible. It's mucky and hot and hard. We don't often get young lasses who'll put up with it.' Margaret did not hesitate.

'I'll give it a bash, Mr Law. I don't have anything else to do except help mi mam clean and wash and cook and I need to be earning some money.'

'Are you sure lass? Well then, report to me tomorrow at six. Gilbert will tell you where,' Alfred said, picking his paper up.

'Thanks, Grandad. I'll fetch you them marrows I've been growing. Gran, you can show me how to make that stew you do.'

'Ok love, see you soon.'

'Bye, thank you Mr Law. I'll see you tomorrow,' said Margaret as they left.

She almost skipped down the road. She had a job. She gave Gilbert a huge hug and started to sing as she led the way back. He laughed, trying to keep up with her.

'Margaret, lass, you're not gunna be this happy when you see job they'll ask you to do.'

'Gilbert, lad,' she mimicked, 'I don't care. If you'd seen what I've just left, it canna be any worse.'

On Wednesday afternoon Gilbert knocked on the door of No 3.

'Hello Mrs Trenham, it's Gilbert. I've brought you a marrow I had spare.'

Before anyone could answer Gilbert walked into the room with the marrow in his hand. Susannah was standing at the sink, Doris and Brenda were playing on the floor while Jack sat at the table. Margaret stood in front of the fire staring at Gilbert with her hands on her hips. Her dress was a grey smudge, her face a black mask with two white smears for eyes, while her hair, covered in ash and coal dust, was sticking up like a stiff brush covered in talcum powder. Gilbert slowly placed the marrow on a chair while all five occupants watched him, gauging his reaction. A smile started to spread across his face.

'Gilbert Law, don't you know not to walk straight in? You don't know what we might be doing!' proclaimed Margaret.

'Well, to be fair, Margaret, I didn't think you'd be practising scaring crows,' Gilbert replied before bursting into pleats of laughter. 'I haven't never seen anything like it. Never.'

Margaret picked up the dishcloth from the table and threw it at him, which only made him laugh even more. Susannah joined in and soon everyone but Margaret was sharing a belly laugh at her expense. She stamped her feet, which brought more laughter until, eventually, she started to join in as well.

'I thought I would nip in and tell you… I've been to me grandad's and he thinks you're a good grafter and he'll get you a full-time job,' he said as the laughter died down. 'But I reckon I ought to go now, 'cos I think it's going to take you two days to get that muck off and I don't want to walk up Hoober frightening kids all along way.' Gilbert ducked and ran out of the door laughing again, as Margaret picked up a plate and raised it above her head.

Saturday morning woke with a weak, sickly sun battling thin clouds, but no rain. Gilbert was up early, in the allotment feeding the hens and watering his plants. Jobs done; he went back inside to find his mother packing ham sandwiches.

'Now, Gilbert, you be careful.'

'Ma, I'm only going for a walk!'

'Yes, but you know what I mean – you be careful!'

'Oh Ma. It's a walk is all. I'll see you later.' Grabbing the sandwiches Gilbert ducked out of the door before she could see him colouring up.

Margaret washed the pots after feeding Brenda and Doris and started putting her shoes on.

'Now Margaret, you be careful.'

'But Mam, I'm only going for a walk!'

'Aye, but you know what I means – you'd best be careful!'

'Oh Mam, it's only a walk is all! I'll see you later,' exclaimed Margaret, rescued by Gilbert knocking on the door, she ran out before Susannah could see her blushing.

As the couple walked out of the Yard, Susannah stood on the top step and watched them go, when she turned to go inside, she looked up the Yard. There, four doors further on, Sarah Law stood on her doorstep, also watching the same scene. Both women nodded to each other before moving inside.

It was only two miles to Hoober Stand but Margaret was astounded at the changes in scenery. The red-brick terraces of Packman Road ended at the Cottage of Content and green fields opened up before them. They turned off Rotherham Road opposite Mill Lane where a small row of workers' stone-fronted terraces hid the mill house behind them. Then they started climbing up America Lane to Hoober Field Lane – Gilbert talking all the while. He showed her the stand of elderberries at the bottom of the lane explaining how he picked them and his mother made jam, or even better, an elderberry crumble.

The lane was only twelve feet wide and the hawthorn bushes at the side were tall enough to arc over, forming a tunnel. The scent of hawthorn and honey suckle mixed with the smell of grass and nettles and the whole world seemed green. Margaret's senses were reeling at smells so strong and so different to the soot and sea salt of Newcastle.

At the top of the hill Gilbert turned off the road, through a gate and followed a path through the trees. They rounded a corner and Hoober Stand emerged in front of them. It was a stone-built, triangular tower stretching up into the sky. The masonry work was so good there was hardly any mortar in between the stones, which were stained black after two hundred years of coal smoke from the surrounding villages. Leaning backwards Margaret looked up; the stone tower seemed to go on for ever; at first the walls were sheer, then they began shrinking, layer by layer as the tower got higher. The effect left Margaret feeling that the tower was falling over.

'Come on,' said Gilbert. 'Let's go for a look,' He opened a huge, green wooden door at the top of three steps.

'But, don't we need to ask?' queried Margaret

'No, this is about the only thing the Earl doesn't lock up. He knows people go up, I think he likes them to see how much he owns. Besides, there's a hundred and fifty steps, which puts most people off, so I hope you're feeling fit,' replied Gilbert, disappearing into the gloom.

Margaret followed him. Inside, a spiral staircase followed the wall around and up into the tower. The inside of the tower was circular in contrast to the triangular outside. While the stone was the same, it was unstained and the warm textured sandstone of Yorkshire felt friendly compared to the black almost brooding exterior. Inside or outside the skill required to cut the stone to such exacting shapes and sizes was obvious even to Margaret as she climbed the stairs.

After two circuits of the tower a window offered some weak light, another circuit brought another window with the same dust-encrusted glass – reducing the pale light, before another three circuits, each with a dingy window, brought them to the top. Gilbert pushed a small door open and light flooded in. He stepped out offering his hand to Margaret. She took it following him out of the door. The view took her breath away. They were above the tree tops, looking down onto the leaves and branches some thirty feet below. As the tower was on the top of a hill, when Margaret lifted her eyes, the view was of a world she could not have imagined.

The horizon was twenty or more miles away and in between were fields and woods with occasional villages and odd plumes of smoke showing where farm houses were. Margaret let go of Gilberts hand and grasped the sturdy metal hand rail running around the edge of the platform. She faced into the breeze and let the wind blow her mind clear; her hair lifting in the gusts. The smell was pure and clean, despite the various clumps of smog in the distance.

'There's Rotherham over there and just behind it is Sheffield,' said Gilbert pointing to a grey smudge in the distance; turning slightly to his left he pointed again; 'you can't see anything other than smoke, but Manvers is over that hill with Wath alongside it. If you keep moving to your left you can see the Yard and your house, at the side of Hallets' chimney.'

Margaret followed him round and, sure enough, there in the near distance was Hallets and Packman Road, the terraces looking like dolls houses on the side of a small hill. Not far away she could see a colliery which she guessed must be Cortonwood, where she knew Gilbert worked, then more fields. The fields, woods and roads were all neatly bordered by stone walls.

This land was one of contrasts: first, the warm, stone-fronted buildings contrasting with the red-brick terraces of Firth Road and Packman Road, the puthering smoke of the factories and houses contrasting with the green fields and woods which surrounded them. From the top of the tower it felt as if, with the exception of Packman, all the buildings and smoke generators were hidden from view, which only seemed to highlight the importance of Packman in her mind.

'Come on,' said Gilbert leading her around the tower. Now she could see that the dome on top of the tower was in fact the top of the stairwell and the stones making the dome were as well-crafted as the interior. The dome was also in the middle of the tower, a lightning conductor at the top seeming to mark the exact centre as they moved around it. It was the triangular exterior which led to the optical illusion that the dome was off centre.

When they approached the last point on the triangle, Gilbert pointed again. 'That's Wentworth Woodhouse where the Earl lives, them's his deer running about in front of it.'

76

Margaret had seen imposing buildings in Newcastle, the large ostentatious Co-op Headquarters had been across from their rooms in Blandford Street, but this was on a different scale. The front of the house was well over one hundred yards long, while two sets of returned stairs led from the drive up to a three-story entrance framed with columns, all built in sandstone. In front of this a herd of deer roamed free in a huge park, with not a person in sight. She looked back over her shoulder at Packman and the contrast, once again, could not have been more stark.

It took a further two tours around the top of the tower before Margaret was prepared to leave. As they descended into the tower the interior was darker but, somehow, friendlier, as though she was in some way more connected to it. They emerged into the light under the trees and started walking through the field.

'There's a cave under them trees where people used to sleep in old days but it's falling in now and there's an old abandoned mine shaft that's flooded alongside, so it's dangerous – which is why it's a great place to hide from gamekeepers.' Gilbert informed her.

'Why would you want to hide from them?'

Gilbert looked at her in astonishment ''Cos you've got a rabbit or something under your coat and don't want to see local Magistrate, that's why!'

'Oh. I see. I've never eaten rabbit.'

Again, Gilbert looked at her in amazement. 'Never ate rabbit? You don't know what you've been missing.'

They walked through the trees onto the lane and started on the way back. Margaret looked at the moon pennies flowering in the fields and enjoyed the novelty of picking buttercups and daisies, while Gilbert smiled at her side. Together they decided to picnic at a spot under some trees, looking over a field with cows and thistles plus a view towards Wentworth. Under the weak cloud veiled sun they sat and ate their sandwiches.

'This is lovely.' said Margaret picking a moon penny and examining the white petals surrounding the golden centre.

'You're not wrong. Can I ask you a personal question?

'Try me.'

'Have you ever been kissed?

'Why, Gilbert Law! What kinda question is that to ask a lady?'

77

Gilbert blushed strawberry red and stuttered 'I just, err just...'

'Well, it's lucky for you, I'm no lady. Course I been kissed, when I was eleven me and Jonny Halford tried it to see what it was like. Didn't reckon much to it if I'm honest.'

'Want to try again?'

'Me mam told me to be careful.'

'So, did mine.'

'Well, we'd better be careful then.' She said clamping her hands behind his head and pulling his face to hers.

Three for a Girl

Saturday 28 August 1937

The weather held fair for several days and, after a downpour the following Friday, another glorious Saturday brought everybody outside. Gilbert and Margaret sat on the low wall talking to Eva while the other kids played in the fields or sat sullenly in the Yard. Jack kicked a stone dejectedly, picked it up and threw it at the clothes post, missing by a mile. Gilbert watched him and realised he was yet to start school and did not really know any of the other kids.

'Eva, you still got that old rubber tennis ball we found up Firth Road?'

'Yeah why?'

'Fancy a game of sticks?'

'Are you gonna play?'

'Yeah, reckon so.'

'Great. Hey, sticks everyone!' she shouted running indoors to fetch the ball.

'Come on Jack we're gonna have a game of sticks.' shouted Gilbert.

'Can I play?' yelled both the Bennett brothers at the same time

'What's sticks?' asked Jack

'Come on, I'll show you,' replied Gilbert as Molly Matlock shouted: 'Me too!'

Gilbert pulled three clothes pegs off the line and led everyone out of the Yard onto the road. He walked down to their house and placed the sticks under the window, two leaning against the wall with one across the top forming a small goal-like frame.

'Right then, Jack, there will be two teams, one running and one chasing. The runners all have to stand at the end of the wall, while one of them comes to the edge of the pavement and throws the ball at the sticks, trying to knock them down. He gets three chances and if he misses all three, he's out. So, the next runner tries. The chasers stand wherever they want but if the ball bounces up and the chasers catch it that runner is out and the next runner tries until all the team are out. If a runner knocks the sticks down then all the team are in play and then, like tiggy, the chasers have to 'tig' the other team but with the ball. Ok? It must be with the ball. If tigged you have to go stand against the wall again. The aim is for the runners to build the sticks back into a frame while the chasers have to tig them all before they do. Whoever wins gets a point and it's the first to three. Ok? Only one other thing if the chasers catch the ball on the throw when the sticks are knocked down then the whole team of runners is out and the chasers get a point. Got it?'

Jack looked at him opened mouthed '…err no.. is it like cricket and tiggy altogether without a bat?'

'Something like, but you'll get the hang on it. Let's just play and see how you get on. Right, we need two teams. I'll be captain of one, you can be captain of other. Being as you don't know how to play, I'll let you have first pick. Who do you want in your team?'

Jack looked at the assembled children and pointed to the eldest Bennett brother.

'Right, you've got Tom. I'll have Eva.'

Jack smiled and picked the other Bennett brother.

'Ok, so you've got Tom and Dan. I'll have Molly.'

At this point Fred Robertson came running up. 'Can I play?'

'Yeah, you're in Jack's team an all. Come on then, let's get started. You can be runners first Jack; Eva you field bottom side, I'll take top. Molly you cover the sticks, who's you're first chucker then, Jack?'

'Go on you start us, Tom.'

The young lad walked out into the road, standing close to the pavement, he checked where Gilbert and Eva were then threw the ball hard at the sticks. On the third attempt he broke them and pandemonium erupted as Eva flew after the ball, picking it up while running and throwing it back to Molly on the turn. The runners fled away from the sticks where they had all collected to try to rebuild them. Gilbert smiled. He knew as soon as Eva was in his team they would win. The girl was lightning quick, with a bullet arm.

Margaret sat and watched from her front door step. All she saw was a blur of motion with kids and Gilbert racing up and down the road, catching the ball and throwing at others, trying to hit them while Molly stood guard at the sticks. As the game progressed more and more children came and joined in until there was a small army of them running around with Gilbert in the middle of a maelstrom. Jack picked up the rules during the first game and for him it became an all-out battle. After half an hour Gilbert's team won, three-one. An exhausted Gilbert collapsed on the door step alongside Margaret, sweat showing through his vest and running off his nose.

'We're going to get a drink and then have a walk to Abdy stream. Want to come Jack?' asked Tom.

'Yeah!' said Jack enthusiastically and the four boys set off, Fred's arm around Jack's shoulders and all of them talking at one hundred miles an hour.

Margaret smiled. 'Thanks Gilbert, it looks like our Jack's made some friends at last.'

'Aye, but I might not last the day, I'm too old for that game – I'm absolutely buggered.'

'But Eva did most of the work for your team!'

'I know, but them young legs don't go down pit and I'm knackered. Fancy a beer at the Cottage?'

'I'm not old enough and you know it.'

'I know, but they don't bother about a few months here or there at the Cottage. Come on, have a shandy then. I don't normally offer twice, but I've gotta have a drink.'

'All right then, a shandy, but only one.'

June 1938

Autumn turned to winter, then to spring and, despite the threat of war with Germany, as summer started the rhythm of the Yard did not change – it was the same whatever the season, maintaining its slow, grinding pace. Barney started work down the pit as an electrician at Wath Main rather than Cortonwood, Margaret continued at Hallets, no longer on kiln cleaning but supervising the loading and the hauliers who took the bricks away, checking their paperwork was correct. Susannah's hand healed and she gave birth to a baby boy much to the delight of Barney who named him Joseph. Jack and Brenda started at Brampton Ellis School, while Gilbert and Margaret became inseparable companions.

Gilbert gave up his allotment and rented half a field from Cadman's where he built a larger hen run and a sty. He bought a piglet and started to fatten it up and dug a large vegetable patch in the remainder of the field. At the side of the hen run he built a shed and, after weeding and feeding, he and Margaret would spend hours talking, sitting on two old chairs in front of a decrepit pot stove with Cortonwood Colliery mysteriously carved into its side.

After one such lazy Sunday morning at the field with Margaret, Gilbert went home for dinner. Margaret went home to help her mother, happy they had arranged to meet later. Gilbert sauntered across the Yard, kicking his boots off on the top step he walked through the door licking his lips at the smell of food cooking. He stopped after only one stride when he noticed a man in his armchair.

'Oh, Gilbert, this is Enoch,' said his mother. 'He's gonna live with us from now on.'

Gilbert stood stock still, uncertain how to react. He was accustomed to being the man of the house and involved in, if not making, all the decisions. It was unlike his mother to spring anything on him, especially something this important. He was aware his mother spent a considerable amount of time at the Plough Inn and knew she was friendly with a man called Enoch, but this was a bombshell. Gilbert never went to the Plough Inn so, to him, Enoch was a stranger who knew his mother.

A tense meal was made even more uncomfortable when Enoch took Gilbert's place at the table and his mother did not ask him to move. Gilbert was relegated to his old chair. The conversation was desultory at best, then non-existent when it became clear that Enoch would be sharing his mother's bedroom. As soon as he was finished Gilbert put his boots back on and returned to the field, his mind in turmoil.

He was still in a sullen silent mood when Margaret arrived and even her appearance did not cheer him up. He explained his predicament but Margaret showed little sympathy.

'When mi Da died I was desperate for Mam to find another fella. I even accepted Barney. I was so scared for her.'

'Yeah, but you was facing the workhouse – I've been providing for Ma for the past seven years since Dad died, I feel put out of place.'

'Well, I think you're gonna have to live with it.'

The day stretched on and Gilbert occupied himself at the field long after Margaret left. He arrived back home late and went straight to bed. Enoch was away early in the morning and Gilbert rose late as he was on 'afters'. He sat outside on the step as usual, smoking his first cigarette of the morning, watching the kids get up for school and the general comings and goings in the Yard. He was almost in a trance when he realised he was watching Dyson's Carters clearing out the end terrace. Mrs Moore, the old lady of the Yard, had died the previous week and Davies was no doubt getting ready for new tenants. Gilbert stopped and stared, an idea forming in his head. He jumped up and started the walk down to Wath.

By the time he arrived at Davies Estate Agents the idea was solid. He marched in and knocked on the glass panel. Davies himself slid it open.

'Morning, Mr Davies, I was wondering if you've got any tenants yet for No 15 Top Yard, Packman? If not, I'd like to rent it from you,' he said, blurting the words out, unsure of the etiquette.

'Ah, and you would be?

'I'm Gilbert Law, Mr Davies. I live at No 7 with me Ma, Sarah Law, it's been me paying rent since me Dad died.'

'Really. And where do you work?

'I'm a hewer down Cortonwood, Mr Davies. I've worked there for past eight years now. Not taken a day off except when I got knocked down by one of ponies.'

'Right… and could anyone vouch for you, Gilbert?'

'Well I'm sure me Grandad would – Alfred Law – he's foreman at Hallets brickyard.'

'Ah right, yes I know Alfred, he rents 38 Firth Road if I remember. Has done for years and has never missed a payment. Right, Gilbert, if you can get your Grandad to come in and vouch for you, you can rent No 15 for twelve shillings a week, with a month's deposit and a week in advance – so you'll need three pounds. Can you manage that?'

'Yeah. Can I just nip to post office?'

'Of course. I'll get the paperwork ready in the meantime.'

Davies was astounded. Top Yard Packman was probably the worst of the terraces he rented but time after time tenants moved around the Yard or left and came back. Though there was a higher than average turnover, it was rare for any house to be left unoccupied for long, he just couldn't understand it. By the time Gilbert returned with the money Davies was prepared, with all the paperwork ready. With the forfeited deposit from Mrs Moore he would have double rent for the house for two full weeks. It already seemed a celebratory drink was due.

'Right Gilbert, if Alfred comes in and vouches for you, the house will be yours from Friday and you can collect the keys from here. But if that doesn't happen, then you can come in on Friday and your money will be returned. Does this seem fair?'

'It does Mr Davies. I'll see you Friday.'

Gilbert rushed home, picked up his snap tin and raced to get to the pit on time. There was no time to see his grandad – he was five minutes late as it was. He volunteered for overtime and luckily someone failed to turn up for the night shift, so he ended up doing a double shift. Absolutely exhausted, at dawn, he stumbled out of the pit yard, walked to Hallets and caught his grandad in their yard. When Gilbert explained the situation, Alfred readily agreed to vouch for him and said he would go to see Bill Davies straight after work. Gilbert staggered home and went straight to bed. He woke just in time to get to the pit for his next shift fighting sleep all the way through the afternoon.

When he got home dinner was ready and Gilbert bolted down his first real meal in two days. As Enoch was at the pub, he took the opportunity to tell his mother he was moving out and he assumed Enoch would now be paying the rent. To his surprise she didn't seem perturbed or upset. *Huh! Can't mean much to her now Enoch is here.*

The next morning Gilbert awoke bright and refreshed. He got up early and took a cup of tea to the back step where he opened a packet of cigarettes. Before he could light one Margaret stepped outside, shaking the crumbs off a table cloth. Gilbert stood up and walked across to her.

'You got a minute, Margaret?

'Yeah, just let me take this back.'

Gilbert walked across to the low wall and sat on it, toying with the idea of a cigarette before thinking the better of it. Margaret joined him.

'Well, you look in a better mood than when I last saw you. Is it working with Enoch?'

'Don't know. I've been working double shifts so I haven't seen much of him.'

Gilbert looked across at the brickyard and the chimney, turned slightly and looked over to Hoober Stand. He let out a big sigh, straightened his back and finally turned to Margaret.

'Margaret, if I can get us a house to rent, will you marry me?'

Margaret reeled.

Although this was completely unexpected, secretly it was all she dreamt about. There was no need for a house, as far as she was concerned, she would have married Gilbert if it meant sleeping in an open field. But, even so, she was not going to make it too easy for him.

'Well Gilbert, you've got a problem. I promised myself I would only ever marry a man if he got down on bended knee and proposed to me, proper like.'

Without a moment's hesitation, in full view of all the whole Yard, Gilbert dropped to one knee and grasping Margaret's hand said:

'Margaret Beadling, will you marry me?

''Course I will you silly sod. Now get up afore you embarrass both of us in front of everybody!'

They sat on the wall until it was nearly time for Margaret to go to work, while Gilbert explained his journey to Bill Davies and how he should have the keys to No 15 on Friday.

'We'll need permission from mi mam,' said Margaret. 'I'm too young to marry without her say-so and you ought to ask permission from your ma.'

'Ok, shall we go in and ask your ma now?'

'I think we'd better, as half the Yard already knows you've proposed to me; let's be the ones to tell her, at least.'

Susannah was delighted, as much with the news Margaret would be staying in the Yard and close by as with the news they wanted to marry. But she was insistent they marry before moving in together. Neither Gilbert nor Margaret were prepared to make a scene so they both agreed instantly. Margaret went off to work with a spring in her step and a promise they would meet when Gilbert got out of the pit later.

Gilbert went to break the news to his mother.

'Gilbert nowt has been more obvious than you and Margaret were in love and going to get married at some point. Why do you think I let Enoch in? He's been asking for months but I always said no until I decided you'd be flying the nest soon. I hope you're both right happy, but there's always a home here if you're not.'

'Thanks Ma, I've got to go to the field and catch up, I'm miles behind. I'll see you later after I get out o' pit.' Sarah held him in a tight embrace before Gilbert bounded out of the house with more energy than he had felt for a long time.

July 1938

The rain came in waves, the windows rattled, the Yard flooded. But nothing could spoil Gilbert's mood – today he was to marry Margaret Beadling and he could think of nothing else he wanted more in the world. He was so happy he almost floated. But still it poured. Though there was a break in the clouds to be seen looking towards Elsecar and Hoober. Gilbert put his jacket on, raced across the mud, jumping puddles, keeping his head tucked into his shoulders. He ran to the door of No 15, thrust his key into the lock – a quick turn and he was in.

For the past four weeks he and Margaret had spent all their spare time cleaning or polishing and generally making good. With the exception of the bedroom they gradually filled the house with cast-offs and bargains until everything they needed to live there was in place. It would be basic at first, but over time they would build upon the basics.

There was a powerful smell in the kitchen – the table and chairs given to them by his brother Jack, which Gilbert had so painstakingly repaired in the shed at the field, were stinking the place out. He had completed the re assembly yesterday and after bringing them from the shed, finished them with two coats of varnish. The varnish was so overpowering his eyes watered. Thinking quickly, he opened the kitchen window and leaning outside the door, grabbed a brick from the quarry wall and used it to jam the window open. It would have to do, hopefully the air would move around and reduce the smell before they got back.

Quickly he checked the rest of the house. All was fine, the new bed in the back bedroom was made and his clothes stacked neatly inside the new wardrobe. The bedroom was their pride and joy. Last week they bought a completely new bedroom set from Cantors in Wath. There was a dresser, a wardrobe, a double bed plus curtains, sheets, blankets and a clock. The walls were freshly papered and the woodwork newly painted. It was a joy to come into the room, but there was a price – the deposit had taken all Gilberts savings and they were committed to pay five shillings a week for the next four years. This meant that well over half of his wages were taken up in rent and hire purchase repayments. But even so, as he stood in the doorway Gilbert's chest swelled with pride – he would be bringing his bride home to the very best.

The rest of the house they had filled as best as they could. The front bedroom was completely empty and the windows covered in newspaper held in place with flour and water glue. There was no need for curtains – the terrace was a dead end and theirs was the last house in the row. As it ended at the quarry wall which formed the boundary to the pond, no one would ever be walking past.

Walking down the stairs, Gilbert opened the door to the front room, which like the front bedroom was empty and also had newspaper on the windows. The front door was ill fitting and Gilbert noticed water coming in from the rain. Cursing he opened the door. The down spout was leaking and the rain water was running down the wall onto the door and some of it coming into the house. Looking at it, Gilbert thought hard and took a hammer and screw driver from his tool bag. Taking his jacket off he braved the rain and a few minutes later had removed the bottom section of down spout. He turned it upside down and by using the ninety degree bend, which had been at the bottom, as a joint he was able to reconnect it onto the top of the wall redirecting the water into the quarry. No one would notice the water flowing into the pond but more importantly, it was not coming through his door any more.

Back in the kitchen the smell was reducing nicely, the table and chairs looked good alongside the two armchairs they bought in the auction. While Gilbert had been busy repairing the table and chairs, Margaret spent hours black leading the fireplaces and polishing the brass fenders in both downstairs rooms. The hob was so clean it sparkled. Gilbert smiled. In two hours time he would be returning a married man. The thought delighted him.

He took a last look around and ran back to the house he now considered his mothers. When he piled in Sarah looked at him.

'Well lad, not long now. Are you going to get ready or are you going to get married in your scruffs?'

'I'll just give me shoes a last polish, then get ready.'

'Gilbert, if you polishes them shoes any more they'll take you to court for cruelty. Get yourself ready.'

Deciding his mother was right Gilbert dressed, for only the second time, in the suit, shirt and tie he had bought for his father's funeral and sat fidgeting at the table. It was painful, every second seemed like an hour but thankfully the rain finally stopped and the sun broke through. At the last moment Shudder barged in.

'Right, Gilbert, I'm 'ere and I've got ring, so you can stop worrying.'

'Bloody hell, Shudder, it were a daft day when I picked you to be me best man.'

'Wrong there, Gilbert, I am the better man. Margaret made a right mistake picking you instead o' me.'

Gilbert shook his head, both born on Firth Road, he and Shudder Madeley were lifelong friends, yet Gilbert could not remember a time when he managed the last word. Shudder had an answer for everything. After a final comb of his hair and an unnecessary brush of his spotless jacket, Gilbert, Sarah, Enoch, and Shudder walked up to Brampton Church leaving the Yard on the top side as agreed. This meant they would not walk past the room where Margaret was getting ready. His grandad, grandma, and his brother Jack with his wife Ivy met them outside the church gates and together they walked inside.

Gilbert fidgeted at the altar, his belly doing flip flops, the priest kept talking to him but he was not listening. Then Susannah, Brenda, Doris and Eva walked in and took their positions on the right-hand side of the aisle. Barney did not approve of the marriage, which he made clear several times, so he was absent on principle. When the wedding march played, Gilbert turned and watched young Jack lead his sister down the aisle.

He could hardly believe his eyes – all his dreams were coming true – Margaret looked radiant. She wore a cream coloured skirt topped with a cream jacket that fastened to the side with one large button. The colour emphasised her hair which gleamed its ginger hue and was freshly cropped in the latest bob style with a small bun behind her right ear. In her hands she carried a bouquet of flowers in which the moon penny was prominent to remind them of their first kiss. Gilbert smiled as he listened to Shudder mutter: 'You jammy sod, Lawman, if only she'd seen me first!'

The service was exactly what Gilbert wanted, quick and efficient but happy and relaxed. Margaret smiled and laughed the whole time, a look of complete contentment on her face. Afterwards everyone returned to Susannah's where they ate sandwiches and drank tea while Shudder and

Jack competed to entertain them with stories of Gilbert's youth, before they both left to go to work.

After an hour, Gilbert and Margaret said their goodbyes. Laughing and smiling they stopped at the door to their new home, both giggling like children. He picked her up to carry her over the threshold, kicking the door open, he readied himself, as the remnants of the varnish fumes swept past them. Stepping through the door, he jumped in alarm and surprise when a panicking cat flew past them. Staggering to the side, desperately struggling for balance he almost dropped Margaret as there was a huge clatter and crash outside the front door.

'Bugger me! That were an entrance and a half,' he exclaimed before carefully placing Margaret on the kitchen floor. Concerned he went to the front door to see what the commotion was and outside; their first load of coal was piled up underneath the window. He returned to the kitchen to find Margaret holding her hands to her mouth. Under the table were three kittens, Mrs Moore's old cat had returned home through the open kitchen window and given birth.

All his dreams of how this moment should happen were shattered, the sparkle in Margaret's eye was gone and the smile on her lips was now a fixed grimace. Still, at least they were married and home. Unsure of how to react he took the practical route: 'I'd best get coal in before it starts to rain again.' He tried to sound chirpy, walking upstairs to change into his pit clothes. Without comment Margaret started to boil water to clean up.

Back in the kitchen, while Gilbert pulled on his boots, still trying to think of some way to make light of the situation, the cat returned, jumped off the wall and stood meowing at the pair of them from the open doorway. Gilbert watched in awe. Margaret did not hesitate – in a flurry of furious motion, she grabbed the pan of hot water and threw it over the cat, which screeched and leapt back over the wall, into the quarry. In the vacuum which followed both of them stopped, motionless, unsure of what to do next.

'Well, she won't be back again!' offered Gilbert into the silence.

'Sorry Gilbert, I'm really sorry, but I can't stand cats. I'm allergic to them. After half an hour near one I can't breathe and come out in a rash.'

He finished tying his laces before pointing at the kittens and said. 'In that case we'd best get rid of these.'

Margaret looked on mute. From the top of the cellar he picked up an empty potato sack, took the brick from the window and placed it in the bottom. Then, with neither of them making eye contact, one by one he dropped the kittens into the sack, tied it, walked to the front door and gently lobbed the sack over the wall into the quarry. The sack landed at the side of the quarry, on the new water chute created by the over flow from the drain pipe, and slid down into the pond. They watched the sack sinking into the filthy water, disappearing within seconds.

'Thanks Gilbert. I should've said something. I'm so sorry.'

'That's ok, you can't help it. So, let's forget it and get cracking.'

He pondered a second or two before adding.

'Margaret, I need to make one thing clear; you've no idea how happy I am, and nothing – rain, varnish, coal, or cats – nothing is going to spoil the happiest day of my life. Nothing. So come on, I'll get coal in while you clear that mess up under table, then please let's start again.'

He smiled as the grin returned to Margaret's face, the sparkle back in her eye. She walked to the bottom of the stairs and just before she started up them, she turned and said.

'Well, I'd better get out of this dress then. Are you sure you want to get the coal in straight away?'

August 1939

It was the longest walk. Each and every step felt painful, his legs were heavy and his arms ached, but his mind held the worst pain of all. Gilbert left the colliery and trudged up Manor Road towards Packman, his thoughts bouncing between the events behind him to the ordeal he faced ahead.

All collieries were steeped in tragedy and every miner knew the risks he took each working day, but when events conspired and you were involved, it became all too real. What began as a normal shift finished in nightmare.

Gilbert had been clearing the ground ready for it to be timbered, his shovel going as fast as he could make it, pulling the lumps of coal and rock free, creating a solid base. The team behind him were working at a feverish pace to keep up with him, while another team readied the timbers. With the ground clear he rolled out of the way and the others moved in, pushing the timbers into place to support the roof. The first hadn't fitted, so they swapped them and placed wedges on top. Joe Brown pushed the last wedge in and gave it a huge belt with his hammer. The wedge slipped and fell out as he hit it and the whole thing fell forward. As Joe moved to reset it, the ground groaned.

There was a creaking noise, like two branches on a tree rubbing against each other in a high wind before they cracked, snapped and fell. With a sound similar to a lorry dropping a load of stones, the roof collapsed, cutting out the light, throwing stones and dust into the air, knocking the men back, taking the air from their lungs, forcing dust and grit into their mouths and noses. Instinctively, all of them closed their eyes and put their arms across their faces. The cloud passed through them like the back draught from a cannon. The larger cobbles and stones hitting them to raise cuts and bruises.

When the roar diminished, to the sound of a few stones rolling down the pile in front of them, the men opened their eyes to see the roadway blocked with no sign of Joe. Although their vision was blurred by a curtain of grime, there was only one conclusion – Joe was trapped and buried beneath the pile of rubble in front of them.

The men threw themselves at the avalanche in a fury. The sound of Joe moaning drove them on through the clouds of black dust which billowed around the fresh fall, making it impossible to see more than a few inches. No one stopped, no one shirked – they all knew it could have been any one of them, if it had been, there was no question that the other men would be working just as hard to free them. Down the mine you lived and died as a team.

Tiny Davidson shouted: 'I've got a gap!' Men pushed wooden timbers to him and he shoved them through, packing them on top of each other to give as much support as possible. Then, slowly, with infinite care, he eased himself into the gap, until only his feet were showing. 'Pull me back lads,' he called. Hands grabbed his feet and dragged him back into the roadway.

'He's gone.'

The men stopped and sat down – there was no need to rush now. They took out their water bottles, slaked their thirst, sitting on their haunches in the gloom, with dust billowing in the silence.

After a while the deputy, Colin Scattergood, took charge: 'Right, lads, there's no need to hurry any more, let's not make it worse by getting anybody else hurt, but let's get Joe out before we finish.'

The rest of the shift passed in a dreamlike state. Slowly the men removed the pile of coal and, carefully packing timbers above them before they made any move, inched their way forward. Sledgehammers and picks were needed to break the largest lumps into pieces small enough to move. Until finally, as they neared exhaustion, they pulled Joe's body clear. Gilbert took hold of Joe's shoulders, then knelt and half-crawled to the roadway where they loaded him onto a stretcher and covered him with a blanket. The whole team took turns carrying the stretcher to the pit bottom. Along the way other miners stopped what they were doing and took their caps or helmets off, standing in silence as the team passed. As they exited the cage at the pit top Gilbert grabbed the deputy: 'Colin, Joe's got a young lass, she lives by us; let me have a word with Margaret and I'll go round to let her know what's happened.'

'Thanks, Gilbert, I'll let Manager know.'

Now Gilbert was facing one of the most difficult conversations of his life and he still didn't know what to say. He walked home, slowly opening the door. Margaret was sitting in the armchair feeding young Alfred. He was only two months old and seemed to need feeding every other hour. Margaret looked up at him.

'What's wrong, Gilbert? What's happened?'

Gilbert explained, his words tripping over themselves as he tried to control his feelings, but the efforts of the last few hours and the tension in his body took their toll. Margaret listened aghast.

'Oh, my God, no! Oh no. Poor Joe. What about Eva? She's gonna be devastated and she'll be all on her own. Does she know?'

Gilbert looked at his wife and shook his head. 'I'll tell her. I wouldn't let anybody else do it – it needs to be somebody she knows.'

'You're not doing it on your own. I'm going in with you. We'll drop Alfred off at your mother's and then we'll go.'

Eva seemed to know that something was wrong the instant they walked in. 'Dad?' Gilbert nodded. 'Dead?' He nodded again. She collapsed in a heap on the floor bursting into uncontrollable sobs. Margaret picked her up and cuddled her in her dad's armchair, while Gilbert stood in the middle of the room, wringing his cap in his hands.

'Christ, Gilbert! You've certainly got a way with words. Do something useful and put the kettle on. Jesus, Gilbert!'

They stayed with Eva for an hour as she insisted Gilbert tell her exactly what happened, again and again. Eventually Margaret said: 'We've got to get back and see to Alfred, but you're not staying here on your own. Come on, Eva, you're coming with us.' The three of them made a sorry procession across the Yard, Gilbert collecting Alfred from his mother's.

Gilbert left Margaret talking to Eva and walked across to the field. Inside the shed as he started to get the feed out for the chickens he looked down at his hands. He was stunned, his left hand and the cuff of his left sleeve were still covered in blood from where he picked Joe up to put him on the stretcher. He jumped up, pushed the door open and was violently sick. Ashen faced, he pulled his jacket off throwing it onto a pile of wood and straw, set ready to burn. He tossed a match into it and stood at the hose pipe, scrubbing his hand until it hurt, while the bonfire took hold. His mood still darker than he thought possible he kicked at the stack of logs ready to be made into sticks. With his shin bloodied and stinging he started to feel better but he promised himself that Eva would not leave them until she was ready.

His black mood partially mollified, he began to tidy up the mess. As he did so, an air-raid siren started its scream, winding up until it rattled his teeth. He stopped and stared. Further away another siren started, then another, then church bells started to ring. There was no doubt now – England was going to war. A day that he'd thought could get no worse somehow did.

Everybody would remember the day Joe Brown died was the day England went to war with Germany.

June 1940

At first the only sign of the war in Top Yard was an increased demand for coal. Any coal produced was moved the instant it left the coal face. The sidings emptied immediately. While the steel works had been taking more and more coal in the build-up to the war, their appetites were now ravenous.

Posters appeared advising civilians on what to do during an air-raid, recruiting halls opened and troop trains passed through Wath Station with increasing regularity. During the Great War miners had volunteered for service in such numbers that coal production had fallen to worrying levels. This time the Government was prepared and declared miners exempt from duty. They were too valuable to the war effort.

In what became a ritual everyone in the Yard gathered around a wireless at news time, discussing the latest developments with increasing scepticism as Poland fell and Hitler turned his attention to France and the Low Countries. Then came the news from Belgium. The Allies faced disaster. Nearly half a million men trapped between Hitler's blitzkrieg and the coast.

It felt as if an unstoppable poisonous cloud was rolling across the continent, devouring everything in its path, destined for Britain. Rationing, tighter than at any previous time sapped the strength of Top Yard, while 'Winnie's' upbeat messages on the wireless fell on deaf ears.

When the efforts of ordinary people, of part-time sailors, fishermen and amateurs in small boats resulted in the rescue of four hundred thousand men from the jaws of the German juggernaut, the Yard cheered. It was a defeat but not the disaster it could have been; then realisation sank in: all that stood between Hitler and the shores of England was a few miles of ocean. Invasion was inevitable.

The wireless rang out its messages with increasing pride and truculence as a small band of pilots fought a war in the sky to deny Hitler the air supremacy he needed. But, at night, the skies were open and bombers had free rein to penetrate deep into England to remind the population it was only a matter of time. Hitler was on his way.

Gilbert first cleared a space in the cellar to act as an air-raid shelter but after stories of houses collapsing and the occupants being trapped in cellars, he built a shelter on his allotment. He dug out a pit and, knocking

98

down his shed, used the timbers to build a frame which he covered with corrugated steel and sand bags. Finally, he covered the whole lot with turf but soon found he needed to dig a soakaway as water filled the bottom.

Neighbours came out to help him and he expanded it so that it could take several families. He put his old stove inside and built benches that could be used to sit or sleep on. With a few rag rugs, when the stove was on, it became almost cosy and the rest of the Yard started to copy his idea. They got permission to dig in Cadman's field and within no time there were three shelters which, between them, could take all the occupants of the Yard. Packman Road was as ready as it could be for the oncoming onslaught.

Margaret busied herself with household chores and the never ending stress of feeding four mouths on war-time rations. Hedgerows were plundered, not only for berries and mushrooms but also feed for the hens whose eggs were now vital.

Imaginative use of the vegetables from Gilbert's allotment varied the diet, while peeling potatoes became an art where only the very thinnest of skins were removed.

Joe Browns funeral was well attended by everyone from the Yard and the pit as he was well-respected. It turned out that, apart from Eva, he only had one other relative left alive, his mother's sister. Eva had never seen her great-aunt who lived in Cornwall, but they started writing to each other and it helped to ease the pain of her father's death to share it with another family member. There were even offers for Eva to go visit or stay with her.

Eva worked part-time at Brampton Ellis School, helping with the nursery children several mornings a week. It was the job she wanted but the war meant she could not attend the night classes needed to gain her qualifications. To supplement her income, she also took on part-time cleaning work. Doctor Moxon had lost his wife and was far too old to volunteer for service, so he did his bit by continuing to serve the district, despite his age. He needed some help at home however and Eva cleaned during the afternoons, then left him a meal ready for when he returned at night. The lack of opportunity to get on in life was eating away at Eva, she confided in Margaret that she was considering volunteering to help evacuees. Frustrating as life was for Eva, she was happy living with Margaret – her best friend and Gilbert the man she most respected.

There were hard times ahead and Eva knuckled down with the rest of the Yard doing the only thing the civil population could do: Wait.

Four for a Boy

Friday 18 October 1940

Stop – **paradise** – stop – **one** – stop – **pan** – stop – **one** – stop – **paradies** – stop.

Harry stared at the message. It was something he had never expected to see, but here it was. He traced the words with his fingers. Words scribbled down in haste as they came over the wireless in Morse. Working in Morse code was not his best skill but he was competent enough and he knew the message was correct. 'Paradise' in English followed by 'one' followed by 'paradise' in Russian followed by 'one' before a final 'paradise' in German. It was a call to meet – from his twin. Billy.

He stared at the words again, it was the coding system they agreed years before, he knew it by heart. The first 'one' meant the first Sunday after the message. The second 'one' meant come alone. Had it been three he was to bring their step-brothers. They had worked out six possible variations to the order of the word 'paradise' by rotating it in English, Russian and German. The order used in this message meant four. So, they were due to meet four days after the coming Sunday. Thursday the 24th of October.

The meeting place and time were already set – two hours before high tide at Man Haven Cove. Harry kept reading the message, his heart pumping. It had been three years since he last saw his twin – when they agreed this code.

He smiled as he remembered how they laughed when they decided upon 'paradise' for the call sign they would use to each other. Paradise. The place where they were born, a place he remembered fondly. Their father, Gottfried, was a German migrant, who, although being a well-qualified man, could only get work at the Paradise cement works and this only because he understood the Russian and German invoices – the factory imported and exported to both countries. He and his Russian wife fled Russia, where they had both been teachers, when he was arrested for sedition and sentenced to three years in exile. Germany had no longer been an option, his wife was permanently banned after being arrested while demonstrating for women's rights in her student days in Berlin. So along with his wife's mother they landed at Newcastle and ended up in Paradise – a tiny hamlet at the side of the Tyne. Together they rented a small cottage on Paradise Row, a run of terraced houses built for the cement factory workers, this was where the twins had been born.

Paradise.

Harry smiled again.

Owned by the Paradise Cement Company, Paradise contained a small industrial complex, falling to pieces and struggling to make ends meet; competing with newer and larger cement works that were vying to build the new industrial Britain. But the boys had grown up happy. There was always food on the table as their father supplemented his income by smuggling – his knowledge of languages giving him the edge over local smugglers. The twins, who learned Russian and German at home, were both respected and resented at school; they were tough and ruthless, you never took on one twin alone. They were one.

Then came the first event that shook their lives: in 1914 when they were ten years old Britain went to war with Germany. Their father was immediately arrested and interned on the Isle of Man. After all they had been through the trauma was too much for their mother, she died of a broken heart so the twins spent the war years living in the tiny run-down hamlet of Paradise with their grandmother. She never learned English, which meant she was almost entirely reliant upon them, they became feral. Because of their distinctive appearance, both were white-haired and blue-eyed with almost transparent skin they could not pick pockets like other youths – they simply stood out too much. As a result they became cunning. Knowing every inch of the docks including the back-alley nooks and crannies, learned from helping their father in his smuggling days, they became skilled thieves and were adept at selling the goods on. They gained a reputation and, despite their age, the community around the dockside came to both respect and fear the twins.

Then came the second shock. After the war ended their father returned home with a new wife and three more children. He met his second wife on the Isle of Man as she, a known German activist, had been one of the few women interned. Somehow, despite the restrictions, Gottfried had managed to father another set of twin boys with his second wife. Then, to balance things out, she had borne him a daughter. He continued the tradition of naming his children after the British royal family but this time, again following the lead of the House of Windsor, he anglicised his surname – from Schwarz to Black. With eight mouths to feed Gottfried set about his smuggling business in earnest. The Armstrong Vickers armaments factory was just down the road; the Russian revolution had been the start of a long-protracted power struggle and this was a prime opportunity for Gottfried. He excelled. The older twins joined him, soon, they too were experts. Paradise was the ideal place for gun-running, but after Lenin eventually took control of Russia they needed to refocus on more traditional merchandise.

So, Gottfried moved them all to the coast at South Shields. Marsden Cottage. Initially they rented it but their gun-running had been so successful they were soon able to buy the cottage and the adjacent, disused limestone quarry, Harton Down Hill. The only access to the cottage was through the quarry, via a tunnel beneath the Whitburn Colliery railway line. This provided them with complete privacy, only yards from the coast. They started to trade in all kinds of smuggled goods: brandy, laudanum, cigarettes, clocks, watches and occasionally, people, from a small cove known as Man Haven – literally fifty yards from their back door.

Harry remembered the day Billy came running to him, yelling in unbounded joy. He had discovered that the stone mined from the quarry was magnesium limestone from the Zechstein group of rocks and was impervious to radio waves at certain frequencies. This meant that transmissions from a niche half way up the cliff at Man Haven could only be received out at sea. Unwittingly the Blacks had stumbled across the perfect place to send undetected messages out to sea.

The third big change in their lives came in 1934, when Hitler came to power – and their father, along with his German wife, returned to Germany and Harry's twin Billy went with them. Harry decided to stay and continue with the family business; his step-brothers and step-sister also chose to remain.

The split from Billy had been hard, but Billy had become increasingly obsessed with wireless and radio transmissions and wanted to join the German research into blind landings at airports. So he volunteered to enrol in the radio navigation arm of the fledgling Luftwaffe.

His interest in radio started out for practical reasons – he first started listening to the coastguard, then Customs and Excise, to forewarn of dangers for their smuggling operation. This gave the Blacks a real advantage over the local competition. Billy went on to develop covert ship-to shore-transmissions from the niche at Man Haven. This cemented their position as the most successful smugglers in northern England.

They continued using the system Billy designed and built for several years, but after he left it was increasingly difficult to maintain. He had to return to repair and improve the system after a local man made a mess of it in 1937 – that was the last time Harry had seen him. Since then, Britain had once again gone to war with Germany and the smugglers used the radio sparingly. It seemed half the world was listening in to all sorts of transmissions and Harry was neither expert nor confident enough to trust the technology under war-time scrutiny. Yet, without fail, he listened every month, at the time and on the channels that he and Billy agreed. It was a habit he could not bring himself to break – his only remaining link with his twin. And now, after three years of silence, here was the signal. They were to meet.

Harry fretted as the days passed slowly. He knew of no reason why his twin would want to meet. The scale of the deception needed to get someone from the German Luftwaffe onto British soil, at the height of the war, was colossal. For Billy to suggest it was breath-taking, but if anyone could do it, he could! The question Harry returned to time after time but could not answer was, why? Growing up they had always thoroughly assessed the risk of any event they undertook. It was what initially set them apart from the competition. This approach grew with them as they moved from stealing apples to running guns. But landing on British soil, in war-time, this was risk amplified one hundredfold.

As the light started to fade on the designated Thursday, Harry dropped his step brothers off at the cottage in the quarry informing them he needed some time alone and did not want to be disturbed. Harry drove their lorry, a dilapidated Morris, into the tunnel beneath the colliery railway line, switched off the engine and removed the keys. He jacked the lorry up and removed a wheel which he hid fifty yards down the track. It was now impossible for any vehicle to pass through the quarry and under the railway. The only access to the cottage was on foot.

Back in the cottage he changed into black clothing. He took a torch and filled a lantern with one hour's worth of oil, placed them on the table and waited. Billy was either lucky or had chosen well. The night was as still as it was black. There was the tiniest of new moons hidden by banks of clouds. High tide was at 3 a.m., so the miners at Whitburn Colliery would either be deep underground or asleep ahead of the 5.30 shift change.

The small cove of Man Haven was accessible from the beach at low tide, but for two hours on either side of high tide the cove was only reachable by boat or via the cliff path from Marsden Cottage. It was perfect for smugglers. Larger vessels anchored off the coast and small boats would ferry illicit goods back and forth before the tide changed. The Blacks turned this into an art during their time at Marsden. Both twins knew every gully, every crevasse, every swilly at Man Haven.

At midnight Harry left the cottage. He walked to the edge of the cliff, his senses besieged by the salt and spray, darkness pressing in on him like a blanket of apprehension. Due to the blackout there was not a light behind him, no stars were on show and the moon was hiding behind a black cover of clouds. Slowly, Harry made his way down the narrow cliff path. It was sixty feet to the surf below, a slip would be fatal. Several times he was tempted to use the torch, but resisted.

Half way down, he found the niche. It was only a crevasse under an overhang of rock, but jutting out as it did, the overhang hid everything from above. Situated in the centre of the cove, the crevasse was also sheltered from prying eyes to the left or the right. Harry took out the sheets they kept hidden there and tied them to bolts fixed into the overhang. This turned the crevasse into a tiny shelter-come-radio room. He lit the lantern and stepped outside, checking the sheets. They hid the glare of the light, but Harry knew from experience that the slightest difference in the shade of black through the sheets would be visible out at sea.

Once his eyes adjusted from the glare of the lantern, he continued on down the path to the tiny beach. He could hear little but the surf rolling around the rocks and sliding through the shingle. Despite watching intently, the ghostly white wave crests at his feet were the only things Harry could see. He checked his watch and the luminous dial seemed like a beacon in the void. At five to one he lit a cigarette. Every twenty seconds or so he took a pull and when it was exhausted lit another from its stub. He knew that the act would seem innocent to any casual observer but to his twin approaching from the dark it was vital – to both lead him in and to let him know it was safe.

Eventually, there was a slight change in the sound of the waves rolling into the cove; then the hint of wood grinding against shingle. Harry peered into the darkness and shadows seemed to move at the edge of his eyesight. He took another pull on the cigarette and his night vision disappeared once again. He heard the sound of hard leather pushing pebbles into each other. The blackness in front of him seemed to deepen as a voice said, 'Harry?'.

He flicked the cigarette into a rock pool where it fizzed and spluttered for a second and held his arms out wide. 'Billy!'

The shadow moved forward and embraced him. He threw his arms around his twin and hugged him, hard and with feeling. 'Long time.'

'Yeah. Hell, of a long time.'

'Father ok?'

'Yeah, he and Olga are fine. You? The boys, Vicky?'

'All fine, though Vicky is a handful.'

'Please don't tell me. I have two girls of my own now.'

'What?'

'Yeah, Martha and Agnes. Eighteen months and two weeks.'

'*Herr Schwarz,* we have little time.' A voice brimming with authority rasped from out of the dark.

'*Ja, Herr Brandt.*' Billy turned back to Harry. 'The Captain has orders to listen to everything we say. I think he's nervous. He's got six submariners, placed at various points to protect us, but even so we need to get down to business.'

Harry froze. A German Captain. Six troopers. He was trapped. Billy was warning him but this was wrong. All wrong.

'Harry, I need you to do something for me. You are the only person I trust. I need help brother.'

Harry noted the change in Billy's voice. He was now all business and there was an edge creeping into his tone, which, while not quite a tremor, was something new – something he couldn't remember hearing before. He waited, trying to peer through the dark to gain some clue from the faint patch of grey he assumed was his brother's face. But it was impossible; it was also impossible to judge his body language now they were no longer hugging each other, so Harry concentrated on the tone of Billy's voice.

'I've convinced the captain that you would never betray me. That you will help me.'

Another warning. Billy took a deep breath while Harry focused as hard as he could.

'I've been working on a blind-landing system for aircraft. We've been very successful, since the start of the war we've moved on and now use the system to guide our bombers. We can direct a radio beam exactly where we want it; a beam so thin it is almost impossible to detect unless you fly through it. Using the beam, we can direct an aircraft to the target. We then send another beam across the first, intersecting it exactly where we want. This makes an X with the centre of the cross exactly over our target. When the bomber has both beams, it releases its bombs, exactly on target. Exactly.'

Harry could hear the tension creeping into his brother's voice and the shuffle of his feet in the shingle. He had used the word 'exactly' several times and each time with extra emphasis. The final time he said it, Billy left no room for doubt. *Exactly!*

'But Harry we're missing the targets. Not by much, but enough to make the raids a waste. There has been an investigation and there are two theories: one, the British are intercepting the beams and distorting them so we miss or the other, that I am deliberately misleading the authorities. You can guess the penalty if this is what they decide.'

Harry now understood the tension in Billy's voice and the need for Captain Brandt to be standing within earshot, listening to every word. Subconsciously he sought the captain. He knew he was close. He needed to know where, but the darkness was complete.

'I'm convinced the British have broken our system… they're playing with us. We now have a new set-up, but we need to test it under conditions where the British will intercept it if they can. If they are intercepting, we need to know. Personally, I cannot afford for it to fail.'

Harry remained silent, knowing there was more to come. There was a whine in Billy's voice. A pleading.

'What I need is a comparison. I need you Harry. I need you to send a signal from a known point, close to the target, as the bombers approach. I can take this signal and compare it with the beams and then we'll know if the British are meddling. Captain Brandt has brought you a transmitter. It's an English version so no one will suspect anything, but it has been adapted by us. The setting is fixed. Harry, I need you to get to a high point within ten miles of Sheffield and at eleven o'clock on the fifteenth of December I need you to transmit your exact coordinates for half an hour. I will measure your signal against our beams and we'll have our answer.'

Harry's thoughts were racing. Suddenly it hit him. Their original conversation had been in English, the language of their youth, Billy had used affectionate Russian terms for their father, his wife and their siblings. But the details of this plan were in formal German. Billy was sending him a message! The meaning of the message remained unclear but the use of German was rigid and unbending.

'Billy, this is not what I do. I smuggle; I work for profit. I do not take unnecessary – make that unprofitable – risks.'

'Harry, I knew you would say that, but I need you, brother. The Reich will also pay you handsomely.'

'How handsomely?'

'Five thousand pounds.'

Harry stifled an instinctive intake of breath – and, after years of negotiating with hard men, he did not let a flicker enter his voice.

'Up front?'

'Up front.'

'I need a cigarette.'

'*Nein!*' The captain took control. 'I have the money and the transmitter here. We need your answer now. We have to go.'

Harry's senses were fully attuned to the darkness and the constant lapping of the waves as the tide crept up the cove. He could see darker shadows in his peripheral vision and took stock of his situation. It was obvious that what he had been told could not go any further. If he said no, he would never be seen again. There was no doubt the captain had orders to kill him and possibly his brother, if he did not agree. He fancied his chances of getting away from the captain in the dark but, with six others around him, escape would literally be short-lived.

Billy's own life or position back home may have been under threat, but by coming here and telling Harry his predicament, he had also placed Harry in mortal danger. He reasoned that Billy's position must be much worse than he was admitting; that he would not have put Harry in this situation unless he was desperate. But he also realised Billy must be confident that his system would be vindicated, otherwise he would not have taken this risk.

'Billy, I've never been to Sheffield.'

'We have maps to help you.'

Harry was in no doubt that Billy had absolute trust in him, he knew from their past that Billy respected his twin's ability to negotiate and keep a cool head in a crisis. He sensed Billy relax as he said

'Travel will be difficult. I'll need passes. I'll need money to bribe people.'

'I told you; we'll pay you up front and you have nearly eight weeks to plan and prepare.'

'Jesus, Billy, you know how to test a man don't you!'

'Does that mean you will do it, *Herr Black?*' whispered the captain, from the side, demanding a committed answer.

'I'll do it.'

The one word response seemed tinged with an element of disappointment. *'Gutt.'*

Billy took control again: 'Harry, to make this work you have to keep transmitting your signal for half an hour. I'll need that long to correlate it with the beams and to realign our signal if necessary. But I realise that is too long for you to transmit safely; the British always have planes flying at night to intercept radio beams and they'll pick up your signal instantly... and your location. So, do not be anywhere near the transmitter, do not send our brothers. This is a suicide mission. If they don't shoot you there and then, they'll hang you. Find someone expendable.'

Harry did not need to see his twin. The emotion in his voice told him everything. Harry was now committed – if he were to show any signs of weakness or hesitation, Brandt might act. Harry sucked in his breath. Inside he was fuming at his brother, but he knew if the situation was reversed Billy would not hesitate to help him. However, he also thought that if he had been in Billy's shoes, he would never have allowed this situation to develop in the first place.

'We need to know where the transmission will be sent from.' Billy continued as if unaware of Harry's discomfort. 'At eleven o'clock on the

111

twelve of December, I need you to transmit the coordinates using our old channel. We don't need the degrees if you are within ten miles of Sheffield just the minutes and seconds. Eight numbers in two blocks of four.'

The old channel was Billy's old system from the niche. Billy was now asking him to potentially expose his smuggling. Fighting the urge to shout at Billy in frustration, Harry refocused. He tensed his body, keeping his knees relaxed, feeling the shingle through the leather of his boots. Billy was in front of him, the captain somewhere to the right. The path was behind him, the lantern would have burned out by now. Whichever way he moved the shingle would shout his location. If the troops were prepared to shoot, the first bullet would not need to find him. The muzzle flare would reveal his whereabouts to the other submariners. No, he was trapped.

Think.

There was only one way forward, that was together with his twin.

Just as it always had been.

'I'll need all the money up front. Whoever I send will need paying and it must be enough for them to keep their mouth shut. *Herr Capitan*, you have my word your signal will be sent.'

The captain turned and spoke in a hurried whisper. A second later, after crisp footfalls on the shingle, Harry felt a large pack being pushed into his chest. He took it in his hands.

'And here is the money you need so much,' hissed the Captain, passing Harry a second parcel. 'Goodbye, *Herr Black*.' The captain turned giving a low whistle and boots rang out on the shingle.

Billy hugged his brother. 'Thank you,' was all he could manage as the captain grabbed him and pulled him away. A few seconds later Harry heard wood sliding on shingle. The sound of the waves returned as he stood alone. The darkness a shroud, the waves a lament, his thoughts a riot.

Back at the cottage, Harry hid the transmitter in the kitchen and counted the money. He sat looking at it for a long time. It was a lot of money, but he would willingly have given it all back if there had been a choice. The risks in sending the signal were huge. His brother was clearly in deep trouble. He took out the map from the case containing the money.

Sheffield. He knew roughly where it was but it still took him a minute or two to find it.

He looked at the scale on the map and took out a needle and thread. He measured ten miles on the scale and cut the thread to suit. Tying one end of the thread to the needle and the other around a pencil he pushed the needle into the middle of Sheffield and started to move the pencil around in a circle, marking the circle on the map. Then he picked the map up and studied it.

Sheffield. Within ten miles he could see Rotherham, Wickersley, Conisborough, Mexborough, Wath-upon-Dearne, Hoyland, Stocksbridge, and Oughtibridge. The names were meaningless, almost foreign. But a dim memory surfaced – Wath-upon-Dearne… where had he heard that before? Harry sat back and poured himself a vodka. Something was struggling to come to the front of his mind, he needed to relax and allow it to surface. Wath-upon-Dearne… He took another sip and looked at the map. There was a high point on the map just outside Wath-upon-Dearne – Hoober. It was the highest point on the eastern side of Sheffield. For some reason he was thinking of his sister, Vicky.

Suddenly everything came flooding back. Barney, the useless radio man who had gone missing. He recalled the night and the wait. The young girl who stood up to him. She had shown more fight than many men he knew which he grudgingly respected. Barney had been gone when Harry returned. He had searched at the time, but all he could find was a reference to a father living in Wath-upon-Dearne and the thought that Barney might have run home to Daddy. He let it all drift away when, a week later, Vicky lost the pregnancy. But now… *Well, Barney, if I can find you, you are about to become Mr Expendable.*

He needed an address – he recalled there was a sister in Benwell, she would do as a start. Then he needed to get passes. Harry finished his vodka and went to bed. There was a lot to do later that morning.

Wednesday 30 October 1940

The smell of baking bread was overwhelming as Eva pushed open the door and skipped into the kitchen. It was fourteen months since her father's death and life was returning to normal. In her eyes, Gilbert and Margaret were simply wonderful and there was always something to do – if not looking after young Alfred, helping out at the field or giving a hand in the kitchen – though Margaret never seemed to need much help – was never flustered, always in control. She was sitting at the table working at some material stretched over a frame while Alfred was asleep in his cot. Eva could see Margaret would soon have to let out her dress again as her stomach was swollen with her second pregnancy.

'By heck, Margaret, you're gonna have to show me how to make bread like that. What're you doing?'

'I'm just doing a bit on a rug for the kitchen floor while I'm waiting for the bread. Got a corned-beef hash ready for dinner when Gilbert gets back from the field.'

'It smells great but the bread smells better. How do you make a rug?'

Margaret pointed to the old potato sack stretched across the frame Gilbert had made.

'It's dead easy, want to have a go? Right. Well, what you do is cut old rags into one inch strips about a quarter of an inch wide, like this. Then you holds one of them in your left hand behind the sack and push the fetching tool through from the front.'

Margaret demonstrated by taking the tool which looked like a circular door knob with a long nail sticking out of it and, after waving it in the air to demonstrate, pushed the sharp pointed spike through the webbing of the sack.

'At the end of the spike is a hook, see, so you catch the rag on the hook and pull the fetching tool back through the sack and it pulls the rag back with it. Then you move a hole or two down the sack webbing and push the tool through again and catch the other end of the rag pulling it through just the same. Now you've got the rag sticking through the sack in a 'u' shape and you pulls the ends even and go onto the next one. Easy. Come on, have a go.'

Eva sat in front of the frame. Margaret made it look so easy. Carefully she pushed the end of the fetching tool through the sack and

114

hooked a piece of rag onto the vicious looking hook at the end of it, slowly she pulled it back through the sack before repeating the exercise on the other end of the rag. It was painfully slow but surprisingly satisfying.

'Keep going while I get the bread. I'll make a cuppa and we can share a bread cake if you want.'

'Yes please!' said Eva with her tongue sticking out of her mouth in concentration. There was a knock on the door and a voice chirped. 'Cantors.'

Without thinking Margaret shouted, 'Come in, Amos.'

Eva cringed.

Amos Trenham walked in, studiously ignoring the girl sitting at the table.

'Here you go, pet,' said Margaret, passing Amos two half crowns. 'How's Barney and the pig farm?'

'Oh, he's alright, but pig farm is coming on slow, Gilbert giving pork away doesn't help. I don't know how he fattened his pig up so quick, but we'll get there. Got ten o' the little sods now and they all eat like there's no tomorrow.'

Margaret smiled quietly to herself. When he slaughtered a pig, Gilbert would give away certain cuts. The pieces they could not eat immediately, or preserve, or cure, he always shared within the Yard. He never charged but everybody gave him their scraps and vegetable peelings which enabled him to feed his hens and fatten the pig quickly and cheaply. Also, as he collected the mash, he sold eggs and sticks, which all in the Yard were happy to buy. She knew Barney and Amos didn't like it, but hey, it brought in some spending money and supplemented the ration book – which was essential now that Alfred was here and she couldn't work.

'There you go, I've put it in book. Thanks, I'll see you next week.'

Amos passed the tally book back, put the half crowns in his satchel and left the kitchen.

Eva breathed normally again. 'I still can't stand that man. What's all this about Barney and a pig farm?'

'Well, since Barney and mi mam got that council house near Amos, him and Barney have been getting on like a house on fire and they've clubbed together to rent a field down Winterwell. They've built a couple of sties and they're fattening pigs and breeding their own, as a business. Debt collecting for Cantors doesn't pay well so Amos needs more money. Barney can't stand the pit and wants out. He's driving mi mam mad, so she's hoping they can make a go of it and Barney will calm down. Mind you, she reckons them pigs is the best company he can find!'

Eva smiled. 'You know what he does when he leaves here, don't you?'

'Who, Amos? No, but I bet you're gonna tell me.'

'Yeah, I am. He goes into No 11 for half an hour.'

'No 11? That's the new people, the Robinsons. They just moved in from Firth Road. They don't have any furniture from Cantors, do they?'

'No, but why do you think he always comes at this time?'

'Cos he knows Gilbert won't be here?' Amos hated Gilbert and could not hide it. Gilbert, mean time did not care a jot, and Eva never spoke a word when Amos came to the door. Margaret kept a diplomatic air not wanting to sour things any further. It would be her mother who bore the brunt if she did. 'You're gonna have to tell me, Eva, 'cos I've no idea.'

'Well, Mrs Robinson works at Catholic School in West Melton doing dinners, so she is always at school at this time, unless it's the holidays and her daughter, Christine, is at home on her own, so Amos pays her a visit like.'

'Pays her a visit like?'

'Yeah, pays her for a visit while her ma's out. You know, Margaret, stop being thick – he pays her for being on her own with him. Do you want me to spell it out?'

'Well I never! The little sod – and I never guessed,' mused Margaret as she took the bread from the oven and left it to cool. She stared out of the window unsure of the implications of this new knowledge. Looking across the Yard her mind was elsewhere when an almost forgotten image walked past her eyes. Confused, she refocused and nearly fainted. There, walking into the Yard, was an immaculately dressed man with white hair followed by two huge men with black hair and black beards.

Margaret grabbed hold of the sink, swayed and held on. Her vision clouded as blood left her extremities and raced to her core. Her head pounded and it felt as though her eyes bulged before hitting an unseen barrier and rebounded back into their sockets.

'Jesus! How the… Why are they here?'

Margaret was sagging, her knees folding and hitting the cupboard in front of her. 'Margaret? What's wrong, Margaret?' Eva leapt to her side, grabbing hold of her.

'See them men, there, Eva? They're the most evil men ever. They're from Newcastle and they're just plain nasty. Jesus! What're they doing here?'

The pair of them watched as Harry Black stopped outside No 3, Barney and Susannah's old house. He knocked on the door; the new tenant, Anne Youel, opened it and started talking to them, she smiled and pointed towards Margaret and Eva. They ducked below the window.

Margaret felt panicked. Her thoughts were racing: *They're here. Why? Wrong question. How? Wrong question. Come on Margaret it doesn't matter – they're here. What to do? They're coming over here. They're evil. They'll hurt us. Come on Margaret. What to do?* The thoughts raced around her head as her eyes flew around the room. At last her brain kicked into action, she stopped thinking and started reacting.

'Eva, go out the front door, run to the field and tell Gilbert to get back here quick. Tell him the Blacks are here, then run to mi mam's and tell her to run, tell her to hide. They'll understand. But Eva fly, run like the wind. Go, girl, run!'

Margaret pushed her out of the front door and raced back into the kitchen, where she pulled the key off its peg at the side of the back door and locked it before leaning against it, breathing hard. *Please, Eva, run. Come home Gilbert, please, please, please!* She heard footsteps on the pavement and saw shadows moving past the window. She stood still, holding her breath. The footsteps stopped. There was a sharp rapping of knuckles on the door.

All went quiet while the men stood outside, waiting. Margaret remained frozen, her back against the door. At least a minute passed and there was another rapping, this time louder and firmer. It made Margaret jump, it also woke baby Alfred who started crying at the top of his voice.

'*Shush! Shush!*' whispered Margaret as she crept across the room and picked him up.

As she held the baby in her arms, the light in the room darkened, a large form looking in at the window.

'She's in there, Harry.' She heard the shadow say.

'Come on then, are you going to open the door or are we going to stand here all day?' came the unmistakable voice of Harry Black, the banging on the door returning, increasing in volume.

Margaret stood transfixed. The shadow at the window waved at her. 'Hello.' it said.

'Just a minute, just a minute, I'll be there,' shouted Margaret. Slowly she walked to the door, the shadow outside the window following her every step. She made a show of rattling the key in the lock, to delay as long as possible and, taking a deep breath and mustering all her nerves, she slowly opened the door, standing on the top step, hugging Alfred, looking down at the three of them.

'Well, well, well, young'un, you are looking well,' said Harry Black looking her up and down, pointing a languid finger first at the baby, then at her stomach. 'What's happening here? Has Barney been up to his old tricks but closer to home this time?'

'Don't be stupid, that's sick!' she spat.

'Ooooh! Still got the old venom, I see. Well, Young'un, me and—'

'Oy! What's all this about?' shouted Gilbert, racing into the Yard with Shudder at his side. The two men slid to a halt in the middle of the Yard, trapping the Blacks against the house and the quarry wall. The two brothers moved, one to either side of Harry as he turned to face Gilbert.

'And who might you be?' he enquired.

'That's my house and that's my wife. That's who I am, so you'd best explain yourself.'

'Ahh! Sir Galahad and Sir Percival come to rescue the fair maiden. Welcome, kind sirs. But, before we get off to a bad start, you should know I am only looking to have a chat with Barney, nothing more. And I do believe the young'un here might know where he is.'

At this point a dishevelled Amos, came out of No 11, tucking his shirt into his trousers. He examined the men facing each other in the Yard and turned around to leave.

Margaret realised that Gilbert and Shudder were in for a beating if anything kicked off and the sight of Amos leaving them to it made her wince. She felt proud as Gilbert stood his ground and could have hugged him when he put her thoughts into words:

'If that's what you want, that's who you need to talk to. Amos, Amos hold up,' he shouted. Amos stopped and reluctantly turned. 'Amos, these men want to talk to Barney do you know where he is?'

'Eh, what? Why?'

Gilbert turned to the three men. 'This is Barney's brother, you're better off talking to him 'cos we don't have a lot to do with Barney. So, if you don't mind, I'd like to go and get my dinner.'

The man pondered for a moment or two, then said: 'Is that true? Are you Barney's brother? And you know where he is? Good! Now if you would be so kind as to lead on, we need to let this young family have their dinner. Thank you, Sir Galahad. Good bye young'un… for now.'

He sauntered past Gilbert and Shudder taking Amos by the arm, leading him out of the Yard. The two bearded brothers walked sideways passed Gilbert and Shudder never taking their eyes off them, a sneer on both their faces screamed the disappointment of moving on.

Margaret watched as the three men and Amos left the Yard. Gilbert leapt to her side and put his arms around her, while Shudder let out the biggest sigh of relief any of them had ever heard.

'Bugger me sideways! What's going off? Mi knees are still knocking!' he said. 'I don't think I've been that scared since me ma caught me with Sarah Longford's knickers in my hand. They're bad men, bad news. Is anybody gonna tell me the story?'

Despite everything, Margaret smiled. 'You blethering idiot, Shudder, I've got the kettle on and bread made. Let's have a brew and a chat.'

They all went inside and Margaret passed the baby to Gilbert while she turned to the hob, Shudder simply collapsed into one of the chairs. The sense of relief was so clear they could touch it in the air.

'Mi mam,' exclaimed Margaret dropping the kettle back on the hob. 'What about mi mam?'

Gilbert looked from Margaret to Shudder and back. 'Calm down Margaret I'll nip to your ma's and make sure she's alright.'

'I sent Eva to warn her, but if them fellas get there first!'

'Easy, Margaret easy, I'll go now. You sit down and look after Alfred.'

'I'll come with you,' piped Shudder, though Margaret was unsure how much help he would actually be.

'Ok, come on then.'

Eva sprinted, her lungs were boiling, as she forced her legs to keep pumping, but she kept going. She had never seen Margaret so rattled and, after the hundred yard dash to Gilbert's field, she was amazed at his reaction. He simply dropped the hammer he was holding, turned and ran. Shudder Madeley was helping him with what looked like a vegetable cloche and he looked at her with his mouth open. Then, shouting, 'What's going on?' flew after Gilbert.

Eva watched them for a few seconds before starting the lengthy run to Susannah's. It was just under a mile but she didn't stop. At the top of Packman Hill she forced her pace taking advantage of the downhill stretch. Her feet smacked the pavement with a resounding echo as she sped past the Bull's Head into the council estate. On she ran, through the playing field, into Susannah's road, racing into the house, breathless.

'Blacks here, got to go. Margaret says run.'

Susannah looked at her in amazement. 'Steady-on, Eva. Take a deep breath. Now what's wrong, pet?'

Gulping deep pulls of air, Eva slowed down.

'Margaret sent me. Some men just come into Top Yard. She says they're the Blacks and you've to run and hide. I've told Gilbert, he's going back from the field. But she says to be quick!'

Eva saw panic cross Susannah's face, noticed her unconsciously rubbing the stump of her missing finger. 'Did you see the men, Eva? What did they look like?'

'There were three of them, one with right white hair and the other two was huge with jet black hair and beards.'

Susannah collapsed into the chair with a moan. 'Oh no, no, no.'

'Mrs Trenham, you've got to go! Now! Margaret says to go.'

To Eva's relief, Susannah controlled her panic, sat upright, taking control of the situation

'Aye she's right. Thanks, Eva, you're a gem. Kids come here now. No arguing, we're going to your Aunty Rita's… now. Eva, tell Margaret we'll be at Rita's until we hear they've gone. Brenda stop it, get Joe and come on, NOW!'

Eva watched Susannah gather the children and leave by the back door.

Rita was Susannah's sister-in-law and lived two doors down on the other side of the road, so they could see her house from there and make sure it was safe before they returned. After seeing them out of the door, Eva left and started on her way back. As she passed the Bull's Head she could see four men walking through the field towards Winterwell. She recognised the three men and realised the other man with them was Amos. What he was doing with them she had no idea but he was leading them in the direction of the pig farm.

She got to the top of Packman Hill as Gilbert and Shudder crested it from the other side. Seeing the men, a smile of relief lit up her face. She ran and jumped into Gilberts arms.

'You ok? Is Margaret alright?'

'She's fine, thanks to you coming to get us so quick. What's happened with Susannah?'

'She's gone to Rita's with the kids for the now but I saw them men again, with Amos, going through the field to the pig farm.'

'That'll be where Barney is. There's nothing we can do now, Gilbert. Barney'll have to sort it out himself. Even if we could do anything, we'll not be there in time if they do want more than a chat with Barney.'

Gilbert looked at Shudder; he was right. Susannah and the kids were safe – his priority was Margaret, and she was on her own. Barney would have to look after himself.

'Come on then, let's get back.'

'Barney, these fellas want to have a chat with you,' shouted Amos as they approached the pig farm. Barney was bending over one of the troughs, filling it with mash, his back to them. He stood up, turned and stopped. Transfixed. He stood stock still, holding the empty bucket of mash in one hand, while the pigs at his feet fought to get into the trough.

'Hello Barney, long time no see. It appears your living conditions have not improved, but still, it is difficult in these dangerous times.' Harry Black leant against the gate and smiled at Barney while lazily looking around at the surroundings. 'It's a nice idea this, but it seems to me you are lacking a little finance.' He waved his hand at the ramshackle building behind him.

'Now, I've travelled a long way, so let's get straight to business – I realise we parted on unfortunate terms last time we met, but if you would care for a little walk, I have a proposition for you.'

Barney looked at Harry ashen faced. Amos could see that a walk with this man was the last thing he wanted. It was obvious that he was terrified of him.

'Now, now, Barney, let's not be shy. I said I had a business proposition and I meant it. This could be very good for you.'

'What about Vicky?'

'Ahh, our little sister. Well fortunately for you she lost the baby, so no one is any the wiser, all's well that ends well, yes? Now, you did me and my brothers a really good job back in Newcastle and we would like to continue our… working relationship, if you would care to listen to our ideas. Why don't you come out here and you and me we can talk while your brother explains the intricacies of pig farming to the boys, hey?'

He gestured to the gate. Barney warily walked forward, opening it slightly, kicking back the pigs who were fighting to beat him out of the sty. He dropped the bucket onto the path and followed the man as he led the way down the track. The other two took up positions either side of the track, while Amos stood motionless by the gate. It was clear they were not going to engage him in conversation, but at least it seemed that they were not going to hurt him.

Amos watched Barney and the white-haired man walk to the corner of the track about fifty yards away and start talking. One of the brothers turned the bucket upside down and sat upon it, while the other leant against the wall of the ramshackle shed containing the pig farm supplies. They made no attempt to talk to him, or each other, he was hemmed in from both sides, so he leant against the gate and waited. He didn't want to get involved in Barney's trouble and needed to get away from these thugs, his satchel contained nearly ten pounds of rent money. But it was obvious he was going to be kept there. At least until they were finished with Barney.

After a good twenty minutes he witnessed Barney and the 'white' man pointing at him, deep in discussion, then they shook hands and returned to the sty. Without a word, the stranger signalled the two brothers and the three of them walked away from the pig farm in the direction of Wath Station.

Amos looked at Barney. 'What's going off, Barney? Who are those men? And what was he on about?'

Barney sat on the upturned bucket, his hands shaking as he pulled two cigarettes out of his cigarette case. He passed one to Amos and, waving his hands in the air, muttered: 'Jesus, Jesus, I thought I was done for.' He leant back against the sty and took several pulls of his cigarette, while Amos hopped from foot to foot in agitation.

'Right, Amos what I'm about to tell must go no further, no matter what, ok?

'Barney I'm your brother. Christ, we've just gone into business together haven't we? I'll do nothing or say nothing, unless it's ok with you.'

'Right. Well up in Newcastle I did a few jobs for them men – the Blacks. They're smugglers and they needed to listen to the coast guard and to talk to their own ships over radio and they were having problems. So, they asked me to repair a ship's radio that were bust and set it up onshore so they could listen to the coast guard, but also to rig it so they could talk to their own ships without coast guard knowing. So, I did. They paid me right well and it were working fine until either the coast guard got smart or the Blacks got sloppy. But whatever, one of their shipments got stopped and I got the blame.'

'So, who's Vicky?'

'Ah, well, you see, I got a bit friendly with their sister and it all got a bit personal. They didn't mind while everything were going well but once things went wrong they decided to make an example of me and we had to run.'

'And now?'

'Well, now they need me again, so they've forgotten about Vicky and made me a proposition.'

'Ok, I've got it so far, so what's their proposition?'

'They want me to set up a transmitter here and send a certain signal at specific times on a particular wavelength. That way, with it coming from here, coastguard won't know it's them. They'll pay me handsomely to do it. Amos, I want you involved because I can't do it on my own. I'll need to get some big equipment and heavy batteries, I'll need somewhere to hide them and someone to help me carry them. We'll share the money half and half. So that's it. Are you in?'

123

'When do we do it and where? And, most of all, how much?'

'Amos that's too many questions unless you're in.'

'If money's right, I'm in.'

'Money will be more than right, I promise you.'

'Ok, if you say so, I'm in. But I need to get rest of my collections done now and get money back to Mr Cantor or else I'm gonna be in trouble of my own.'

'We'll go for a pint at the Bull's Head when you're finished and I'll fill you in on the details.'

Amos took a long drink of his pint and passed Barney a cigarette. After they both lit up, they sat back looking around the pub. The tap room was noisy, so they had chosen the 'best' side which wouldn't get much traffic until later, when couples would come in for a quiet evening drink. At the moment they were the only customers.

'What's your idea now you've had time to think?' asked Barney.

'Oh, I'm in, alright,' replied Amos. 'Cantors don't pay much and our pig farm has emptied me of all my cash. My worry is, I don't know anything about radios.'

'Look, it's dead easy, but leave that side of things to me. I could build a receiver now with some bits I've got, but a transmitter is more difficult especially with a war on.'

'Why?'

'Well loads of people have got wireless sets, but Government isn't worried about them – it's good 'cos they can get their message across... you know, good old Winnie giving us a gee-up and such like. But they don't like people to transmit 'cos they could send messages to the Jerries, so getting hold of them parts is gonna be tricky.'

'How we gonna do it then?'

'I can nick a lot of what we need from pit. They'll never know 'cos there's only me uses it. Next, I'll need to go to Newcastle and get bits from places I know around the docks. Harry – the older brother I was talking to, is gonna set that side of things up, the rest I can buy as though I'm repairing a wireless. Then we put it all together and 'cos we've got the parts from three different places nobody will ever know. Harry has promised me he will pay us when I go up to Newcastle, so we only meet once and nobody knows we're working with them.'

'How much?'

'It's a good job you're sitting down. Five hundred pounds.'

'What? Five hundred quid? Jesus, Barney, what's he smuggling? Gold dust? Two hundred and fifty quid each?'

'No, Amos, five hundred pounds each.'

Amos sat open-mouthed staring at Barney, oblivious to the cigarette butt burning his fingers.

'I told you the pay would be right – but, Amos, there's a downside to it. If you let him down, Harry Black'll take five hundred pounds out of you, physically and enjoy doing it. And he expects you not to mention him – in fact, he expects complete silence, no matter what'

'I'd punch Hitler on the nose for five hundred pounds. You don't think he's doing something with the Jerries do you?'

'Get real, Amos. He's a gun smuggler and times like this he's in demand and making good money. Do you care which side he's selling guns to?'

'For five hundred quid he could sell them to the devil for all I care. Mind you, Adolf isn't far off being the devil, is he? Look, I've said I'm in and I'm in, ok? What do you want me to do?'

'Nothing for now. I'm gonna have to think of a reason to go back to Newcastle – Susan's bound to ask questions.'

'She'll know the Blacks have been, 'cos Margaret and Gilbert have seen them.'

'Oh Shit.'

'Yeah, they knocked on Margaret's door looking for you. That's when they saw me and Gilbert tells them I'm your brother and that I'll fetch them to you.'

'God he's an interfering sod and that bitch, Margaret, she's wound me up since the day I met her.'

'I shouldn't worry too much, they're about to get into deep trouble.'

'How?'

'Well here's where I trust you, Barney. You know young Christine at number 11? Used to live on Firth Road? No, well never mind. I've been seeing her like and paying her to keep quiet about it. Trouble is, I don't have enough money and I didn't want Rita to notice. So, I've been using Margaret's rent money to pay Christine and not putting it down in her book. She thinks I have, but I've changed the pages in her book without her noticing. So now they owe Cantors five pounds and that's the amount where Mr Cantor always takes them to court. They haven't got a fiver, even if they have, the court'll want the full amount paying – and that's near on twenty quid. So, they're in big trouble.'

'Oh yes. I love it. That'll teach em and it'll stop him stealing our business. Love it, Amos, that's a beauty you randy sod. But now I'm gonna have to spin Susan a yarn.'

Susannah sat with her arms crossed at the table. There was a cold plate of stew waiting for Barney. Her scowl would have frozen volcanoes as he sat down and picked up his fork.

'Well?' The word came across the table like a bolt from a crossbow.

'Love, I've had a bad day, please don't make it any worse.'

'Obviously, not as bad as the day I had when we last met the Blacks.' Susannah waved her left hand in the air gesturing at him. 'Barney, the Blacks don't travel this far for the good of their health and you don't seem to have lost any body parts. In fact, you look in fine form. So, what's going on?'

'No, I haven't… yet.' Barney placed his fork on the table and leant forward on his elbows.

'Susan, I told you, I've had a bad day and I meant it. Harry Black wants me to do a job for him. If I do it, he'll forget about us – if not, his brothers'll be back and I don't fancy my chances of seeing the end of the day when that happens. If I do it, he'll pay me thirty quid.'

'No way, Barney. What can you do to earn thirty quid?'

'It's illegal.'

'Never, not Harry Black.'

'Listen, Susan, he wants me to go back to Newcastle and repair his wireless, the one he listens to the coastguard and his ships on. The fella who did it for him has been called up and he doesn't know anybody else. I also have to make him a spare and that's it. He promises he will leave us alone after that.'

'And do you believe him?'

'It doesn't matter whether I do or not, does it? If I don't do what he wants, he'll send his brothers back for us.'

'Go on then, suppose for the first time in my life I believe you. How do you plan to do this?'

Barney pulled a piece of folded paper from his pocket.

'Well he's given me a pass to go up to Newcastle on Friday. I can be back on Sunday with the job done, the Blacks are out of our hair and we've thirty quid to spend. I'll have to pretend to be sick and you'll have to cover for me.'

'You've done this afore haven't you?'

'Don't ask questions I can't answer, Susan. Let's just do this and get Blacks out of our lives. Yeah?'

'I want a new coat for me and new shoes for Doris when you get back.'

'Yeah, yeah, whatever you say. I just want them Blacks gone.'

Five for Silver

November 1940

Margaret tore off the bus and raced down the street. Her coat and hair flapped behind her, while her shoes slapped the ground angrily. She ran straight passed her mother's house ignoring Jack as he called out, 'Hey sis, what's up?' She flew into the house two doors down, battering the door open and screeching in. Without hesitating, she stormed inside and grabbed the figure sat eating his dinner by the back of his collar.

She pulled Amos off his chair dragging him through the kitchen and into the back garden. There she threw him to the floor and, as he started to get up, screamed: 'You lying, cheating, bastard! Do you know what you've done?'

Amos struggled to his feet, while Rita stood at the door looking on in amazement, a furious Margaret yelled again at Amos: 'You had that money! You know we paid it, yet you lied, you scum bag.'

Amos found his feet and opened his arms in a defensive gesture so Margaret threw a punch at his stomach. Amos leant forward and put his hands down to cover the blow but Margaret adjusted and launched a right uppercut at his chin. It connected with all the force she could muster, lifting Amos off his feet and onto his back once again.

'Get up, you piece of shit! Get up so I can knock you down again. And don't think it'll end there. Get up. I said, get up!' Amos held his face in his hands and rolled over onto his stomach.

'Get up!' Margaret managed once more as Jack and Susannah raced around the corner.

'Margaret, stop!' shouted Susannah. 'What's going on?' Jack jumped between Amos and Margaret and held his arms out wide.

'What's going on is, I'm gonna beat this miserable piece of turd to within an inch of his life. Then do it again tomorrow and the next day and the next, until Gilbert gets out of prison.'

'Whoa, what do you mean, prison?' Susannah joined Jack between the two of them, while Rita jumped from the door and cradled Amos on the floor.

'Gilbert has just been sentenced to four weeks in the debtor's prison at Wakefield for not paying our Cantors' repayments, when I've been paying them to this turd every week.'

Susannah looked at the figure on the floor. 'Amos?'

'She's lying. I recorded every payment she made. If Mr Cantor sued them, they haven't paid.' Margaret leapt at the figure on the floor as Rita scrabbled to one side. Jack grabbed his sister from the front while Susannah pulled her from the back. Slowly they steered a kicking, screaming Margaret back out of the garden and onto the road.

'Margaret you can't go around decking people, no matter how much you think they deserve it. You'll be arrested too, where'll that put Alfred and Eva? Come on love, calm down. Come home, let's have a cuppa and a chat.'

'I want to break his face, I want to see him bleed. Don't you ever come into the Yard again, Amos, do you hear me?' she yelled over her shoulder as her mother and brother maintained their grip on her. 'If you do, you'll regret it. I haven't done with you yet. I'm not finished!'

'Margaret, come on, easy, easy love. Let's go home.'

A few minutes later they were sitting in the back room at Susannah's, mugs of tea in their hands. Jack said: 'Wow sis! That was some punch. I didn't think me and Mam were gonna be able to hold you. Bet his chin is sore for the next week.'

'It'll be even sorer if I see him again!'

'Calm down love. You'll end up having that baby early if you carry on at this rate. Now what's happened?'

'Cantors have sued us for not paying the weekly payment on the furniture. The one that Amos collects. I've paid it every week but the tally book doesn't show it. Amos hasn't been recording it. Gilbert went to court and told them that we have paid. But the judge just said the book doesn't say so and sentenced him to jail and they carted him straight off to Wakefield.'

Susannah gasped, Margaret never lied, never. No wonder she was furious. Amos was a snake and always had been, but this was atrocious. She looked at her daughter, the flashing eyes, the way she twitched and shuffled. There was a lot of her father in her – he was never able to disguise his feelings either.

'Come on, pet. Me and our Jack'll walk you back home. Eva's on her own with Alfred and you need to get him fed. Come on.'

The whole Yard was depressed as reports of the London Blitz continued. But Margaret was disconsolate. Alfred couldn't distract her; Eva couldn't

132

make her smile. A cloud settled over the household, thicker than soot and heavier than a lead blanket. Margaret could hardly bring herself to talk and wouldn't eat as she tried to work out how they would manage for the next four weeks. Putting lack of money to one side life without Gilbert was intolerable.

Two days after her fight with Amos, Shudder Madeley appeared.

He sat down at the table looking more miserable than Margaret could ever remember seeing him. 'I've just come back from Wakefield. I've been to see Gilbert.' He hesitated, took a breath then looked at Margaret across the table, locking eyes with her. 'Margaret, he says we've got to get him out –we've got to find a way to pay the money. He can't do much longer in there Margaret. He's, he's… well, he's been beaten up and he doesn't look good. He says we've to get him out, whatever it takes.'

The look on Shudder's face shocked Margaret. He was drawn and pale with a harried expression of concern, a stark contrast with the usual happy-go-lucky Shudder. Margaret flopped down opposite him, a new, even deeper sense of discomfort, spreading through her.

Tears began falling down her cheeks, her nose ran, her hands shook. 'I can't take any more. What're we going to do, Shudder? I haven't got twenty pounds.'

'Neither have I, Margaret. I could give you a quid at a push – but that'd be it.'

'Aye me an all. Jesus, that man's a lot to answer for. How could anybody do what he did?'

The still stinging anger burst inside her. She fought to crush her feelings of fury and concentrate on what Shudder was saying.

'I don't know, but he did. Margaret, Amos's got a streak in him, like his mother, she was mad, completely doo lally. He'll get his come uppance, don't you worry about that but why don't we do the rounds, you know, see what we can raise from everybody. It's got to be better than just sitting here! Come on, lets at least try. Everybody likes Gilbert and knows he's as honest as day is long.'

Margaret agreed. At least it was something and they had to do something. But the feeling of inadequacy raged, the hollow in the pit of her stomach tightened, knots grew and the tremor in her chest threatened to shake her into spasms. Shudder was right – she needed to act, to move, to see progress. To forget Amos. To find hope. He said he would start there and then, jumping up and going off to see if he could catch any of the lads from the pit. His action invigorated Margaret and she decided the first person to call on was her mother. It needed to be straightaway, because she had to do this while Barney was at work, but mainly, while Amos was out collecting. Her nerves were still raw and if she saw him, she was concerned she would not be able to control herself.

Susannah was surprised to see her daughter, mentally she checked the whereabouts of Barney and Amos before she examined Margaret with a critical eye. She had lost weight, her eyes were red-rimmed through crying, underpinned by black bags from lack of sleep, her shoulders slouched –her spirit seemed defeated.

'I didn't think things could get worse, but Mam, Shudder's been up to see Gilbert and he's been beaten up in jail. He says we've to get him out, no matter what it takes. According to Shudder he's in a bad way.'

'Oh Margaret, what're you going to do?'

With tears running down her face and falling from her chin, Margaret replied: 'Well, me and Shudder have put our heads together and we've got all our cash together and we're asking folk for anything they can lend and hopefully we'll have enough to buy him out.'

'How much do you need?'

'Nearly twenty quid. We've got two already, anything will help.'

Susannah looked at her daughter, she had seen her down before, when her Da died, when they left Newcastle and again when they were living in Blandford Street; but she could see this was different. This was inside Margaret, it was eating away at her and she was diminishing before her very eyes. Susannah thought back to how much of a support Margaret was during the bad times with Barney; how strong she had been standing up to the Blacks; how she had taken charge in the flight from Newcastle; how she had never complained and always done what she was asked. She made a decision. She couldn't stand by and see her daughter suffer like this. She also liked Gilbert and knew that if Margaret said she had paid the rent, then she had paid the rent.

'Margaret, let's get this sorted. You go to the back door and check the street, if nobody's coming, slide the bolt across and I'll do the same in the front room. Come on.'

134

Confused but intrigued, Margaret did as she was asked and followed her mother into the living room. Susannah started talking as she knelt down in front of the fireplace and began looking up and reaching inside the chimney.

'Barney hides his gun up the chimney in case the police ever search – he doesn't have a licence. He also hides his stash up here. He thinks I don't know, but whenever he gets something and hides it, he leaves soot in the grate and it's me what cleans it, so I know. Now a couple o' weeks back, when them Blacks came down, he said he needed to go to Newcastle to mend a radio for them. He said he'd give me the money. But there's a new tin in the chimney, one he thinks is even better hidden because it's further up.'

Susannah was almost inside the chimney as she reached up and lifted out a grey tin box. She gently placed it on the rag rug and after wiping her hands, carefully opened the lid. Inside were bundles of five pound notes all neatly wrapped and bound in paper bands and placed on top of each other.

'Jesus, Mother and Mary! How much is there?' exclaimed Margaret.

'More importantly, what did he do to get it?' answered Susannah. 'Keep an eye out on the street, Margaret. What I'm going to do is take out twenty pounds and give it to you. I'm going to take it from the bottom bundle and if Barney ever finds it missing, I'll just deny I know anything. You get Gilbert out of jail and this'll be our secret. Forever.'

Susannah carefully lifted the bundles out of the box and took four notes from the bottom one. She put everything back and replaced the box back up inside the chimney. Then she got out her pan and brush, cleaning the hearth and surrounding area thoroughly. She passed Margaret the four notes and said: 'Come on, let's have a drink.'

Margaret stood, silently crying, tears falling down her face as she held the notes in her hands; the relief consuming her. The weight had been so heavy, with it released she felt as if she was floating. She followed her mother back into the kitchen, watching dumbfounded while she unbolted the door and put the kettle on. Eventually she found her voice: 'Mam, I'll never be able to thank you enough.'

135

'You don't need to, girl, you've done enough for me over the years. Let's just say we're both happy, Gilbert can get out of jail and Barney's none the wiser. But we need to forget it ever happened.'

Amos watched Barney as he turned knobs and tapped out the message they were to send – testing the system.

'Well that's it,' Barney said.

'So, what do we do now?'

'We've still got ten days, so first off, you're going to have to learn the code so you can take over from me if needed. Then we need to go and test how long it'll take to walk up and get to the top of Hoober Stand. We need to decide if we should take anything up beforehand and, if we do, where we can hide it. Next, we need to plan where we transmit from and we need to plan an escape route, 'cos I'm not planning on getting caught. Then we're done until the night.'

'What happens on the night?'

'We connect up and make our signal at exactly one hour before midnight. We do it for exactly thirty minutes. Then we ditch the transmitter somewhere it can't be found, that's it. Until then we keep the transmitter hidden – no one is gonna question a wireless.'

'Are we still keeping it here?'

'Yeah, for now. No one ever comes down, I think the smell puts em off! But we've to go up to Hoober and check it's all ok up there. Remember we've to make sure this signal can be heard in Newcastle, so we need to broadcast from a height. Harry says Hoober Stand is perfect.'

'How does he know?'

'He saw it when he went to Packman you dim wit! He asked me about it when I was up in Newcastle. He agreed, in fact he insisted, that's where we transmit from before he give me the code. Look Amos, it's perfect, nobody goes up there after dark and with the blackout nobody can see anyway.'

'So, how're we going to see to transmit?'

'No need to see; once cables are connected, I can operate it in the dark. It's only a repeated code and anyway the transmitter will make a bit of light. No one will see it from more than ten yards away. But we'll take torches, just in case.'

'I can't believe he paid us before we do the job.'

136

'Yeah, strange for him, but he won't want to be seen down here again and he don't want us up there again, so how else was he to do it?'

'It's a lot o' money Barney. What you gonna do with yours?'

'Nothing 'til after war. Got it stashed nice and hidden where nobody'll find it. When war's finished I'm gonna go somewhere with a younger woman and live me days out in luxury.'

'What about Susannah?'

'What about Susannah. She never cared about me; all she ever wanted was for her kids to be safe and happy. So, she can have her turn and look after them, including that bitch, while I enjoy myself.'

'She is some girl, Barney, she didn't half give me a smack. I know she jumped me from behind, but it was still a punch and a half.' Ruefully Amos rubbed his chin where a large blue and green bruise was spreading.

'Yeah, her Dad were a boxer.'

'What a boxer dog?'

'Ha, good 'un Amos. No, he were a bare-fist fighter.'

The night was drawing in as Shudder walked through the trees. With rain dripping from their branches, he placed his feet carefully and quietly between the puddles. The traps he and Gilbert had set were known only to the two of them, but the gamekeepers were always on patrol and Shudder didn't want to get caught with two rabbits under his jacket. The brooding menace of Hoober Stand dominated the skyline as he used it to guide him through the wood towards the road. He stopped, frozen, at the sound of voices. Slowly sinking to the ground, he moved behind the cover of the wall, close to the road at the side of the wood. He placed his back against the wall and, breathing slowly and softly, checked for the best way out if he needed to run for it. If they had dogs he might have to throw the rabbits to them, but that was better than getting caught.

The voices came closer; boots walking briskly on the tarmac. They stopped ten yards past him, by the gap in the opposite wall leading to the cave below Hoober Stand.

'There. How long did that take us?'

Shudder was stunned to hear the voice of Barney Trenham. What was he doing up here? The furthest he ever walked was to the Red Lion in Wath. Barney Trenham wasn't a poacher and it was nearly dark, so what else could he be doing?

'Thirty-five minutes,' came the reply.

Shudder nearly gasped in disbelief. The man with Barney was his brother, Amos. He never came up this way. He lived his life on the other side of Brampton and always went into Barnsley. Apart from his debt-collecting activities, the nearest to Hoober he ever came was the bus stop to Barnsley, by the Bull's Head. Shudder moved further along the wall, the damp from the long grass seeping through the seat of his pants.

'It'll take us longer with kit, so we'll need to set off well before ten o'clock, or maybe even earlier so as to miss shift change then we need to find somewhere dry for the heavy stuff – somewhere we can get at it in the dark. Come on, we haven't got much time left afore it goes dark and I wouldn't mind a beer after we finish.'

The footsteps sounded muffled as the two men passed through the gap in the wall opposite; they were obviously heading up the rabbit track to the cave below Hoober. Shudder let out a sigh of relief. He waited for five minutes then slowly moved along the wall at the edge of the wood, he kept going until he was well away from the Stand and felt he could climb the wall unseen, making use of the road for a quick walk home.

Amos stood stock still. A gentle breeze fluffed up his fringe, revealing a forehead that was wrinkled with frowning concentration. He had asked Barney to go on ahead, sensing something was wrong and was now hidden behind a tree, screened from the road by low bushes. His eyes roamed up and down the way they came. Was he mistaken?

There was a movement; a head with a flat cap pulled fiercely down, slowly raised itself from behind the wall. Amos barely breathed. The head looked everywhere until it was satisfied and dropped back down behind the wall. Amos was tempted to move but stayed still. His patience was rewarded when he saw the head appear again, further along. Then it became a head and shoulders. The figure climbed over the wall and jumped onto the road. Shudder Madeley.

Amos sucked in a breath. You interfered once before Shudder, you still owe me for that. He remembered Shudder and Gilbert jumping on him, the ropes around his chest, the old bitch talking to his Dad. He'd made her pay, oh boy, had he made her pay; he'd made Gilbert suffer too, not enough and there would be more to come for him; but Shudder,

138

somehow, he'd got away unpunished. *Well, I've not forgotten, Shudder. No sir, I have not forgotten.* He turned slowly, thinking hard and set off to re-join Barney.

Despite marching at a good lick, it was dark by the time Shudder reached Gilbert's. He knocked on the door and waited until Eva pulled the blackout curtain back before going into the kitchen. The atmosphere was quiet. Subdued. Undeterred, like a magician on a stage, he produced the rabbits from under his coat with a *da-daa!* and passed one to Margaret. She took it with a grateful but gentle thank you. Gilbert was in his chair, cowed, looking smaller than Shudder remembered. Shudder tried to lighten the mood.

'Well Gilbert, I thought we would celebrate your release with a stew. Them traps we set before you went in have been bob-on and Earl's storm troopers have no idea where they are.'

Gilbert managed a tired smile. His left eye was bloodshot and swollen, his nose obviously broken; his lips were cracked and there were teeth missing. When he moved the pain in his ribs caused him to wince.

'Thanks Shudder, I need something to eat, something I can really taste – snap in there were awful.'

Margaret looked at Gilbert ruefully as she stood over the oven, taking out hot bread. Realising her discomfort, Shudder changed tack: 'You're not gonna believe who I just saw up Hoober.'

'Let me guess, Adolf and Winnie having a picnic?'

'Bloody hell Gilbert, good guess – close, but no coconut. Amos and Barney.'

Gilbert, Margaret and Eva all turned and looked at Shudder at the same time. Never one to miss the chance of an audience, Shudder took his coat off and, sitting down at the table, looked across at Gilbert.

'I got the rabbits from them traps we set towards Wentworth, on other side of Hoober and took long route back through Bluebell Wood thinking there wouldn't be any gamekeepers about tonight. So, I makes my way towards the road near to Hoober – you know – near that gap leading to the cave? I was just getting near the road, when I hears these voices. I'm crapping myself, 'cos if it's game keepers, if they've got dogs, I'm done for with rabbits up my jacket. I thought I'd had it, so I legged it to wall and got down real low. Two fellas walk past me and stop about five yards away. Any road, they start talking – I can't see them, but I know it's Amos and Barney…' Shudder paused for effect.

'Go on, Shudder, what was they doing up there? What were they saying? asked Margaret.

'Well, this is the strange bit; they were timing how long it took them to get to Hoober and they was talking about coming back but with something heavy and that it needed to be kept in a dry place.'

'And that's it?'

'Honest Margaret, they didn't say owt else, after they went, I took off and come here.'

'Tell us again, Shudder, from the start, from when you first saw them.' Gilbert had suddenly become more like his old self.

'Well, I didn't see them, I only heard them. They were walking up top of Hoober Field Lane when I heard them and I hid behind the wall 'cos I thinks they were gamekeepers. Then, they starts talking and I recognise both voices. I'm so close I can hear every word they said: "It took thirty-five minutes; it'll take longer with kit." Oh yeah,, they need to set off before shift change at ten. That were it.'

Everyone in the room looked at Gilbert. 'They could've been doing anything, but I think we all know what a pair of bastards they are.'

'Look, we don't know what they were doing and they can walk to Hoober whenever they want, just like the rest of us. Now, I'm gonna make a stew with this rabbit but I've got some soup and bread ready if you want to join us, Shudder.'

'Get in, Margaret! I thought you'd never ask,' said Shudder.

After Shudder left they sat in front of the fire, Gilbert smoking, Margaret and Eva chatting while taking turns at rag-rugging.

'Margaret, can I ask you a question?'

When Margaret nodded encouragingly, Eva poured out her thoughts: 'Barney and Amos are up to something. Think about it. Barney's an electrician who used to make and mend radios for a living, Harry Black's been down to Wath to see him. He didn't attack Barney then Barney goes up to Newcastle and is suddenly interested in Hoober Stand. There's something going on, but I don't understand what.'

Margaret looked hard at Eva – the girl was unusually perceptive and whatever Barney and Amos were up to, it was obviously bothering her. Thinking about Barney and Harry Black suddenly a forgotten memory came back to her: 'Eva, what does schwarz mean?'

'Black. It's German for black. Why?'

'When Harry Black attacked mi mam back in Newcastle, the old lady who helped us called him *Schwarz*. She said: "Schwarz very bad man."'

'Was she German?' Eva was bristling with excitement.

'I don't know, I don't know why I only just remembered it. Even if she was German, she would have called him Black, wouldn't she? I mean, that's his name.'

'But don't you get it? It could mean Harry Black is German and that Schwarz is his real name!' Eva exclaimed

'Ok, let's imagine the worst, if Harry Black is a German and Barney repairs radios and he's been up to Newcastle to do a job for him – and is now interested in Hoober Stand, something dangerous is going on. There's also something you two don't know and you can't tell anybody. If you do, mi mam will be in big trouble.'

Gilbert watched fascinated as the two women built a case out of hearsay. But now he leant forward, his interest doubled at the serious look on Margaret's face. She paused to take a breath and continued

'I told you I borrowed the money to get you out of jail. Gilbert, I said we all chipped in – but most of it came from mi mam… well actually, it all came from mi mam. She took it out of Barney's stash without him knowing. He's a pile of cash like you've never seen which he hides and thinks mi mam doesn't know about. He got it after he went on his trip to Newcastle to see Harry Black. And guess what? When he were up in Newcastle, he told mi mam that it was to do with radios – he either made or mended a radio for him!'

Gilbert and Margaret jumped in surprise as there was a burst of laughter which Eva could not hold back.

'So, Barney got Gilbert out of jail and bought your bedroom furniture without knowing it. Ooh that's good,' giggled Eva. 'Shame it's a secret, 'cos I'd love to be the one to tell him!'

Gilbert looked at the smile on Eva's face and laughed for the first time since his release. The action made him wince and hold his ribs.

'Bloody hell, you're right Eva. That's made my day!' he turned serious again and still rubbing his painful ribs, he continued 'Amos still has a lot to answer for and I for one, am not going to forget in a hurry. But that aside, I still don't get why the pair of them are suddenly interested in Hoober Stand? What's it got that's so important? Go on use your imaginations, you've been doing good so far. What's it got?'

'Well, it's the highest point around here, until you get the other side of Sheffield. It's empty, it's unused. It does nothing, but everybody knows it. I can't think of anything else.'

'Nobody goes up there after dark, yet it were nearly dark when Shudder saw Barney and Amos,' Margaret joined in.

'It'd be a good place to hide something. It's dry.'

'But Barney's hiding his money at home.'

'Yeah, money's different, but you could hide a tank up there,' said Eva.

Gilbert sat upright in his chair – Margaret and Eva stared at him as his facial expression went through several different emotions in a few seconds.

'Radios! Empty, high places – dark, lots of money and Harry Black could be a German. He's paying Barney to send radio signals off top of Hoober Stand!' he declared. 'Didn't you say Harry Black were a smuggler, Margaret? What if he were a gun smuggler? Smuggling guns to the Jerries? He'd pay lots of money for that wouldn't he?'

'Hang fire. Just hang fire. This can't be right. We're taking our dislike for them too far. No. No. We're making too many jumps and anyway, what're we gonna do? Tell the police the man who put you in jail is a German gun-runner 'cos his brother mends radios, has a lot of money and likes Hoober Stand? No, they would laugh right at us. We'd look proper idiots.'

Tuesday 10 December 1940

Amos poked the fire. Rita left them for bed an hour ago but he and Barney were still roasting chestnuts. He placed a cigarette in the corner of his mouth and poured the last dregs from a bottle of pale ale into his glass. He looked across at Barney whose feet must be frying as he sat in the armchair with his boots resting on the cast iron fender around the hearth.

'Barney I've been thinking' he started. 'Something's wrong. Why do we need to send a signal at eleven o'clock on Sunday? No one is telling us to send a message, or if this happens say this, if that happens say that; just a signal in Morse, at a certain time. Why? Everybody knows it's eleven o'clock on Sunday, so why do we have to tell them?'

Barney looked across at his brother. He took his boots off the fender and pushed the soles onto the floor. The heat they had absorbed singed his feet, which tingled with a pleasing pain. A kind of Hail Mary to his sins or a hair shirt to his conscience.

'I know Amos, it's been bothering me too. And I can only come up with one answer…'

The brothers looked at each other while Barney pulled the skin from a chestnut, dipped it into the small pile of salt they had tipped onto the table and popped it into his mouth.

'We're not sending a message' he said, talking around the chestnut, 'we're a directional beacon.'

'What the heck does that mean?'

'We've got to send a message in Morse and keep repeating it. Like you said, we're not responding or reacting because it's not a message, it's a signal. The signal can be picked up all the way to the North Sea. If you pick it up and know beforehand where it is supposed to come from, you can work out where you are. Amos we're transmitting from a known location and the only people what need a signal from a definite location, from a distance, in a blackout, are the Luftwaffe, coming in to bomb.'

'Jesus, so we're guiding them onto their targets.'

'Yup.'

Barney chewed his roast chestnut, while Amos lit his cigarette. After a long ten minutes in silence, Amos flicked his stub into the fire and went down to the cellar for more beers while Barney peeled chestnuts. They refilled their glasses, lit fresh cigarettes and chewed on the chestnuts.

It was Amos who broke the silence: 'Barney, people are gunna die.'

'Yeah, I know.' Barney took a pull of his cigarette and blew smoke up to join the grey blue cloud hanging above their heads. 'But Amos, we were happy when we thought it was gun-running and guns kill people.'

Amos threw a handful of chestnut shells into the fire, where they crackled and popped in a miniature imitation of gunfire.

'There's more. When I was up in Newcastle, Harry didn't want me to build a transmitter, he gave me one and instead got me to set up a receiver to the exact frequency. He's going to be listening in so if he doesn't hear the signal he's going to know straight away. And, Amos, he promised to do things to us what are not very nice and to keep doing them for a long time.

'What's more, we've taken Harry Black's money. On top of that, if we don't do it, it isn't just going to be the Blacks looking for us. That's why he give us the money up front. It isn't his and he knows that by taking the money we're guilty whether we do this or not. It were a German transmitter he gave me, Amos. Even if the message isn't for Luftwaffe, if we get caught with that, they'll think it is. If we do this, the Army'll be after us and, if we get caught, we'll hang for treason. If we don't do it, Harry and the Jerries will be after us.'

Amos digested everything Barney said. They were in trouble – no doubt about it – and he felt angry that Barney had kept this knowledge to himself. But it was too late now. It had already been too late, before Barney's trip to Newcastle.

As if reading his thoughts, Barney said: 'Right. So apart from us, only Harry knows what's planned. Bombing will go ahead whether or not we send his signal. I don't see any way out – we've been set up good and proper. So, we do this and make sure we get rid of all the kit and maybe we're in the clear. Harry says it'll take army at least an hour to work out where signal is coming from and get somebody up to Hoober. We'll be well away by then. Harry'll have his signal; we're in the clear and bloody rich.'

Amos looked at his brother. He was in the same place. There was no way out. They must send the signal, destroy everything and keep quiet.

He knew Barney would not say a word to anyone. *If you can't trust your brother, who can you trust?*

'Barney we do this. We get the money. People die – so what? It's a war. I 'ain't running. Let's do it.'

Barney reached across and the brothers clinked glasses. 'Thanks Amos, I knew I could rely on you. We'll get this done and the pig farm will make money which we can use as cover for what Harry has paid us. Here's to sending a signal and living a long and wealthy life.'

The brothers clinked the glasses again, smiled and both took a deep drink.

Thursday 12 December 1940

'Come on Eva, fancy a walk?'

'What? It's only seven o'clock!'

'Yeah I know, which is why I've made us a breakfast picnic to have when we get there.' he patted the satchel he had ready packed. 'Come on, there won't be many more nice mornings like this and we can let Margaret and Alfred have a nice slow start.'

'So, where're we going then?'

'Hoober Stand.' Gilbert grinned across at Eva. 'We're not only having a breakfast picnic we're going to solve a mystery.'

Eva looked at him and smiled 'Ok, now you've got me interested.'

'Eva, you were right – Hoober is the perfect place to hide something. Barney and Amos are up to no good. So, let's have a look and see what they're doing.'

'Sounds like a plan to me.'

The two of them set off. It was a wonderfully clear autumn morning, there was little breeze and the sun dared winter to show its face. The last few leaves of the oak and beech were lit up by the low light, their rich gold and bronze colours ablaze between the drab leafless branches of the sycamores. They walked the two miles chatting casually about the Yard; Margaret's pregnancy, which was near full-term now; Eva's plans when she left school; and how they could fatten up the next pig with everyone on rations and there being hardly any scraps. In next to no time they arrived at the Stand.

Walking through the gate, they did a full circle of the tower without saying a word. Stopping outside the door, they examined it. Gilbert had not been here since the war started and was surprised. The Earl was obviously determined no one was going to use the tower or even get inside. Not only was the door secured, with the glass removed and wood boarding inserted in its place, there were huge screws through the door into the frame. It would take at least an hour to undo them all and the evidence would be obvious to anyone passing by. But even then, another layer of chicken wire covered the whole door and frame, tacked to the wood with dozens of tacks. And to make sure, there was a large notice which stated 'No Entry. By Order of His Majesty's Government' nailed in the middle.

'Well, it appears we're not welcome inside,' Eva observed. 'Come on, let's have our picnic, I'm starving.'

They sat on the grass at the side of the tower. Gilbert got the jam sandwiches out and poured them both a cup of well stewed tea from the flask he filled earlier.

'Eva, I'm not happy. Those two are up to something, I need to know what. It's like… well, it's like it's eating away at me. I need to get into the tower.'

'Gilbert, look at it! We would need a pound of dynamite to get through that door the way they've nailed it.'

Gilbert smiled. *We…?* 'See the window above us? If you look, it doesn't lock. It's not even fully shut and notice how the lintel sticks out like a dormer over it. Well if we get a rope and throw it over the dormer, we could use it to get into the window'

Eva looked up and could see a stone lintel sticking out like a roof gable over the top of the window 'maybe….' she said hesitantly.

'Let me show you.' Gilbert cleared a patch of ground by their feet and drew out the angle of the lintel with a stick. He drew a looped rope over it with both ends touching the floor. 'I hold this end, you climb up,' he said, pointing. 'Once you get onto that window ledge, you attach the rope to the window and I climb up after you.'

'First we need a rope, then we need to get it over the lintel; then your plan might just work.'

Gilbert dipped into his satchel and pulled out a rope and a torch. 'Might not be a bull rope, but will Margaret's washing line do?' he said with a grin.

They cleared the picnic away, hid it under a bush and started on the job of getting the rope over the lintel. The first fifteen feet of the tower rose vertically, then there was a small ledge and the tower started to lean inwards as it shrank on its way up. The window lintel was about six feet higher than the ledge by Gilbert's estimation and they needed to throw the line over the top and catch the end when it landed. First, they scurried round for fist sized stones and selected several which they put into a pile. Selecting the one they felt was the best, they tied it to the end of the rope. Gilbert took aim and threw the stone over the window but as it came down the line missed the dormer and all the rope fell to the ground. After three more tries Gilbert looked exasperated and dejected. 'This is harder than I thought,' he said.

'Here, let me have a go.' Eva wound the slack of the line into a coil and held it in her left hand, the stone tied to the rope in her right. Standing close to the tower she threw the stone over the dormer while throwing the coil after it at the same time. This time the stone did not have the weight of the rope on it for most of its journey and sailed over the window dropping down at the far side. Eva stamped her foot on the end of the washing line to stop it following the rest over the window. They watched as the stone slid down the wall at the far side of the window, bumping on the ledge. For a long second it seemed as if it would catch and stay on the ledge, but it rolled and slowly slid down the remainder of the wall bringing the rope with it.

Eva grinned at Gilbert with an 'I told you so!' chortle, holding on to the end of the rope. She looked at the tower above her and said, 'I think it would be better if both my hands were free as I climb up. Can we tie a loop in this end of the rope? I'll put my foot in it and if you pull the other end you can pull me up the wall until I'm high enough to grab the ledge.'

Gilbert tied the loop and Eva stood with her foot inside it. Gilbert took up the slack. The washing line grew taught and straightened above her head as Eva grasped it with both hands. Slowly Gilbert heaved, pulling the rope and Eva up the wall. His damaged ribs screamed at him every time he raised his hands to grab the rope before pulling it down towards him.

 The stone looked smooth, but whenever Eva's hands and knees brushed it the stone acted like sandpaper, rubbing her skin off, until her knees and knuckles were grazed and bleeding. Thankfully, it only took a minute and Eva was at the ledge. She grabbed the window sill, first with one hand then the other; balanced herself, pulled herself up, first sitting, then standing on the ledge, she pushed the window open and disappeared inside pulling the rope after her. She opened the other window and tied the rope in a double loop around the middle stanchion and signalled to Gilbert.

He tested the rope, putting all his weight on it, before starting up the wall. It was only fifteen feet before he was able to grab the ledge and pull himself up and through the window, but his ribs were on fire by the time he sat inside the tower, sweat pouring off his forehead. He sank to the floor gasping for breath. Eva pulled the rope in behind them and closed the window. They sat in silence, flush with success, while Gilbert got his breath back.

After a few minutes, with Gilbert fully recovered, they stood up and looked around. Before the war both of them had been regular visitors to the Stand and knew it intimately, but this time they viewed it completely differently. The light coming in through the window was dimmed by grime. There was nowhere for anything to be hidden, the only breaks in the stonework were where local youths had scratched their initials. They checked the stones around the window, the alcove and the stairwell, as far as the light let them. Anything stored here would be obvious.

Gilbert led the way down the spiral staircase towards the door at ground level. At every step they stopped and checked the stone work. Not knowing what they were looking for, they inspected everything, encouraging each other to look overhead and under foot. But the beautifully fitting stones revealed nothing. As they reached the bottom the light from the window above hardly penetrated, while the wood over the glass in the door blocked the light from below. Gilbert took out his torch and switched in on, running the light around the walls, then around the back of the door and along the floor. He stopped, turned and shone the beam back up the stairs behind them. He could see their foot prints in the dust. He turned the beam back to the floor in front of them. Nothing except a thick layer of dust accumulated over the past two years.

'Eva,' he whispered, 'there's no foot prints, no one's been down here since it was boarded up. Look at the ones we've left.' Eva followed the beam of the torch while he repeated the search. 'Come on, let's look up top.'

When they reached their starting point by the window, they stopped, looking at the stairs going up. There was no sign of entry, while their foot prints showed clearly behind them. 'Let's look anyway,' said Eva, and they started the climb. Up and round they went, a window on every circuit enabling them to see without the torch until they got to the top. The door to the platform at the top of the Stand was unlocked, but Gilbert stopped – if they ventured outside, they would be in full view of anyone looking at the tower and the tower could be seen from miles around. While he was debating, Eva pushed past him, opened the door slowly and, almost on her belly, crawled in a full circle around the platform.

'Nothing.' she reported on her return. 'Come on, let's get out of here and quick in case anyone saw me.'

They ran down the stairs until they reached the window. Opening it slowly, they checked that no one was around and threw the rope out. Gilbert slid down it and waited at the bottom. Eva untied it and threw it after him. Closing the window behind her, she climbed out onto the ledge, grabbed the edge and slowly let her feet down the wall until she was hanging by her hands. Gilbert stood beneath her, raising his arms as high as he could, but there was still a gap of several feet to her shoes. 'Go on, Eva. I've got you,' he called. She let go and started the fall.

There was a wild second when she was airborne until she felt Gilbert's strong arms grab her and pull her into his chest. He let her down to the floor, holding his ribs, trying not to breathe so hard, his chest pounding. They stood rock still, Gilbert still panting; looking around and checking for any one passing.

They were clear.

Eva picked up the rope, wrapping it into a coil, but walking away from the tower her foot caught in a root and she tumbled to the floor, dropping everything.

They both laughed as he said, 'Good job you weren't as clumsy on that window ledge, else you'd have had a right bump! Come on, let's get back.'

Smiling Eva picked up the rope and followed Gilbert making his way around the Stand. It was still a delightful but crisp morning and, with the sweat from his exertions now cold on his back, Gilbert was keen to start moving to generate some warmth.

He realised that Margaret was right when she said the police would laugh at him, but he was certain they were onto something. Something was going off with Amos and Barney and the throbbing in his ribs would not let him forget it. He led the way through the trees towards the cave behind the Stand, his curiosity would not allow him to leave without at least checking there. He and Shudder had once hidden inside the cave when chased by the Earl's gamekeepers. Gilbert grimaced at the memory. They had been close to being caught that day. One of the gamekeepers actually got hold of Shudder by the hair. In the struggle that ensued both pulled violently and a large handful of Shudder's hair was ripped out. It took weeks to grow back properly and Shudder looked a proper Charlie in the oversized hat he needed to wear to hide it.

They approached the cave from above, straight away Gilbert could see that this was also a wasted journey. The cave had collapsed. All that was left was a pile of stones at the bottom of a hollow in the ground. There was so much mining in the area, it was unsurprising. Most houses suffered from some form of subsidence and the cave had been unstable for years. He walked past, to the edge of the old mine shaft some twenty yards further on and looked back. Hoober Stand stood stark and majestic above the hill. Its lop-sided appearance ominous as it stood sentry over the pile of rubble that had once been a cave. Gilbert shrugged his shoulders and started the walk back. Eva stopped at his side, bent down and picked up a rope from the ground. It was tied tightly to a young birch tree at the edge of the flooded mine shaft.

'What's this for?' she asked Gilbert.

'No idea' he replied 'It'll be some kids messing'

Eva let the rope play through her hands while they trudged up the hill. All the spring left their stride, the disappointment of failing in their quest leaving them frustrated. The rope continued to slide through Eva's hands, rising from the long grass where it was loosely laid and hidden. Every now and then it would be curled around the base of a tree but it followed the path up the hill. They reached the open ground around the Stand with the rope continuing towards the tower. Gilbert gathered the picnic from under the bush, while Eva followed the rope to the tower where it came to an end, tied to the lightening conductor, where it sank into the ground. This was what Eva had tripped over. Clueless as to what it meant Eva stamped the conductor back into the ground and helped Gilbert with the picnic before they rounded the Stand and set off on the pleasant walk down Hoober Lane.

'Ah well, there goes that theory,' Gilbert grunted to Eva. 'Glad we didn't tell anybody, we'd have looked proper daft.'

'Yeah, but be fair, Gilbert, the picnic were great. It made a real change and you needed the exercise for your ribs. Come on I'll race you back.'

'Fat chance o' that. A snail would beat me, the shape I'm in.'

'Come on then, Grandad, let's get you back to your pipe and slippers.'

'Why you cheeky little sod—' Gilbert started, before Eva burst out laughing and began to skip down the hill.

Oberleutnant Riesling sat hunched over his receiver while the pilot and co-pilot concentrated on their instruments in their seats ahead of him. The bomber thrummed and throbbed. The massive engines burning gallon after gallon of fuel to keep the machine in the sky. He listened; watched the dials and turned knobs, guiding the bomber along the radio beam. As part of the Nautikerkorps he was trained in the civilian Lorenz blind-landing system and its war-time bombing equivalent, Knickebein. The British, however, had blocked the effectiveness of the Knickebein system after finding parts on a downed German bomber.

So, a new system had been developed – X-Gerat. This was the brainchild of Capitan Schwarz, a genius who had worked on civilian systems before moving onto the military programme during the build-up to the war. Riesling worked closely with Schwarz and was one of his star pupils, so he was honoured when he was chosen to fly on a test mission to see if the British were once again interfering, as they had with Knickebein.

While the mission was being planned, the Luftwaffe had concentrated on London – the distinctive shape of the Thames shining in the moonlight guiding the bombers to their targets, despite the blackout. But now it was time to take the blitz to the rest of England.

They were nearing the target. X-Gerat sent out a thin directional beam from Bergen in Norway and, if the pilot strayed from it, Riesling would hear a change in tone from his receiver. The tone varied depending whether the pilot moved to the left or right. Riesling's ears were super sensitive and over the months he had always been the first to detect the slightest variation in the beam. It was his job to pull the pilot back on line. Then as they approached the drop zone a new beam would cut across the direction beam forming an X, with the centre of the cross over the target, giving the instruction to drop.

The beam was holding steady when the cross beam came in. He listened hard. The signal was good its message clear and loud. From the corner of his eye, Riesling could see the bomb bay was open and the bombs were starting to roll out of the hatch, the cross beam triggering their release. The signal was strong despite having travelled all the way from the transmitter station outside Kleve in Germany. Riesling began to relax and leant back in his seat, but as he did a faint echo of the cross beam sounded in his ear piece. He could not say for certain that anything was wrong but it did not feel right. Why an echo? Anything that gave rise to doubt would be questioned, and an echo was definitely a doubt. He knew the ultimate test was needed – a direct comparison with a local land-based signal, he also knew that in three days' time that test would be run.

The blackout curtains shut out the light completely and, once the candle was blown out, the darkness became as thick as treacle. Gilbert woke slowly, his thoughts as dull as the light in the room. Then through the stupor something bullied his senses into action. A scream, which kept building in intensity, until it could not be ignored. A wailing increasing and dying before rising again. The scream of an air-raid siren.

Gilbert grabbed the sheets on the bed and threw them back, shaking Margaret he fumbled for the torch on the bedside table. Without a word, he grabbed his trousers and yanked them on. Wrapping her dressing gown around her, Margaret picked up Alfred from his cot, while Gilbert banged on Eva's bedroom door. She was already awake and dressed in her overcoat. Quickly, the family ran out of the house, through the Yard and across the road to the shelter. Other bodies hurried over the road throwing coats or blankets around themselves, but in the dark, it was unclear who they were.

Inside the shelter Gilbert lit the hurricane lamp. Their next-door neighbours, Howard and Mary Arnold, were the oldest and frailest, so Gilbert gave them blankets, shouting instructions as both were nearly deaf. He wondered wryly if it could be something of a blessing, with the siren screaming and the kids yelling. Only five minutes after the siren had begun its wail, five families were huddled in the shelter: the Laws, the Robinsons, the Limers, the Masons, and the Arnolds – the fifteen residents of the top row of houses in Top Yard.

At first there was hustle and bustle as everyone tried to get comfortable; kids complained while tired nervous parents vented their feelings, but slowly a different sound began to grow. A deep grumbling groan, initially low, it increased – drowning the siren until everyone in the shelter sat mesmerised by the approaching clamour. The gruff bass roar vibrated the shelter, shaking dust from the ledges, chests throbbed to an unnatural beat as a swarm of angry throated German bombers flew directly overhead.

The tension inside the dugout reduced all the inhabitants to silence. Margaret hugged Alfred close to her chest. Gilbert sat in between her and Eva with his arms around them both. The shelter was airless under normal conditions, but now it seemed the German planes were pulling the air and the very ability to breath from inside, up into the sky. Every eye was wide with terror. Slowly, the cacophony began to lessen until it was a mere distant buzz. But, as the roar lessened, they heard the crump and thud of bombs exploding somewhere in the distance. At each crash a small tremor passed through the ground in a subversive echo of the destruction falling from the sky.

Gilbert wondered if the men working underground at the mines would have felt the tremors. He wondered if there had been any damage to the pit infrastructure, or worse – if they had caused any collapses which might trap men. It was not a welcome thought, but they had all seen the photographs of the blitz in the newspapers and knew that somewhere buildings were being destroyed. Under that devastation death or horror was being inflicted on innocent people. They sat avoiding eye contact, all knowing that for the moment, they were safe. But while they were grateful, their imaginations also shared the pain of those elsewhere. Those suffering the misery of the whirlwind of fire falling from the sky.

After an eternity the siren changed its scream, sounding the all clear, and the weary inhabitants of Top Yard almost fell out of the shelter. Their silence deepened when they looked into the night sky. As fires burned, Hoober Stand stood out on the horizon, a deep-black silhouette framed against the yellow glowing sky – a serene backdrop to the carnage raging below. No one could think of anything to say so they silently made their way back to their respective homes. Shattered, sombre and scared.

Back inside, Gilbert made a hot drink and Eva made toast while Margaret settled Alfred back into bed. There was little point in Gilbert going back to bed, his nerves would not have allowed him to sleep. He could see that Eva was a wreck, remembering how her body had trembled in the shelter.

154

'What can we do, Gilbert?' she asked. 'We can't just sit there in our holes in the ground and pray. We've got to do something!'

'Eva, there are a lot of brave men and women trying to stop this and we can help by sitting tight and producing the coal they need. It'll end, and those of us who survive have got to believe that life will be better for the efforts of them fighting on our behalf.'

Dawn was starting to break and a dim light filled the sky. They turned off the gas mantle and pulled the blackout curtains back, looking out at the fires still burning behind Hoober. Now the light was growing they could also see huge clouds of smoke over Sheffield. Gilbert turned the wireless on and they listened to the story of the night's events. A staggering number of German bombers had targeted Sheffield and though they had largely missed their intended targets – the armaments factories, huge numbers of civilians had been killed, injured, or made homeless.

'So, was it all a waste of time?' Margaret stood behind them as they all looked at Hoober.

'Yeah, we even checked the cave, but nothing.'

'No, not that, the bombing. They missed, so like I said, it was a waste of time. So, they'll be back.'

'They've been bombing London for two months. So, I guess Sheffield has more coming.'

'Aye well, on that note, I'm going back to bed. One of us has got to be awake later for Alfred.'

Gilbert took out a cigarette and stared at the plumes of smoke staining the morning sky. There was little wind so they rose straight up. Like fingers pointing the blame. He looked at the mantelpiece and remembered the photograph of his father in his uniform still on display at his mother's. A bright youthful looking man with a hint of mischief in his eyes. Then he remembered him as he was after the war. Crippled, in permanent pain, with a shuffling walk which made anyone watching him wince.

He wondered what he had seen, sitting in the trenches at the Somme, with German soldiers less than fifty yards away. Bullets flying through the air; bombs crashing all around; men dying in front of him; the constant sound of guns, large and small, with flares at night, all happening in clawing, claggy mud. The scars on his stomach and back testament to the charge his company made on a machine-gun nest. Then, three days and nights lying injured in no man's land, watching the ongoing carnage through pain-misted eyes before stretcher bearers could get to him to carry him out. And after all that, he went back. To Ypres.

A few hours sitting in a well-built air-raid shelter with the enemy fifteen thousand feet over head aiming for a different target and he was already badly shaken. During the raid Eva's thin body shivered constantly with fear and shook like a dog getting rid of water every time a bomb exploded. Margaret had been predictably calm, constantly muttering soothing sounds to young Alfred as she locked her focus onto the baby, her swollen near-term belly making it difficult to hold her son in the confined space.

Gilbert sighed and turned to Eva

'Here I am looking at a city burning and all I'm thinking about is Amos and Barney. They might be up to something, but it's not important. That...' he pointed at the smoke, 'that's what's important.' He continued staring out of the window as he lit his cigarette, his thoughts weeping.

Friday 13 December 1940

Barney sipped his beer impatiently, waiting for Amos to sit down. Last night was still playing on his mind – the mad dash from the house; grabbing the kids and wrapping them in blankets, sitting waiting for the worst – praying it would be someone else, not them. Susannah had been frantic. Jack as cool as a cucumber while Doris, Brenda and Joseph had been terrified. Like most he had not been able to get back to sleep, so the day shift down the pit was a long and tired affair. After dinner he sorted the pigs, then walked to the pub to meet Amos when he came in after his Friday collections for Cantors.

Eventually he was sitting opposite Barney with a fresh pint in front of him.

'You alright? Rita?'

'Aye, your lot?'

'Yeah, but I hope they don't come again tonight, I could do with a good night's sleep.'

'Puts paid to the idea that we're guiding them in, doesn't it?'

'I don't know. Wireless says they missed factories and hit the city. Perhaps they need a bit of help.'

'Jesus, Barney. It's a bummer this. If we're thinking right, we're helping to make them more accurate. They get the factories and war is a lot harder, but they miss Sheffield and fewer people die.'

'The Government will build more factories.'

'Maybe they will, but I've got my call-up papers. Yorks and Lancs on fourth of January. It's alright for you miners but I've got to go and fight these buggers.'

'Jesus. Sorry, Amos.'

'So, what shall we do? '

'Amos, being in army won't save you… Harry will still find you if we don't send that signal. Anyway, you could always try for an office job with your qualifications.'

'So, we carry on?'

'I don't want to see them Blacks down here again. I say we carry on.'

'Ok, I agree. I want to keep that money… I can't stop counting it to be honest, but what are we going to tell Rita and Susannah when there's an air-raid on Sunday and we're not in the shelter? They are not going to be happy.'

Harry Black put the newspaper on the table and thought hard. The raid on Sheffield last night had been a surprise – he was fully expecting the first raid to be on Sunday. That was the day Billy had asked for the signal to be sent, so why a raid last night? It didn't add up. He had transmitted the coordinates from the niche exactly as instructed. But the bombing began only half an hour later. There was a small crumb of comfort in this. If he was confused then British Intelligence would also be struggling to understand.

Everything was set up for Sunday – Barney was primed, along with his brother. The wireless behind him was tuned in and he would know exactly when the signal was sent. He would monitor it and have a tense wait until he knew Barney had managed to get away in time. Harry looked again at the map, the one he had kept for himself rather than giving it to Barney. The one showing where the army camps were. The map was dog-eared, as he was constantly consulting it. Since Barney had agreed to send the signal, Harry poured over the map every day. Billy had been right to warn him not to go himself, he simply couldn't work out how Barney could get away. The only advantage Barney had was that he was local and would know the back routes, which, from experience Harry knew could make all the difference.

As the crow flew, the nearest troops were in Chapeltown, only three and a half miles away from Hoober. True, the roads were narrow and winding, speed would be difficult in the blackout, but unfortunately, the army would already be on standby to help with the effects of the bombing and if they received the order to race to Hoober to stop the signal, they could be there well inside the half an hour that Billy needed.

He thought about Barney. He was obviously terrified of Harry, but was he terrified enough to keep his mouth shut and how much had he told his brother? Harry knew he must assume the worst. He must plan for Barney and Amos being caught and for them to give the authorities his name. He needed an escape route already set up plus the ability to disappear. He smiled; not that hard for a smuggler to disappear. He would head to Ireland and sit out the war in neutral territory, happy in the knowledge that Billy would be safe. He already had the war-time travel

158

passes sorted – that had been his first priority after Billy left. The money he had built up over the years would be more than ample – but even so, he decided to collect some more debts. There were still two days to go and a robust debt collection might even yield enough to pay for the trip. Stop him dipping into his savings.

Still the early raid bothered him. He could only trust the plan had not been changed, that Barney would go through with the signal and Billy would be fine. Contact with Billy or with Barney was impossible so he had to carry on, but plan for the worst.

Six for Gold

Sunday 15 December 1940

Sunday broke dismally with skies grey and heavy with the threat of rain as Margaret kneaded her dough. The bombers had not returned after their raid on Thursday, so while the wireless reported bombing in other cities it seemed that Sheffield had been spared for the time being. For Eva sleep was getting easier, although Margaret heard her nightmares – calling for her mother and father – on both nights since the raid. Margaret's growing belly was slowing her down while Alfred's demands increased. Her own sleep patterns were disturbed without the bombing. Still, she reminded herself, compared to some they had a lot to be thankful for.

Winnie went on defiant walkabouts in London to show he was still with the people, suffering as they suffered, not cowering in some concrete-lined safe house miles from anywhere. Margaret wondered what Hitler was doing. Bet he wasn't in a bunker. Bet he was living it up while everyone else suffered. That was the way of the world – those on top lived to the full, while those underneath lived any life they could grasp.

Margaret punched the dough instead of kneading it, twisting her hand like her da had taught her. She smiled at the memory. When he had tried to show her how to hit the punch bag she practised on her dough. Hit with twist; hit with twist. Not the recommended way to make bread according to her mother – but it worked and the more she had practised on the dough the easier it became on the bag.

Her da had always said to get what you can, when you can, but to do it honestly and without hurting anyone. When she had questioned his boxing he simply replied: 'When we go into the ring, we both know what we're doing, putting on a show for them as wants to pay for it. I'm not intending to hurt my opponent, only beat him. God made me not only poor, but large and quick and if I can use that to improve things for my family, I will. Remember all you can do is try to make the problems you face now easier for those who follow behind you.' *Well, Da, I don't know how to make this problem go away or how to make it easier for Alfred and Eva, but I do know how to bake a loaf and if that improves their humour then at least I've tried,* she thought, punching the dough. Hit with twist, she smiled, leaving the dough to rise.

Amos was twitchy – he had been all day. It was no good, he could not look at Rita for another second; he must get out. Grabbing his cap and coat he grunted, 'not be long' and walked out of the door, grimacing as he saw the relief on her face. There was still light, but it was dimming with less than half an hour before total darkness. He and Barney had agreed they would meet at the farm at seven, three hours into the blackout and two hours before the shift change at the pit. But he could not sit still.

After fifteen minutes of walking aimlessly, Amos realised he was turning in the direction of the pig farm. It was too early but still he continued on. He stopped at the edge of the road to light a cigarette and blew the smoke into the air, savouring the taste. He looked over the field, ready to take a second pull, when a movement caught his eye. Someone was coming out of the sty. He leaned forward, casually resting on the fence and watched. It was Shudder. He'd been inside their building! An indignity started to well inside Amos – he was trespassing. Why?

The indignity turned to panic – the transmitter was inside the shed, along with his money. Shudder could not be allowed to see either of them. He flicked the cigarette away ready to jump the fence. But Shudder wasn't coming his way; instead of taking the short route out, he was going the other way, away from Brampton. Amos watched Shudder move away with brisk, purposeful strides, at no stage did he look back. Amos had not been seen.

He turned and started to jog down the road. It was easier going and he was hidden by the hedge. At the bottom of the road he stopped and watched Shudder again. He wasn't going to Brampton, he was headed towards Darfield. Confused, Amos thought it through. The only thing in Darfield was the Conservative Club where the Home Guard gathered. Wait, there would be a meeting tonight, Sunday, and they had a telephone. A direct link to the army. Shudder was going to raise the alarm!

He looked back, there was no time to get Barney; he needed to act now. If he ran down the road, he could cross the canal at the lock, while Shudder was headed for the bridge. A sprint through the path, over the culvert, and he should be ahead of Shudder. After that it was anyone's guess… would he cut over the railway line or continue to take the long route? Amos took a gamble – Shudder was not a long-route man. He ran, his heart pounding, his breath ragged.

At the railway line he leapt down the embankment and looked around. He'd seen no one the whole time and the dark was settling in. It was a single-line track with an old speed limit sign at the side, its brick support crumbling. He grabbed a brick from the support and pushed himself back into the shadows, into the weeds and scrub, at the side of the embankment. He had guessed right. Shudder appeared, easing himself down the embankment, taking care with his footing in the rapidly dimming half-light.

The second Shudder's feet reached the railway ballast, Amos jumped out of the scrub and, with all his might, smashed the brick into the back of Shudder's head. Shudder stumbled but stayed on his feet. Amos brought the brick down again and Shudder fell to his knees. Amos hit him a third time. Shudder fell flat onto the rail ballast. Amos stepped over him and smashed the brick into his face again and again and again.

Panting, exhausted, Amos threw the brick away. He glanced up and down the track. It was a pit service-track moving coal wagons from the collieries at Darfield and Wombwell to the collection point at Wath Hump. There was a bend in the track to his right, he grabbed Shudder and dragged him onto the railway line. He laid him over the track as if he had fallen, carefully placing his head with its battered features directly on the track. It was close enough to the bend for the engine driver to have little chance of seeing a body on the line, especially in the blackout; and, in the race to produce coal, trains were running all night long.

Amos brushed himself off and climbed back up the embankment. Darkness was closing in with every second. He had not gone more than four hundred yards when he heard a train pass through on its way to Wath Hump. Without stopping or slowing his pace he raced to the pig farm. First, he checked the transmitter and his cash before he washed the blood off his hands and face. The stains on his trousers and jacket were impossible to clean, so he hid his jacket at the back of the shed for later disposal. He would change his trousers when he got back home.

Reassured that the transmitter and his cash were safe Amos regained his composure in time to be casual as he walked into the kitchen where Rita was knitting by the fire. 'I'd love cup of tea before I go back out, love. It's gonna be a long night.' He went straight upstairs and changed his trousers, placing the spoiled ones in a bag, to take with him and hide at the farm.

Back down stairs he moved through the kitchen to the cellar top and pulled his shotgun from its shelf. He took half a dozen cartridges from a box, stuffed them into his pocket and warmed his hands by the fire, waiting for his drink. Inside he could feel every twitch of his nerves; his fingers throbbed, expanding with every heartbeat. But a clammy cloying echo inside his chest was slowly relaxing. A need, a craving had been eased. The old image flashed past of Shudder grabbing him on Pontefract Road, the pain of his arms tied to the post, both quickly soothed by the sight of a brick meeting flesh. The old cow and the accomplice were both gone now. The main offender had somehow escaped lightly – but there would be more for him, and now there was a new insult to be avenged. The boxer. She had to have it.

The bread was the success of the meal. Margaret contemplated how she could have made a few old potatoes, a straggly leek, three bent and twisted carrots, a shrivelled turnip, two ounces of milk powder and a spoonful of flour any more edible. There was no answer apparent, unless you added ingredients she simply did not have. Tomorrow her ration book would open for the new week and she could join the queues to boost her larder, but today they ate exactly what they had.

After the meal they turned off the gas mantle to save gas and sat by the light of the fire, storytelling. Gilbert was the master of stories. Give him a subject and he would invent a situation and an adventure would begin. Eva always sat enthralled while Margaret tried to challenge his stories and outguess him with twists and turns he could not get out of. Inevitably it ended with the three of them collapsing in heaps of laughter at the ridiculousness of it all.

They were at the point where Hitler's moustache needed cutting but the barber's scissors were blunt, when there was a knock at the door. The habit of people walking in had ended with blackout curtains. The curtain hung across the door, which could not open until the curtain was pulled back, so someone inside needed to let the visitor in. Margaret watched as Eva pulled the curtain back and opened the door. The clouds had finally burst and her brother Jack almost fell into the kitchen, sodden and wet

166

through. He raced to the fire where he stood shaking, brushing off the rain.

'Blimey, Jack, what's going on?' asked Gilbert. 'You smell worse than a wet dog that's rolled in fox grease.'

'Ha ha very funny Gilbert, I've just gone arse over tit in Barney's pig farm,' he replied turning around and showing them a long streak of mud down his back.

'Jack!' yelled Margaret 'Don't you dare get any of that muck on my rugs!' Jack looked forlorn but bent down and moved the rug out of the way, standing in front of the fire dripping mud-coloured rain water onto the flags instead.

'Come on then, Jack, give us the story 'cos I've got a feeling this is gonna be good.'

'Yeah, yeah, you all have a laugh,' a disconsolate Jack muttered. 'Look, Barney and Amos have told our Mam and Rita that they're out all night tonight and won't be back when the siren goes, but they've both taken a torch, so we haven't got a light. So, Mam sends me to the pig farm to get a torch back off them, in case we have to go to the shelter.

'So, I sets off to the bloody farm and I've just climbed over the gate when I sees a light shining over the style on the way to Manor Road. I thought that's got to be Barney and Amos, cos I can see two blokes carrying a box between them. Any road, I shouts them at the top of mi voice but their light goes out and I can't see them. So, I think if I'm quick I can catch them, I jumps at the gate and slips in all that mud. When I gets back up, I can't see anything of them, so I shouts back at pig farm, but still gets no answer – so I thinks maybe they've come here, or gone to your allotment. So here I am.'

'Did you check the allotment?'

'No, I come straight here.'

'Jack, you know Amos wouldn't come here,' Margaret counselled.

'Yeah, I know, but if I'm honest, I thought maybe you'd have a spare torch and would lend it. Save me any more effort, 'cos I've got to go back and make sure our Mam is alright.'

'I've got a spare at the allotment. Come on let's go get it, we can wash that muck off you as we walk across in rain,' said Gilbert, barely disguising the grin on his face.

167

Jack looked at him with a rueful grimace. 'You can laugh Gilbert, but mi Mam's got to wash this lot and she's gonna give me hell. Aw stuff it. Come on, before I get comfy.'

Gilbert shook himself dry and stood in front of the fire, exactly as Jack had done some ten minutes earlier. Margaret could hardly contain herself: 'It's tonight – they're gonna do something tonight! Did you hear what Jack said? There's gonna be a raid tonight.'

'What do you mean, tonight?'

'Didn't you hear what he said?' snapped Margaret, 'Amos and Barney won't be at the shelter tonight when the air-raid siren sounds! It's happening, Gilbert and it's happening tonight!'

Gilbert looked between the two women they had obviously been talking while he had been out with Jack. He looked at their animated faces – it was a long time since he had seen Margaret so convinced of anything or so passionate about it.

'Ok, Ok, calm down and explain to me what the pair of you have decided is happening tonight.'

Margaret glanced at Eva for support, took a deep breath and started: 'Jack said Amos and Barney said they wouldn't be back when the siren goes – so they believe there'll be a raid tonight. They're staying out all night, he's seen them carrying something; and when he shouted, they switched the torch off and didn't shout back. They obviously didn't want to be seen. They must have been headed towards Hoober. Look, if they cross Manor Road from Winterwell Fields and go down the back of Cadman's field behind your allotment, they can get to Hoober Lane without being seen. They're doing it now, because if they wait any longer it'll be the start of the night shift and they'll have to pass the men going to Cortonwood. They're taking a wireless up to Hoober – they know there'll be a raid tonight. Gilbert, we have to do something!'

Breathless, Margaret almost stamped her foot in impatience. Gilbert knew she was frustrated and that she could sense his doubt and disbelief. Even so, he tried to be logical: 'Margaret, Jack might have heard them wrong, or might have said it wrong. They're just doing something that needs them to be out all night – but it could be anything knowing those two!'

'Don't be stupid, Gilbert, would you be out if you knew there was going to be a raid. No, you'd want to be with your family! Our Jack is looking after two families down there because them two is up to something. Well I'm not having it! I'm going to find out what they're doing, I'm going to put a stop to it!'

Margaret strode across the room and grabbed her coat from behind the cellar door. Eva, who had been nodding at Margaret's every word, jumped up and grabbed her coat as well.

'Whoa. Nobody's going anywhere in this weather, especially not you Margaret in your condition. Stop it, the pair of you! Let me have a think about this. If anybody is going do anything, it'll be me. So, sit down and let me think.'

All three froze. It was rare for Gilbert to raise his voice and even rarer for him to be so firm. While both women wanted to move, they were frozen to the spot. They looked at him and waited. Gilbert thought hard. Margaret and Eva had had more time to think this through, even if only ten minutes. He replayed everything Jack said and considered the implications. The only conclusion he could reach was that Margaret was right – something was wrong.

'Gilbert, do you remember that rope we found lying on the floor?' Eva spoke for the first time, urgently. 'That weren't kids. That were a guide. If they go by the route Margaret says, they can go past the Stand using the road and go through the gap in the wall from the other side. That'll bring them to the old mine shaft. They pick up the rope from there and that leads them to the Stand. They'll know their way, even in dark!'

'It isn't just a guide, Gilbert,' burst in Margaret, 'it's an escape route. They can use that to get away in a hurry, in the dark. Eva says that rope were tied to the lightening conductor which was pulled out of the ground. Gilbert, what if they connect the wireless to the lightening conductor – they can send a signal from that. There's no need to even go inside the Stand. They can do it from the outside!'

Gilbert looked at both women in amazement and knew they were right. Amos and Barney were intending to send a signal, but unless they were caught red-handed, there would be no evidence. If he were to go to the police, Barney and Amos would simply get rid of the evidence and be able to talk themselves out of it. He would look a fool.

'Ok you're both right; something stinks, so let's find out what it is. But you, Margaret, are going nowhere. I'll go up to Hoober and see what's what. Eva, if you want to help, you can come with me, but if a siren sounds, everything stops and we get back here to Margaret and Alfred. Is that clear?'

Agreement made, Margaret took her coat off and hung it back up. Eva wrapped herself even tighter into her coat and put on a headscarf. Gilbert shook out his old waxed jacket which was still drying by the fire, screwed an even older, even wetter cap back onto his head and wound a fresh scarf around his neck. He refused to take the torch, saying that if Margaret was right, then there would be a raid and she would need it to guide herself and Alfred to the shelter. With a huge sigh he pulled back the blackout curtain and once again strode into the downpour.

Barney looked at Amos in amazement. 'What the hell do you think you're doing? We don't need no shotgun – first, we're not shooting nobody and second, we've got a lot of delicate stuff to carry.'

'But if somebody sees us, they're gonna wonder what we're doing. If they see the gun they'll think we're poaching.' seeing Barney hesitate, Amos pushed on: 'And they're a lot less likely to challenge us if they see a gun!'

Barney relented. There was little time to argue. They needed to get past Cortonwood before the night shift started. It would mean a long wait at Hoober before they sent the signal, but that was better than being seen. The battery and the accumulator were fully charged and he had packed the transmitter as carefully as he could. The delicate glass valves were wrapped tight and would need unpacking and checking when they got there. The connection to the lightning conductor was a brute of a thing because Barney was taking no chances. This signal would be heard in Moscow! The rain was still pounding down, so he had carefully wrapped everything inside a blanket then in a waterproof tarpaulin that he had been intending to use to cover one of the pig sties. He hadn't been able to think of anything else.

'Come on then, let's go. But you do your share of carrying. Just 'cos you've got that gun, doesn't mean you do less.'

Gilbert marched purposefully down Packman Road. He passed the Cottage of Content without saying a word, ignoring the sounds of a game of dominoes being played behind the blackout curtains. Eva was almost running to keep up with his stride, until, leaving the shrouded lights behind, he was forced to slow. The rain was incessant, it kept coming straight down. There was no wind to divert it so it landed on their head and shoulders and ran down their coats. Even before they left the boundary of Packman Road they were soaked.

The rain was falling from the blackest sky Gilbert could remember. Not a star and no moon. The blackout provided the final backdrop, sucking all the light out of the air and leaving them without a landmark to guide them. They walked down the middle of the wide expanse of Rotherham Road, its surface only just visible, a dim and gloomy shimmer reminding Gilbert of the pewter mugs once favoured by drinkers. Dull and grey.

With the rain in his eyes Gilbert watched the hedgerow on his right-hand side grow darker. When it vanished altogether, he knew they were at the bottom of America Lane. The lane was only twelve feet wide and the hawthorn hedges on either side were so tall they fell over the lane making it a wonderfully scented green tunnel in the summer, but tonight it was a dark blotch, dimming the edges of his vision. Just a hazy notion of an entrance, as if to a discarded mine, or sett, or lair.

Gilbert stopped. He knew that when they entered the lane they would see even less but at least it would give them some shelter from the rain. He walked to the hedge and pulled several branches towards him. The ones which spiked his skin with thorns he dropped – they were hawthorn. He felt the immature stems of an elder and pulled them free, snapping two of them off close to the trunk. In the dark he ran his hands down the thin branches and pulled away the offshoots.

Quietly, he called to Eva: 'Here take this, it's an elder branch – when we get into the lane, use it like a walking stick. Swish it in front of you, you'll be able to tell if it's brushing the road or if you're moving to one side into the verge. Use it to try to keep in middle of road and just so's I don't get lost will you hold my hand?'

Despite the dark, Gilbert could sense Eva's smile as they set off again holding hands and moving up the lane, stopping several times to redirect themselves when one or the other felt their stick hitting the grass verge. After an age of fumbling in the tunnel they felt the air getting lighter, although it was the lack of cover from the downpour which first indicated they were moving out of the lane. They stopped when the road in front of them turned as they reached the bend. Gilbert led them on to the grass verge.

Once again Gilbert started feeling in front of him. His left hand was almost numb despite the warmth from Eva's hand the cold and rain stripped the heat from his and he swore as he stubbed his fingers on the gate in front of him. He knew exactly where he was. This gate was the entrance to the cow field alongside Hoober Field Lane and the start of the approach to Hoober. He rummaged around on the floor in the dark and picked up a large stone from the crumbling wall at the side of the gate. He placed it at the foot of the gate and turned to Eva.

'Eva, when we get up to the Stand we're going to have to split up. You go to the left, around the bottom side and I'll go to the right. If no one is there, we'll meet up near the path to the cave. If them two are there and up to something, just watch. If they are there, I'll shout at them and get their attention. That's all we can do. Distract them and hope we put them off whatever it is they're trying to do. If they chase after me, don't worry – I'll get away. But while I lead them a merry dance you run back and warn Margaret then get the police to come. Ok?'

'Ok.'

'Now. If we don't meet after walking round Hoober, you come back this way. If you're the first to get here, take this stone and put it on top of this gate post – here.' Gilbert held her hands and showed her where the stone was and where the post was. 'So, whoever comes second knows that other one has gone and knows they are safe. Understood?' without waiting for her reply, he continued 'If they're up there, I expect I'll be last back, so don't worry. I've been chased by better than them through these woods and fields. Eva, I can lead them a merry chase or I can hide from them but I can't run like you. I need you to get back and raise the alarm. That's your job. You ready? Come on then.'

They both left their sticks by the gate and started up the hill. The dark was a shade paler than under the hawthorn but still impenetrable. After four hundred yards they stopped. Despite the brisk walk they were now wet to the skin and freezing cold. The sense of foreboding intensified while an invisible menace seemed to emanate from the blackness ahead.

172

They could feel, rather than see, the oppressive, brooding Stand – watching them from above as they drew near.

After a couple of hissed words of encouragement from both of them, accompanied by pats on the back, they separated. Gilbert made his way slowly up the lane. He held his right hand out at the side and kept in contact with the wall. His knuckles were scraped several times and the cold bit into his fingers but he kept on. He knew he was close. The Stand looming unseen overhead. He crossed the road and leant against the wall, shivering and wiping the rain from his eyes – he was sure there was a patch of grey ahead. A small vague break in the dark at the base of a blackness that continued into the sky. Gilbert held his breath and strained to see, trying to use his peripheral vision to break the void. He watched and waited.

Eva let go of Gilbert's hand and turned into the field. Immediately she realised she had drawn the short straw; even though the grass had been beaten down by the rain, it was still above her ankles, her shoes and socks were soaked within seconds. She moved around the edge of the field, keeping the deepest black looming above to her right. The cold pierced the skin on her face while strands of her blonde hair were plastered across her features, as if stuck in place by glue. The head scarf, long abandoned, was in her pocket.

Desperately trying, but failing, to keep herself orientated to the road, she slowly manoeuvred through the grass, her eyes darting left and right seeking any break in the gloom. At first it was just an impression then it became the dimmest glimmer, until, she turned, realising she was actually seeing light. She slowly sank to her haunches and watched, trying to understand the smudge of illumination at the base of the tower.

A match struck and suddenly all was clear. Two figures were sitting hunched over a box underneath a blanket or sheet of some kind as they tried to keep the rain away. One of them lit a cigarette and offered the match to the other. He pulled life into the cig and she saw it was Barney. The match went out, along with Eva's night vision. Darkness engulfed her once again. She shut her eyes and waited, after a count of three, reopened them. The dim blur at the base of the stand was back. It had a golden tinge to it. As one of them pulled on his cigarette, Eva realised the golden glow was from the display panel on a radio. The two men were huddled over it – seemingly waiting for something.

Eva moved forward, she needed to do something. Where was Gilbert? Slowly she crawled through the grass, the damp clawing its way through her clothes, the cold smothering her with indecision. Her knees slid through the mud while she pushed her hands forward in a crawl – stalking her prey. The brothers were still smoking, cowering under their blanket. Eva's hands hit a pile of stones. It was the pile she and Gilbert had collected to throw over the stone lintel. They rattled as she inadvertently moved them. She stopped and held her breath. She was only ten yards from them now and the rattle sounded like a drum roll. Watching their every move she realised they hadn't heard the clamour – the rain beating on their blanket drowning out the noise.

Where was Gilbert? Eva knew she could move faster than Gilbert, but even so, he should be in place by now. Any minute now, he would shout and distract them; she would watch for a second or two then scoot back to Margaret.

She was still on her hands and knees when her hand located a stone underneath. Eva felt it – smooth and round, almost a tennis ball. She felt around and found another. Similar. Slightly smaller and not quite as round, but very throwable. She placed this in her left hand and picked the first stone up in her right, an idea forming in her head. Slowly, she pushed herself up onto her knees, then her feet. Carefully, she made sure her feet were well planted, one in front of the other, her body side on. *Come on Gilbert! It's now or never!*

Gilbert pulled himself slowly up the side of the wall. It had taken an age to reach the Stand. The dark, the rain, the cold all nagged him as he clambered along the grass verge. He dared not risk walking on the road, the metal segs on his boots would have made the most fearful noise. But scrambling along the verge had been slow work. Brambles had ripped his hands and face, twigs sprang back and whipped him, while roots and sods constantly ruined his footing. But he was finally in place. He looked at the Stand, its dark mass ominous in the gloom above. The first thing he saw was someone smoking a cigarette. By, they were confident if they could do that! Even when they thought they were well clear he and

Shudder never smoked while poaching. It was almost the first rule of poaching. Do not smoke.

He could smell the tobacco and felt an instant craving, but he shook rain from his eyes and watched. The next time one of them sucked on their smoke, the glow revealed their forms. There were two of them under some sort of cover with a box between them. He could make out Barney, who was facing him, but the other man was a silhouette with its back to him. He assumed it was Amos. It was clear that Margaret had been dead right. The box between them had a faint golden glow – and was exactly in the place where Eva had fallen. He was sure they had already connected it to the lightning conductor.

Gilbert knew from experience that the glow of the cigarettes would temporarily take away most of their ability to see in the dark and decided he would shout at the next glow. But first he needed to ensure his feet were on firm ground and check where he was going to run to if they chased him. He took a quick look around and made his decision, but before he could turn back a glow came from the base of the tower.

Barney – she was sure it was Barney – took a deep pull on his cigarette. The whole scene lit up in front of her as if street lights had been turned on. Eva's mind was made up. Taking aim at the box by Barney's feet, Eva pulled her arm back and let fly, throwing the stone with all the force she could muster. Without hesitating she swapped the second stone into her right hand. The glow was still evident when the first stone hit the wireless with a solid impact. The world seemed to go into slow motion, the box tumbled over and Barney turned to look at it. Darkness returned as Eva heaved the second stone and was rewarded by the sound of a crash as it hit its target full-on. She turned darting into the trees, taking shelter behind a large oak thirty yards behind her, off to the right.

She placed her back against the oak breathing deeply and leant her head back to rest on its trunk, readying herself to run and get back to Margaret. Without warning there was a loud boom and a flash of light. A shotgun rang out and pellets ripped through the trees around her. One of the brothers had brought a shotgun and fired it into the place where he thought the stone came from. Eva pushed herself closer to the tree, the cold and rain all forgotten – the terror of her situation sending bolts of cramp through her body. A sharp boom and another blast of light

175

signalled another shot as, either Barney or Amos fired blindly into the void. Pellets flew about her and Eva felt the sharp pain of fast-moving lead in her shoulder and hip. An involuntary yelp escaped from her as she fell into the woods and started to run. There was no thought of exposing herself to more shots – in sheer panic, she bolted.

Gilbert's subconscious witnessed a blur at the edge of the wood then he heard a crack as the box between the brothers jumped. He grabbed the top of the wall harder watching as something else hit the box and the feeble circle of golden light vanished. He realised Eva was throwing stones. Both brothers seemed to be as transfixed as he was for a moment, before two small red ends fell to the floor. He heard a scrabbling sound but could see nothing until suddenly the whole scene was lit up by the flare from a shotgun fired from the other side of the Stand.

In its light he caught a glimpse of Barney bending over the box, but before he could react the shotgun rang out again. Gilbert tried to see what direction Amos was firing in, but the light from the explosion was gone too quickly for him to take in the scene. He had to be aiming at Eva.

'Barney. Stop it, Barney. We know what you're doing!' he yelled at the top of his voice and sank behind the wall. 'Do you hear me, Barney?'

Barney stopped. His whole system frozen. Gilbert?

He vaguely felt Amos whirl around and face the direction the shout had come from. The glow no longer came from the radio, their cigarettes had died the instant they hit the damp grass. The darkness was complete. He knew without looking that the transmitter was broken. The delicate glass valves he and Amos had taken so much care with were smashed. He did not have to see it. He had heard enough under the din of the rain to know. His thoughts racing, he squatted motionless.

Despite someone out there shouting he needed to be certain that the damage was terminal. The image of Harry Black returning terrified him more than he would ever admit to Amos. He took out his torch and, pulling the blanket around him to shield as much of the light as possible, flicked it on to inspect the transmitter. The circular frequency display in the middle of the front was smashed to pieces but when he turned the transmitter over, he heard the rattle of glass falling inside. There was no light from any of the valves.

176

It was over.

There would be no transmission from this set tonight. He had no spares and it would take him several days to replace the parts. He flicked the beam of the torch quickly around the area in front of him. Amos had now reloaded and was starting towards the wall where the shout had come from. Barney was certain it was Gilbert who shouted. Damn that interfering sod.

'Amos, Amos, here!' he rasped loud enough for Amos to hear. 'Amos get back here quick! We've got to get rid of this, then you can go hunting.'

'But there's somebody out there, I can chase them off.'

'No, we get rid of this first – its knackered do you hear, knackered, but we can't be caught with it. Stick to the plan. Give me the wrench.'

Amos pushed Barney to the side, dug a wrench out of his pocket and uncoupled the bolts connecting the transmitter to the lightning conductor. When it was uncoupled, Barney wrapped the set in the blanket they used for sitting on and picked up one end. He flicked on the torch while Amos picked up the other end of the blanket, putting the torch in his pocket, he felt for the guide rope and let it run through his hand moving towards the cave. Taking care, they followed the rope past the cave and at the point above the mine shaft they stopped. Getting into the positions they had practised they swung the set back and forward then on three flung it into the pond. A splash and they were clear; all they needed to worry about now was Harry.

'That were Gilbert weren't it?' spat Amos 'I'm going back for him!'

'Don't make it any worse – nobody's going to believe him! Let's get back and worry what we do about Harry.'

Just at that point another shout went up, from the direction of the road. 'Barney I know you're there. Come on Barney, stop whatever you're doing. The police are on their way!'

'Bugger this, I'm having him,' declared Amos as he strode away from Barney towards the road, the shotgun pointing forward from his hip. He marched out, through the wood and fired in the direction he imagined Gilbert to be. The sound echoed off the walls of the Stand with the pellets ripping through the trees.

Suddenly in the field beyond the woods, two powerful flashlights came on. Then they heard a brusque voice shout out: 'Oy! Stop.

Fitzwilliam gamekeepers. Stop what you are doing and put that gun down. You're on Fitzwilliam land. If you shoot again, we'll return fire. Do you hear? Stop now!'

As the flashlights started moving towards them, Amos turned to run blindly into the woods, almost knocking Barney over.

'Turn round, run,' hissed Amos. 'It's gamekeepers.'

Barney grabbed Amos by the coat. 'Stop, you silly bugger. If they catch you with that gun up here, you'll be done for poaching, or worse, shooting at them. Come on, chuck it in pond and let's run.'

Amos couldn't see Barney in the dark but he knew he was right. They scrambled around and found the rope again. This time, Amos hurled the gun into the pond and, using the rope, they both hurried back to the Stand, away from the approaching flashlights.

'Barney, you'll not get away with this. Do you hear, Barney? They'll catch you, Barney.'

Gilbert's voice echoed around the woods as Barney and Amos found the road.

'We can't use this road. If police are coming it'll be this way. We've got to go back the way we came, across them fields.'

'You go back to the farm; I'm gonna sort Gilbert out for good this time. I'll see you back there.' Without waiting for a reply, Amos turned around, pulled the wrench from his pocket and started away from Barney, in the direction of Gilbert's voice.

Gilbert crouched behind the wall, his knees resting against the stones; with both hands holding onto the top, he poked his head over just enough to see what was happening. Apart from two pools of light bobbing up and down, the entire scene in front of him was black. He orientated himself: the Stand was directly in front of him, Barney and Amos were to the left, presumably heading back to Brampton, while the gamekeepers were approaching the Stand through the woods from his right, following the path taken by Amos and Barney.

Eva should be gone by now, her athletic stride carrying her away from danger. But he needed to check. Amos had fired the gun into the trees – albeit blindly and high from what Gilbert had seen, but he still might have injured the girl. Gilbert had to check the far side of the Stand

– where Eva had been; the area the gamekeepers were headed for right now.

The gamekeepers turning up had been an unforeseen stroke of luck. Poaching must be rife if they were out in this weather! But Gilbert was certain that whatever Barney had been planning was over. Firing the shotgun had been stupid. It showed where they were and attracted unnecessary attention in what had otherwise been the perfect night for their venture. But as soon as the shot had been fired the gamekeepers had to investigate and, from its flash, they had an idea where Barney was.

Gilbert thought hard. Once he circled the Stand, if he couldn't find Eva, he needed to get to the junction of Hoober Field Lane and America Lane to check she had left the stone and was away. But Amos and Barney were between him and the road, to say nothing of the gamekeepers. Gilbert decided to go the opposite way, to his right, cross the road and head towards the old mine shaft – following behind the gamekeepers. He would pick up the rope and find his way to the Stand. From there he would turn away from the Stand and Brampton, loop around the cow field to get to the gate with the stone. When he was sure Eva was safe, he would once again head away from Brampton and take the path through the fields towards Newhill. From there he could cross the Grange back into West Melton, then on to Packman. He was adding a good mile or more to his route, and following the gamekeepers might be foolhardy, but at least the last part of his journey wouldn't be on Fitzwilliam land and Amos and Barney would be nowhere near.

Decision made Gilbert set off. Cautiously he followed the rope up to the Stand. The gamekeepers, some one hundred yards ahead, were helping him with the continuous light from their torches. There was no sign of Eva and he dare not shout. He decided to check the gate and return to the Stand if the stone was not in place. At the patch of grass by the base of the tower he turned and followed the fence around the cow field. Dark shapes lay or stood in the field their backs to the rain as the wind now started to pick up. The rain was still pounding down and he stepped in a cow pat which splashed around his ankles, his segs stopping him slipping. Okay he was going to smell as bad as Jack but right now he was more concerned about disturbing the cows and giving his position away.

He crept on, his cap was gone, torn from his head by the branches as he stumbled through the woods below the Stand. His clothes were drenched and heavy with the rain joining the river of sweat cascading down his back. Gilbert's breath came in pants, wheezing through the gaps in his teeth; his face, fingers and toes numb with cold.

Finally, he reached the gate. He no longer saw the lights from the gamekeeper's torches. Barney and Amos could still be around. He slowed almost to a standstill, ears, nose and eyes all working overtime as he tried to find any clues to the whereabouts of the other four. He reached his hand out, his heart pumping madly. He touched the gate, then moved his hand to the right, across the top rail – then up onto the gate post. He smiled so wide he almost burst out laughing. The stone was on top of the gate post. Eva was away and safe.

All discomfort forgotten he turned and headed away from the lane, on the long route back. At the far side of the next field Fitzwilliam land ended and the gamekeepers would not be able to follow him. Barney and Amos would be walking the other way, so caution wouldn't be necessary meaning he could step up his pace.

While the adrenalin had been pumping through his system, Gilbert hadn't noticed the pain in his ribs; but he knew once he calmed down, he would start to hurt once more. However, for now, all there was between him and home was a long walk through the fields, with a bitterly cold wind pushing rain into his back.

Amos turned away from Barney and started towards the voice, a dark rage building inside his chest and thudding at his temples. A deep breath calmed him while he watched the torches bob up and down to his left. He pushed his hand inside his coat and grabbed the handle of the wrench tucked into his belt. He held it in his right hand and slowly tapped the top of the wall at his side, making his decision on the way forward. Straight down the road, past the gamekeepers – Gilbert was down there somewhere.

Slowly, he moved down the road keeping one foot on the verge and the other on the asphalt to make sure he knew his position. He moved past the gamekeepers, their lights flicking around the base of the Stand. He stood, listening – something was different. There, a noise, steel upon tarmac. Gilbert was on the road in front of him, his segs echoing off the surface. Amos listened. Gilbert crossed the road then it went quiet again – he must be on the grass verge now. Amos began to move, realising that when Gilbert entered the woods, he would be harder to catch. He started to run, but immediately, his boots slipped on the slime at edge of the road and he crashed to the ground in a heap. The grass verge cushioned him but its angle threw him back into the road, where he lay in a puddle. He thought it was impossible to get any wetter but the water ran through his clothes, straight to his skin.

He placed his hands under his shoulders and pushed; pulled his knees up beneath his belly and grimaced. Every action added water to his already waterlogged body. From his knees he stood up. A light flashed past him. The gamekeepers were coming back this way. They had obviously given up the hunt. He looked left and right for an escape route, but to no avail – everywhere in front of him was black, pitch black. One light started down the road behind him the other flicking through the woods and trees towards the Stand.

There was no other option – he moved towards the roadside wall, as soon as he felt the brambles growing along it, he jumped and attempted to throw himself over to the other side. He was neither near enough, nor good enough at jumping, and landed solidly on the top of wall, knocking every ounce of breath out of his lungs. Gasping, he grabbed for a hand hold and pulled himself over the top of the wall, collapsing on the far side into a ditch full of mud. He lay wheezing as a torch beam flicked along the top of the wall. He rolled onto his back and waited. His world seemed to shrink to the two beams of light moving slowly down the road. He was unaware of the rain falling onto his face as he licked his lips.

They must have seen him. They must have heard him!

The beams moved past.

He waited.

After a full five minutes he slowly raised himself and looked over the wall. The beams were tiny blobs in the distance. He looked up, Hoober Stand scrutinised him from above, a solid black edifice frowning its disapproval from the miserable sky.

Shaking water from his clothes he clambered back into the road. Gilbert would be long gone now; Barney away across the fields, and the gamekeepers were half the way back to Wentworth.

181

What was the point of hiding anymore? He wiped the rain from his hair, pulled his collar up high, put the wrench back in his pocket and started to march down the road. The rain was now driven by the wind coming from behind the Stand, the dark still impenetrable, but Amos's anger was blazing. It was the only thing burning within two miles, yet if it could have given off light, the whole of Hoober would have been a wall of flames.

Once again Riesling sat hunched over his receiver, the vibration of the aircraft pulsing through his bones, his world condensed into the beeps, dots and static of radio waves. A spotter plane had flown over their previous raid and checked the accuracy of the bomb placement. The bomb craters were within one hundred metres of the X-Gerat directional beam, but unfortunately, all of them anything between half a mile and a full mile short. The British must have interfered with the cross beam. The echo he heard after the bomb's release had been the real cross beam directing the bomber to drop its cargo. But it was too late, the British interference had already triggered the system.

Not this time, he thought. They already had the information from the earlier raid, a control test run. Tonight, a decoy was flying ahead of them and would record the timing of the cross beam. When the decoy reported back to Bergen, the ground crew, including Capitan Schwarz, would be listening in. A ground-based local signal would also be transmitting from a known location – somewhere called Hoober. The full team would do the necessary comparison calculations and a new directional beam would be sent. Riesling smiled. The British were damn clever but this time they had been too clever for their own good.

Once again, his ears had been chosen to listen to the beams, to understand the impact of the British interference. If this raid failed, there was a chance that the whole of X-Gerat would be scrapped, this would be a personal disaster for Capitan Schwarz, so Riesling listened with extreme care. The Capitan was a hard man but one who, in the past, had helped Riesling to promotion. Now it was his turn to help his Capitan.

The void below swept past in complete darkness just as before. Although he could not see them from his position behind the cockpit, there was nothing visible but clouds. The bleeps and static were constant, the pilot was flying a perfect course. First following the beam from Stollberg then in the middle of the North Sea picking up the new even thinner beam from Bergen. This beam would lead them directly towards Sheffield. Riesling was impressed, the deviation from the line was minimal and there was very little to do.

But now he was getting irritated.

The decoy was twenty minutes ahead of them and would soon be needing the land-based signal to allow the comparison, but so far there was nothing but silence. He kept glancing at the second receiver he was to listen in on when the dial registered a signal – it needed to be active soon. The pilot flashed the overhead lights on and off. This told everyone inside the aircraft they were about to cross onto the British mainland, the North Sea behind them.

Where was the signal?

Riesling kept watching and listening, but there was nothing. There were getting closer and closer – soon the chance to make any adjustments would be gone and they would be back to relying upon the cross beam from the old system. He felt his heart thumping above the vibration of the aircraft. *Come on! Come on!* For the first time he dared think the worst. No signal meant no comparison and if the bombs were off-target, Capitan Schwarz would be blamed and there were plenty of places much more uncomfortable than the one the captain occupied at the moment.

Seven for a Secret

Sunday 15 December 1940 – 11 p.m.

Margaret paced in front of the fire. Trying to distract her mind she had washed all of Alfred's dirty clothes, cleaned the hob, filled the coal scuttle, mended the fire, and even tried rag-rugging – but she couldn't sit still. The wait was agony. She ran her hands over her belly – with only two or three weeks to go it was now pushing even her biggest dresses. She knew it had been the right decision for her to stay behind, but she was frustrated; she was a doer and this waiting was not in her make up.

She put a full kettle on, they would need a warm drink when they got back. She drew the blackout curtain from over the door, resisting the temptation to look out, but leaving the curtain back so they could get in more easily. She poked the fire. It was a bitterly cold night and they would be wet through. Best be ready to warm them up and dry them out. Towels! She got them ready by the sink. She went upstairs, checked on Alfred and brought down two blankets, folding them over the back of a chair. Food! Would they be hungry? She took out some cheese and resumed her pacing.

There was a clatter at the door. It flew open. Eva plunged through it; she turned, pushed the door to and collapsed onto a chair at the table. Her hair was plastered across her face, huge drops of water falling from it. Her coat was a sopping wreck, her socks down by her ankles and her shoes unrecognisable. She was panting for breath, taking huge gasps of air as she looked at Margaret with wild eyes.

'They were there... wireless. Hit with a stone. Gilbert shouted... ran, like he said. Got to tell police... Gilbert following me.'

'Steady, Eva,' Margaret covered her shock with an air of confident calm. 'Let's get you dry and warm and wait for Gilbert. After that we can decide what to do. Now, take your coat off.'

Eva was too tired to argue – she stood up and pulled her coat off, handing it to Margaret. Margaret took it and didn't even bother to try to dry it. It weighed a ton, was torn and scratched and covered in brambles so she hung it on a peg at the back of the cellar door. She turned back to Eva gently pulling her in front of the fire. Her cardigan and dress were wet through – she was drenched to the skin and her shiver was starting to grow into a shake.

'Off with that cardigan and dress – let's get you warm and dry.' Margaret unbuttoned the cardigan and tugged it from Eva's shoulders. The girl winced and held her left shoulder. Margaret looked at the cardigan there were holes in it and blood stains. She turned Eva round, and there, on her shoulder, was more blood showing through her dress.

'Eva! What happened? You're bleeding!'

'Shot. Behind a tree. Shot.'

The girl was shaking so badly her whole body seemed to rattle. Her eyes were receding while a puddle of water was forming around her feet where the rain dripped from her hair and her dress. Margaret grabbed her to hug her but she recoiled, whimpering. Margaret realised some of the water on her face was from tears not rain.

'Right, pet, let's get this off and see what we've got.'

She grabbed one of the towels, undid the buttons at the top of the dress then pulled it down while Eva stood shaking but compliant. Margaret wiped her face and placed the towel over her chest turning her around to look at her back. There were three holes in her left shoulder and she could see another under her left hip. Margaret snatched a blanket, wrapped it fully around the girl, pulled a chair in front of the fire and sat her down. She bent over and examined the shoulder more closely – the pellets were visible in the flesh – Eva's sodden wet coat must have cushioned the impact and, while they had entered the flesh, they had not gone deep.

Margaret put a pot on the stove and heated some water. She took out her sewing basket and found the tweezers, dropping them into the water. Next, she made a drink passed it to Eva, taking the girl's shoes and socks off, placing them by the fire to dry.

'Drink slowly, Eva. I'm going to take them pellets out of your shoulder; so why don't you tell me what happened while you warm up?'

Margaret lifted the sterilised tweezers from the water, allowed them to cool then lowered the blanket from Eva's shoulders and looked at the wounds. Talking all the time and slowly drawing the story from the girl, she carefully inserted the tweezers and pulled the pellets out. She gasped in horror when Eva described how she had been hiding behind a tree when they shot at her. She could not believe either Barney or Amos could fire a shotgun at Eva. Although they couldn't have known it was her, to shoot at anyone sang of desperation. Margaret's thoughts momentarily turned to Gilbert – he was still out there, and now there was every reason to worry. Once Eva was settled, she would go and get the police.

She covered Eva's shoulder wounds with antiseptic cream, stood her up and tackled the pellet in her hip. With only one wound here, it was a matter of seconds before the pellet was out and the wound smothered in antiseptic. Eva didn't flinch while the pellets were removed, but continued to shiver with cold. Margaret ran upstairs, pulling a fresh dress from the wardrobe, along with thick socks and a clean cardigan. She helped Eva dress and she was just pulling her socks on when the door crashed open and Gilbert tumbled inside.

His cap was gone, his scarf wrapped around his head to give his ears some cover. His coat was torn and his heavy, wet trousers hung down over saturated boots. His face was red from the wind and the rain but his expression lit up the room as soon as he saw Eva.

'God girl! Am I glad to see you!' He beamed as her grabbed her off the chair and gave her a bear hug.

'Gilbert, stop—' Margaret intervention was too late to avoid the inevitable cry of pain from Eva. Gilbert stood back and looked at her in confusion.

'I've just taken four pellets from her back.'

Margaret gave Gilbert a long hard look.

'Come on let's get your stuff off and get you dry. Then we can decide what to do.'

Gilbert did not answer immediately, but the grim expression on his face spoke volumes. He moved to the door, his body once again tense. 'I'm just nipping to the loo first – I'll take this lot off when I get back in.'

Harry sat in front of the fire. The bitter North Sea wind lashed the rain it carried against the window. With the blackout curtains in place the rattle should have been muffled, but the battering against the glass sounded as if the elements wanted to get inside and take shelter themselves. The wireless was set up and ready. It provided a gentle backdrop to the rain, with its crackles and buzz of static seemingly in tune with the pop of the fire as rain fell down the chimney.

189

The signal would come soon. Harry took a sip of his vodka and ran the fluid around his teeth and gums. It was a habit picked up from his father who believed the alcohol killed the germs in his mouth and sterilised his gums. Whether or not this was true Harry could not break the habit and enjoyed the gentle warmth as he held the fluid in place. What it did to his insides or his humour in a morning however was purely determined by the amount of vodka he consumed and tonight he was already a third of a bottle down.

He hunched over the wireless – still just static. He wondered what Billy was doing right now. No doubt he would be hunched over a set somewhere on the continent, listening as hard as he was, the tension in the room electric. What Billy did not know, however, was that the success or failure of their mission depended upon a terrified Yorkshireman with a propensity for the ladies. Harry grimaced. Barney – what was he doing now? Harry knew what he should be doing – sitting at the top of Hoober Stand with the equipment set up and ready. In two minutes time he should be starting the transmission.

Two minutes passed and the static rumbled.

Ten minutes.

Twenty.

Harry looked at the bottle of vodka, perhaps a third full now. Thirty minutes. The signal should have been sent and Barney should be on his way, but nothing.

Absolutely nothing.

Harry raged. Billy would be facing the consequences of this failure.

It was rare for Harry to lose his temper, he generally considered violence with a cool head and little emotion but right now he wanted Barney. If he had him right there in front of the fire, he would take every ounce of life from him in the worst possible way. He grabbed the poker and smashed the coals. He should go, stick to the plan, but his temples pulsed, his neck reddened – bugger the plan – he needed to get to Wath; to see Barney one last time. He grabbed the bottle and emptied it into his glass. *Get ready Barney, Harry Black is coming.*

Amos approached the Yard, his coat dripping mud behind him, boots squelching at every step. Wiping the rain from his face with numb hands,

190

he stopped to think. He didn't know if Gilbert was home yet, and even if he knocked on their door, there was no way they would let him in. He stood at the end of the row of terraces his resolve diluting with every drop of rain that hit him.

Then, the door to the end terrace opened and Gilbert walked out. In the shaft of light falling from the door he looked as bedraggled as Amos felt. Watching Gilbert cross the yard Amos felt the rage pounding, expanding, growing inside him. Amos realised that without thinking he had moved into the Yard, and was holding onto a clothes post. Memories flooded back: the young German slag; Gilbert tying him to the post; the feel of the magpie bitch's fist as it smashed into his face. Amos's head screamed and his heart raced. His anger beat at the storm, casting away the wind and rain, his rage grew from fury into a frenzy.

The thought of revenge was all-consuming and he wanted it now. Tonight.

He slid, noiselessly, to the edge of the toilets where Gilbert had gone and waited behind the wall, pressing into it as far as he could – pushing himself into the shadows. Gilbert was in the end toilet. He heard it flush and the door open. Gilbert's dark form emerged from the opening and started back across the Yard.

Amos stepped out from behind the wall, with the wrench raised above his head. He took two quick steps forward and swung. Some extra sense seemed to warn Gilbert that something was wrong. He started to turn – too late. The wrench caught him a sickening blow on the side of his head and Gilbert tumbled to the floor, motionless.

Amos stepped over the limp body and raised the wrench again. There was not a twitch or sound from Gilbert. A huge gash on his head poured blood down his face, turning the puddle around his mouth and nose dark red. Amos stepped back and kicked the lifeless bundle in the ribs and again, harder. Not a sound, not a stir.

He took a quick look around.

Nothing.

Time for the bitch and that pup.

He moved to the door, a thin band of light around its rim, but as he put his hand on the handle, he looked back and checked Gilbert again. No movement. Just blood. The dark puddle under his head growing

191

larger by the second. He smiled, turned the handle and pushed the door open, wrench in hand.

Eva had moved away from the fire to make room for Gilbert and was at the table, while Margaret was busy making him a hot drink at the gas hob. Neither paid too much attention when the door opened, but both turned and looked when they heard the key turn to lock it closed.

Amos spun from the door, wrench in hand, smiling at the women. His coat was wet and covered in mud. His hair was stuck down with muck and sludge. His face was wind blasted and raw, his mouth a vicious slash across his face. Flashing between the two women, red-rimmed eyes glared with evil menace and deranged violence.

Before anyone could talk, he lunged toward Eva, taking a huge back-handed swing with the wrench that swept through the air with a whoosh. Stunned though she was, Eva pushed against the table and threw the chair backwards. The wrench whistled in front of her face as she crashed to the floor. Amos stepped over, put his hand on the table and took another swing at the girl. Scrabbling on the floor, she darted under the table pulling the table cloth and all the contents onto the floor, the wrench smashing into the chair above her.

Margaret watched transfixed. Instead of Gilbert appearing through the door, a filthy apparition had jumped in, spraying mud and water as it leapt and swung. It was a long second before she realised it was Amos. But at the end of that second, she moved. Picking up the mug she was filling for Gilbert, she hurled it at his head as he bent down to swing again.

The mug missed but hot tea covered his face, he swivelled in anger.

Leaving Eva, he moved towards Margaret. 'So, bitch,' he hissed, 'I've not got my back to you this time. You're gonna howl, do you hear?'

Amos moved slowly around the table – Margaret retreating from him, suddenly he leapt forward, swinging wildly. Margaret tried to get away from him, but was trapped by the armchair at the side of the table. She turned and threw herself the other way, only for the wrench to catch her on her shoulder and send her falling. She fell across the hearth, her back into the fire, the coals searing and scorching through her clothes.

Frantically she rolled away, her apron bursting into flames.

Before she could recover Amos was on her. He grabbed hold of her arm and pushed it up her back, bending her over and forcing her face towards the fire. Margaret threw herself left and right, flailing her free arm, trying to grab his face. Amos dropped the wrench and grabbed her with both arms. She was much stronger than Jane Thicket, but he could smell her hair burning. He could hear it shrinking from the heat as the flames singed his fingers.

He moved his feet to get a better purchase, ready for the final push. From underneath the table, Eva pulled on the rug, hard and fast. It slid from under his feet and he fell, bouncing off Margaret as she scrambled away from the fire. His shoulder hit the coal scuttle, throwing coal across the room. Screaming in anger, he rolled, picking up the wrench from the hearth, pushing himself up. Margaret was on her back, pumping her legs to get away from him.

Amos laughed, stepped forward, moving towards Margaret, raising the wrench again. As he did so, still hiding underneath the table, Eva put both her feet on a fallen chair and pushed it with all her might. The chair hit him fully on the shins, catching him off balance. He fell, grabbing at the wall and fireplace, dropping the wrench, pushing himself away from the fire. He lay on the floor looking across at Eva, now moving under the table, scrabbling away from him, the wrench in her hand.

Margaret was on her back slapping her burning apron, her hair seared on one side, tight curls burned close to her scalp from the heat of the fire. Her face was red and flushed, sweat running in rivulets down her face. Amos looked around, picked up the poker and started to rise.

Margaret kept her eyes fixed on him and felt around the floor. Her hand closed on the spilled contents of her empty sewing basket. From her position on the floor she picked up the basket and threw it at Amos. He grinned at her, pushing himself to his knees. Margaret rolled onto all fours and started to stand, her feet and hands on the floor as if in a sprinter's starting block.

As she started to rise, her right hand slid onto the fetching tool. She grabbed it, holding the bulbous end in her palm, the spike protruding through her fingers.

Amos was on his feet standing over her, the poker in his hand, smiling confidently.

'Here, doggy, doggy,' he purred

193

Margaret acted first. Springing into action, launching her heavy body up, pushing with her legs, throwing herself forwards and upwards, she led with her left shoulder, catching him below the ribs. He staggered back, she continued to push, he slammed against the wall. Margaret kept pushing with her legs, holding him there. He raised his arm with the poker in his fist.

'Howl bitch' he cried

Margaret took a small step back, got her feet planted, and punched up. It came from below her waist, an upper cut that raced towards Amos's chin. When she stepped back his head flopped forward slightly and she hit him on the top lip. The long spike of the fetching tool extended beyond her fingers and slid into his nostril. She continued to punch, all her weight behind it, seeking to follow through as far as she could. *Punch through the bag.* She kept the punch going.

The spike hit bone and pierced it.

Amos's head snapped back hitting the wall behind him. There was a sickening crunch as bone met masonry, the fetching tool followed, smashing through flesh, bone and brain. Still Margaret kept on with the punch. The fetching tool kept going, its spike relentlessly pushing through his face until, with his head trapped against the wall, there was nowhere left to go. Eventually Margaret's fingers reached his lips and nose and face.

The punch stopped. The four inch spike embedded in his face.

She kept the pressure on, pushing through her legs. Her left forearm in his chest, her right fist in his face. Amos looked at her, his grin gone, his expression wide with shock. Margaret glared at him, her hazel eyes flashing lightning bolts, her lips peeled back in a snarl. Baring her teeth, she growled, her words spitting into his face.

'Woof, fuckin' woof!'

Amos watched her barking at him, a wolf at his throat.

Margaret twisted the fetching tool. *Punch and twist.* The hook on the end of the spike turned inside his skull, tearing brain cells apart. Margaret pushed with her left forearm and pulled with her right. Yanking the fetching tool back from his face. The hook on the end grabbed brain tissue, then nerves, severing the optical nerve to his left eye. Still, as it withdrew, it grasped anything in its path, bone, splinters, tendon, sinew, until it came out of his face. Ripping the flesh from his cheek as it exited.

Leaving a gaping hole. Amos whimpered as electricity raced through his nervous system, his fingers, his feet sparking, muscles twitching involuntarily, then everything was still.

Margaret held him against the wall. Staring into his eyes, daring him to say something, daring him to wriggle or fight. His weight increased as he no longer supported himself, his eyes glazed in a faraway stare, blood welled into red tears, forming at the sides of his eyes. Margaret relaxed and let him fall. He slid down the wall and sat in a crumpled heap on the floor. His head dropped backwards, his mouth fell open, while above the vile hole in his face, his left eye sagged at the lack of support. Blood trickled around it, down his face, mixing with mud and rain, running into his open mouth.

Margaret started to breathe again, sucking air into her lungs. She turned around, Eva was on all fours crawling out from under the table, her eyes fixed on Amos.

Taking two shaky steps backwards Margaret looked at her hand. She was still holding the fetching tool, a lump of grey red mush stuck on the hook. A shiver ran down her spine making her shake. When it reached her hips the shiver seemed to gain energy, she shuddered, shaking violently. She dropped the tool into the fire, where the contents spat and hissed as the flames caressed them.

Margaret fell to her knees and held her arms out to Eva. Eva crawled across and threw her arms around her, wailing in sheer terror. Huge sobs racked their bodies as they knelt, hugging and crying in front of the fire. Steam rising from Eva's socks on the side; tendrils of smoke spiralling from Margaret's apron. They continued holding each other, neither of them looking at the body on the floor, their world condensed; concerned only with each other. At the same instant, they pulled apart, looked each other in the eye and Margaret said, 'Gilbert!'

Margaret flung the door open, careless of the glare, unconcerned about the blackout. In the pool of light that fell from the door they could see Gilbert lying prone, in the mud of the Yard. A pool of red still growing beneath his head. They jumped down the steps and picked him up, one under each arm. He was breathing but it was shallow and slow. The blood running into the rain came from a nasty wound on his head.

They pulled him to his knees and got their heads under his shoulders to carry him, when another beam lit up the Yard.

'You alright, Margaret?' a voice called from next door, it was Howard Arnold stood on the top step next door. 'Can I help?'

'We're fine thanks, Mr Arnold. Gilbert had a fall is all.'

Howard simply stared at her vacantly. Remembering he was hard of hearing she repeated herself, shouting as loud as she could, trying to be heard over the rain.

Still he was not put off.

'Here, let me help you carry him in.' Howard reached behind himself and pulled a coat out. Margaret froze. There was a dead man slumped against her kitchen wall.

'No! We're all right thanks,' she cried. 'Come on, Eva, get him in, quick!'

'Don't be ridiculous!' came the voice of Mary Arnold who was now standing on the door step behind her husband. 'You're nearly nine months pregnant, you can't be doing that! Go on, Howard, help them.'

The rain pounded down, Margaret's hair was dripping, her dress soaked through. She stood motionless. Howard could not be allowed to help, but how could she stop him? Nothing came to mind. She glanced at Eva, seeking inspiration, but she was open-mouthed, on the verge of panic.

Just at that second, the alarm sounded. The siren began its mournful wail, ramping up to a scream, to warn of an imminent air raid. Everyone stopped and looked at the sky. The rain beat into their eyes. Margaret pulled on Gilbert, heading for the door.

'Please Mr Arnold, we're ok. Get everybody to the shelter. Gilbert can't do it this time – you need to take charge. We'll see to Gilbert, we'll come when I've patched him up… please, Mr Arnold.'

Howard stood, dithering, the siren screaming at the top of its voice, demanding a reaction. He turned and looked over his shoulder seeking his wife, but she had already gone back inside. That made up his mind for him. He turned and ran back to the house, shouting instructions to anyone who was listening.

Barney shoved newspaper and sticks into the battered old stove. He threw a match in and stood shaking, water running from every part of his clothing. The walk back to the pig farm, though cold and wet, had been uneventful. The skeleton Sunday shift was home, the night shift already underground. He marched through the fields unseen.

He tried to take a cigarette from his case but his fingers were wet and shaking too much. He closed the case and took a sheet of newspaper, using it to draw the front of the open fire. Holding it in front of the grate, restricting the air flow, making it rush past the kindling, whipping it into life. He held it too long, the newspaper burst into flames; cursing, he threw it into the fire. The sticks were ablaze now and after he had thrown more on, he started to feel the heat.

His hands were no longer shaking, his fingers were starting to dry. Barney pulled a cigarette from the case and lit it. Their problems were only starting. Harry would be down wanting revenge, as well as his money back. The shakes this time had nothing to do with the cold or rain it was the terror of thinking what Harry would do.

They should be planning, but Amos was running around the countryside looking for a fight with Gilbert. He should be the last of their worries! He sat on a bale of straw and sighed. Then the siren started its baleful wail and Barney's shake grew until he had to stand up and move. Harry would know by now.

He would know the signal had not been sent.

Margaret and Eva hauled Gilbert through the door and onto a chair. His head flopped back, his chin fell forward and his mouth opened in an expressionless gape. Margaret grabbed a towel and wiped the wound on his head. It was deep and long, but the rain had washed it clean. She held the towel in place and turned to Eva who was staring into the fire, her back to Amos as he lay slumped against the wall.

'Eva pet, I need you to hold this here, while I get stuff to seal it. Come on, Eva! Lend me a hand, please!'

The girl looked at Margaret with a vacant expression and, without saying a word, slowly rose and held the towel in place. Margaret put yet another pan of water on the hob and rummaged around on the floor. The contents of her sewing basket were strewn everywhere, difficult to find in the rag rug. Eventually, she found some thread and a needle. With shaking hands, she threaded the needle and dropped it into the pan on the hob.

Eva was still looking into space while she held the towel to Gilbert's head, a red stain slowly growing on the white material. Margaret moved the armchair out of the way and opened both the doors at the bottom of the stairs into the front parlour. She came back and grabbed Amos under her arms. She dragged him backwards, his arms and head flopping from side to side while his legs stretched out behind him. She pulled him into the parlour and dropped him unceremoniously onto the floor.

Closing the door behind her, she ran up the stairs and gently picked Alfred up from his cot. Taking him downstairs she placed him in the armchair. Miraculously, despite the disturbance downstairs and the scream of the air-raid siren, he was still fast asleep. Margaret turned back to the hob and, using the tweezers that were still there from earlier, took the needle and thread from the boiling water.

'Ok honey, let me take over now. Thank you.'

She carefully eased Eva away and delicately wiped the open gash. Next, using the sterilised cotton, she stitched the wound. She tied every stich off in a simple granny knot, her fingers deftly remembering her net-mending days. Fifteen stiches later she patted the wound dry and smeared antiseptic cream across its length.

Eva had crawled into the armchair and was curled up with Alfred on her lap. Margaret picked up her sewing basket, gathered as many of the items from the floor as she could, replaced the table cloth and moved the chairs back into place, her brain racing all the while. The siren was still screeching as she heard planes pass over head, the sounds echoing as her ears pounded with every beat of her heart.

She jumped at a knock on the door.

'Margaret are you all right? Do you need a hand?'

It was Howard Arnold again.

He stepped into the doorway, out of the rain.

'Mary sent me to help. You all need to get to the shelter.'

Margaret watched as Howard looked around the room. Eva was with Alfred in the armchair. Gilbert was leaning backwards in a chair with his head tilted back, as if asleep, the large wound on his head smothered in cream with drops of blood still oozing from underneath. There was a huge smear on the far wall where someone in a muddy jacket had slid down.

'Thanks Mr Arnold. It's really good of you to come and help, but we need to stay a few minutes longer. Gilbert can't be moved just now. We'll be along, just as soon as I can move him, but please go back to your family now, and thank you. Thank you.'

Margaret tried to emphasise her point by moving to shut the door. Howard looked at Gilbert uncertainly.

'What about Eva and Alfred then? Do they want to come with me?'

They both turned to Eva who shook her head violently. 'No, I'm staying with Margaret and Gilbert. I'll come when they do.'

Howard looked at them, then, reluctantly, he turned back into the rain.

Riesling kicked the floor of the aircraft then punched the frame of his receiver. There could be no checking – the signal had never arrived. The bombs had been dropped by the beam from Bergen but he guessed they were off-target. This spelt disaster for Capitan Schwarz. He imagined him now, being led away in disgrace, facing a radio-operator posting in some god-forsaken outpost with only bombs and bullets for company. It was a sad end to a brilliant career but Riesling didn't want to follow him. He knew on landing he would be quizzed and knew that, for his own sake, he wouldn't hold back the truth.

Again, he punched the frame.

The plane was in a steep climb and turn, his stomach churned before the pilot finally levelled out. He returned to his head phones, they were off line, he signalled the pilot to veer starboard. They still had one last job to do: there was one last bay full of bombs – these had been saved for the return journey. When they flew back, they would fly over Hoober, where the signal was supposed to come from. Capitan Schwarz was adamant the transmitter must be destroyed, so twelve fifty kilo bombs were saved to drop on the site. After the raid the operators below were supposed to continue transmitting their location, without realising that, once the raid finished, they were the next target.

But the best bit was the directional beam. Someone had either been very clever, or very lucky, because if you drew a straight line from Bergen to Sheffield, Hoober was directly beneath the beam. By returning down the beam there was no need for landmarks or a land-based signal.

Riesling forced a grim smile. Hitting the target was simply a case of correctly timing the bomb release.

That had been close. If she hadn't moved Amos, Howard would have seen everything and she would most likely be in front of the police, accused of murdering a man she assaulted in public only three weeks ago. In the distance she could hear the crump and thud of falling bombs. The windows rattled above the rain, and dust rose from the mantelpiece and pelmet. *Huh, you haven't cleaned this place as well as you thought!*

But sound of the bombs spurred her on – this was her opportunity! Even Howard would not come back now the bombs were dropping.

She went to the top of the cellar, grabbed her washing line, and using the carving knife from the table drawer she cut the line into five-foot strips. She looked at the others – Alfred was asleep, Gilbert unconscious and Eva paralysed with shock. She marched into the front room with new-found determination.

Laying the strips of rope on the floor in a ladder pattern she pulled the blackout curtain down, placing this on top of the rope. Pushing the settee out of the way she rolled Amos onto the curtain. Getting him onto his back, she placed his feet together. Then she lifted the cast iron fender from the hearth and laid it on top of him – the top on his chest – the bottom on his knees. She took his arms and folded them over the top. Next, she folded the top of the curtain down over his head, feeling a sense of relief as she did. She folded the bottom in, then both sides. She pulled each end of a strip of rope together and tied them tightly over the top. She did this with every strip until Amos was firmly tied into the curtain.

Margaret opened the front door, the rain and the cold and the sound of the siren raced in. Backing up she grabbed the top rope around Amos and started to drag him to the door. The weight of the fender made it all the more difficult. Realising she couldn't do this on her own, she returned to the kitchen. No one had moved. She knelt in front of the armchair. Eva's eyes were closed, her arms holding Alfred tight.

'Eva… Eva,' she said softly. 'Can you help me, please? I need your help just one more time.'

Riesling knew there would be no cross-transmission, so he was going to have to release the bombs manually. The pilot skilfully found the beam and settled on it – now it was all about timing. Riesling watched the dials and the clock timer which came on the instant it located the cross beam during the raid. He thought about the British interference. One mile. Right, he would adjust for that. He was not going to let the Capitan down, the imbeciles who failed to send the signal would have a good bye present from Capitan Schwarz – half the bomb load on the planned release and half adjusted for the interference.

He watched the clock linked to the beam and read the wind meter and speedometer – now! He pressed the first release, eight seconds later the final one. He watched the bombs fall out of the aircraft's belly, feeling personal attachment for the first time.

Go on, he thought, go and get them.

He turned back to the receiver and stared at the dials. The clock ticked and something registered inside his head. They were flying back. He had used the timings from the flight forward. The bombs were off-target. They would land somewhere between a mile and two miles north east of Hoober Stand. He stared at the receiver in horror – an error even a junior operator wouldn't make!

While the bombs fell out of the sky, towards who knew where, he twisted the dials and recorded the correct setting on his flight pad. He realised this act of deception was probably the final indignity and the one which would cement the Capitan's fate. But Capitan Schwarz would not survive this mission and he was not going to join him.

Eva slowly opened her eyes, looking dully at Margaret, her spirit crushed. Her movements were sluggish, but she laid Alfred carefully down on the armchair and stood. Margaret took her hand and led her through into the parlour. The drop in temperature was dramatic with the wind and rain beating in through the open door.

'Eva, can you get the bottom and help me drag it out,' Margaret shouted, pointing to the foot of the parcel while she picked up the rope around the shoulders once more. They struggled out of the door, the weight bending both their backs, wind whipped the rain across the pond, lashing it into their faces. They placed the wider heavier part of the bundle on the top of the wall. The throbbing drone of a single plane passing overhead, on its return to Germany, added its roar to the cacophony of wind, rain and siren. She pushed the bundle along the wall until it was over the water chute underneath the down spout. Eva stumbled along lifting and dropping the legs to help.

Amos's body was now balancing half over the pond, half in the Yard. The world suddenly lit up. A series of huge flashes shattered the dark, as bombs exploded less than two hundred yards away, behind them, somewhere on the Grange. The crash roared at them, repeated time after time – the bombs exploding in close formation. Margaret screamed, 'Now!' and pushed the body with all her might; it fell off the wall into the chute, where the water picked it up and channelled it down the side of the quarry. She did not see or hear a splash; the light was gone and darkness had returned. Eva stood frozen, her hands clasped to her ears and screamed – a sound absorbed by all the other sounds, a silent echo of the siren as it belted out its warning.

Then came another flash of light as more bombs exploded – this time on the Winterwell side of Packman. The whole night lit up again, and Margaret could see that the filthy pond water below had pulled another secret into its belly. There wasn't even a ripple on the surface. Amos was gone. Earth and debris started to fall from the first bombs behind them as the flare from the bombs in front diminished. But before it did, Margaret saw huge mounds of earth leaping up into the sky.

Margaret grabbed Eva and pushed her indoors, yelling for Alfred. She slammed the door behind them and, gathering Eva, raced into the kitchen. Alfred was screaming and Gilbert was sitting, awake, but dazed, trying to take in his surroundings, his head swivelling around; a look of pure bafflement on his face. The windows rattled, and Margaret heard slates falling from the roof, dust flew up from everywhere. Muck and debris hammered the roof and windows, competing with the rain for attention. The double blasts were detonating waves of concussion from either side, seeking out every weakness in the terrace. Margaret sat Eva in the armchair and put Alfred into her lap. Her screaming had stopped but tears were falling in rivers from her eyes, her lips quivering as she cuddled the young child. Margaret turned and hugged Gilbert by the shoulders. He put his arms around her.

'What's happening love?' he asked, a strangely innocent expression on his face.

'Nothing much,' she heard herself say as her waters broke. 'Nothing much.'

Wednesday 18 December 1940

Margaret sat in the armchair, baby Miriam feeding at her breast. Alfred was at her feet playing with the wooden blocks Gilbert had made for him, while Gilbert was washing pots in the sink. It was only three days since the bombing but things were already feeling more normal. She doubted they would ever feel the same again but at least it was better.

Gilbert couldn't remember a thing about the night of the bombs. She would tell him in time, but for now she watched him stacking the pots, barefoot, his trousers pulled up by bracers over the top of his vest. The scar on his temple was still red and vivid. His hair was too long and flopped over his forehead, she knew he liked it like this but wouldn't admit it. His broken nose offset his features and the gap in his teeth made his grin comical, while the strapping on his ribs limited his movement. But she wouldn't swap him for the world.

There was a pounding noise as Eva came down the stairs, hauling a suitcase behind her.

'How about a cuppa afore you go? You've got loads of time.'

'Ok, thanks.'

Eva had hardly spoken since that night. Her nightmares were long and loud. Whenever she went to the toilet she made a point of not looking over the wall towards the pond. It was heart-breaking to watch her being destroyed from the inside as the trauma ate away at her. It was a long time ago when she had only been a young girl herself, but Margaret recalled watching her step-sister being destroyed from the outside in. TB took Martha and it was a scar Margaret could never erase. She would not let it happen again – nothing was going to ruin the life of another beautiful young girl, and there was no doubt about it – Eva was beautiful.

Margaret watched Eva pick Alfred up and hug him. She hoped her Aunt Beth would be able to arrange for Eva to have some contact with children. Eva had decided to go to her great-aunt and live with her in Cornwall. The Yard was no place for her now. Margaret knew that there were too many ghosts. But Eva had never met Beth, she only knew her from the letters they exchanged after her father's death. Margaret looked across at Gilbert. He stood with two cups in his hands, also watching

Eva. The love in his eyes was plain to see. Eva sensed him looking and turned to him. Margaret saw a matching look in her eyes.

Gilbert looked at Margaret. They shared an understanding without needing to speak. Eva was so precious, but in a few minutes' time she would be gone, on a journey he could only imagine. From Yorkshire to Cornwall. A couple of buses, several trains and lots of changes. Two days of crossing England. An adventure he would have loved to try, but he had lived all his life in the shadow of Hoober Stand and he doubted that would ever change.

He knew Margaret felt the loss as much as he did, but Eva was not the only loss – Shudder had fallen under a railway wagon on the night of the bombing. He had been on his way to his mother's in Darfield when he took a short cut and slipped. On finding out Gilbert was distraught.

Apart from Margaret, the two people he loved most in the world were gone. Within three days. One for ever, the other to the far side of England.

But that was not the end of it – Barney and Amos were gone. They were, apparently, inside at the pig farm when bombs landed directly on it. All the military might of Adolf, to blow up a pig farm. Pathetic. Barney had only been identifiable because of his cigarette case while other than a few scraps of a bloody jacket nothing was found of Amos. There were several body parts and lots of blood and flesh but no one knew what was human or what was pig. Amos must have been completely annihilated by the bombs. Rita was distraught and planning to go back to her family in Barnsley, Susannah however seemed to accept the situation with calm and grace.

Gilbert remembered the cups in his hands. He placed them on the table and took a drink from his own. Why couldn't he make a decent cup of tea? Margaret only had to flick at the hob and a drink fit for a king appeared. He laboured over it yet it still tasted like rabbit droppings strained through straw and this was Eva's last cup in the Yard.

He watched as she sipped. She grimaced and looked up sharply to see if he had noticed. He had. He shrugged his shoulders. She smiled and for the first time since the bombing, laughed.

'I'm going Gilbert, there's no need to poison me now,' she joked.

He looked at Margaret who beamed and laughed. He joined in. Seems his tea was so bad, it was good.

Harry stood staring at the hole. It explained everything. A young lad, passing on his bicycle, told them the story. Two brothers were at their pig farm when the German bombers flew over, several of the bombs made a direct hit. The brothers were gone. Completely destroyed, only recognisable by a cigarette case.

Well Barney, you got away with it. A quick and painless death was the opposite of what Harry had planned for him. Three days of anger were built up inside and he could feel it sloshing around his body. It came all the way from his bones, an ache which needed soothing, an itch which needed scratching, and now a void which needed filling.

His thoughts once again centred on Billy. What was he going through now? Harry had done his best but fate intervened. German bombs killing German collaborators. You could not script this stuff.

He looked to his two step-brothers and signalled. They walked up the hill towards Packman, crossed the style and headed up Manor Road. At the top where it joined Packman Road he stopped looking down. The road fell steeply then rose again, up the hill to Hoober Stand on the horizon. It stood there watching him. It's lop-sided look curious to see how he would react. He stared at it for some time. The day was crisp but bright, and the sunlight reflected off the still damp road. The trees were leafless and grey but the sun shining behind the Stand made it seem darker, more dominating.

Harry pulled his eyes from it. At the crossroads by the pub a bus pulled in and a young girl with blonde hair walked towards it carrying a suitcase. At the door she stopped, waving to a couple with a baby and a young child, standing on the pavement. They waved back until the bus disappeared around the corner. The woman turned, facing up the hill. It was the young'un. She looked up the hill at him. He could see the defiant stance and gleam in her eye from here. Yes, she was really something.

He raised his hand then touched his forelock, mimicking taking a hat off. He waved the imagined hat to one side and bent forward in an exaggerated bow. Straightening up, he put his hands into his pockets and turned. Without a word to his step-brothers he walked away from

Packman Road and Hoober Stand. He had some debts to collect, a void to fill, and Jarrow was calling.

Margaret dragged her eyes away from the bus and turned, looking up the hill. At the very brow of the hill there were three figures. One slim with white hair, the other two large and dark. She stared at them. The slim one mimicked a theatrical bow, stood still for a second, defying her, then spun on his heel and walked away. The two giants followed.

Gilbert followed her gaze, but they had gone.

'What's up love? What are you looking at?'

'Nothing. I thought I saw a ghost is all.'

'There's no such thing. This is all there is. Life's hard, then you die.'

Seven for a Secret

Never to be Told

Echoes

'I refused to get into the car at Margaret's funeral.

No one rode. We all walked. It seemed fitting.

There were dozens and dozens walking behind the hearse and when we got to the church all the pews were full; apart from the ones left for the family. It felt like the whole village turned out. Not being church goers, the vicar had never met me or Margaret and even if he had he could hardly have talked about the day the magpie barked.

Eva came, bless her. Travelled all the way from Perranporth in Cornwall. She stood looking at the grave for a long time. When our eyes met it was clear she was back in the day, reliving that time, we were the only ones to share the secret.

She bled to death, my Margaret. She suffered a miscarriage which started a massive haemorrhage and her organs packed up. She was not quite forty years old. But in those forty years she shone like a beacon through that coal-grey landscape. Everyone who met her remembers her laugh, her sparkling hazel eyes, her wicked sense of humour, and the kind, generous woman she was.

Trying to be positive, I suppose she'll always be remembered as youthful, her looks remaining as she was in her prime, but I regret not having the chance to grow old with her.

Me? I've grown old.

Forty-four years working down Cortonwood Colliery while smoking forty Woodbine a day has taken its toll. My lungs struggle to meet the demands of my body, though truthfully, I don't demand too much of it these days.

I've got a finger missing on my left hand and a vivid blue scar around my right eye. Both mementos from the pit. Fortunately, National Health specs hide a lot.

I've never carried much weight, but even so, I've been losing some recently. I suppose my eating habits don't help. You know… it's funny how things change. We used to pick blackberries and Margaret would make jam which I would smother onto her bread scufflers. Now I buy Bramble Seedless – 'cos I can't stand pips under my dentures – and scrape it across Mothers Pride.

Yeah, the old days were poorer, harder, but much, much better.

They've just flattened Top Yard. A crane with a ball and chain smashed the terrace to the ground and a dozer pushed it all into the quarry pond. I sat and watched as memory by memory it fell apart. Then it was gone. Afterwards I walked home past the cemetery where I stopped at the grave and had a chat with Margaret, telling her what happened.

'Bloody good riddance,' I heard her say.

Unable to think of a decent reply I retreated to the Crown Inn. After two pints, I surprised my old dog by getting up early and walking the two hundred yards home. As usual I made myself two slices of bread and dripping, opened a bottle of stout, switched the telly on and, after lighting a fag, slumped into the armchair while the dog crawled into his basket.

As you can probably tell, I miss the old days, the bustle of the Yard, the noise of the kids running around the house, the clatter of dishes, even the spluttering of the fire. But without a doubt, most of all, I miss Margaret.'

The Magpie Barks is fiction. However, the places mentioned exist or existed at the time of the story. Some of the people were real and some of the events actually happened.

For more information go to themagpiebarks.co.uk

Printed in Great Britain
by Amazon